# The Exile of Gibbo

### ANNIE OWEN

**The Exile of Gibbo**

First published in Australia by Annie Owen 2025

*A catalogue record for this
book is available from the
National Library of Australia*

ISBN: 978-1-7638709-0-1 (pbk)
ISBN: 978-1-7638709-1-8 (ebk)

Typesetting and design by Publicious Book Publishing
Published in collaboration with Publicious Book Publishing
www.publicious.com.au

For Peter

# Contents

# Prologue

## Speaking from the Heart

I am the spirit of the Great Southern Land - I am the earth, the rock formations - the source of life and death. My greatest strength is that I can feel - I feel the pain of dying people, animals and plants. I can feel their joys and anxieties.

I don't know 'time' but I felt the separation of my land mass into the sea to form an island. For many thousands of years, I felt the people on top of me and was not pleased or bothered by their existence, although I did admire their resilience when I became covered with floods or dried to a crisp with scorching conditions. I felt the pain of these people as they bunkered down against the elements that could hit me — scorching fires, gale force winds, snow, ice, and intense heat. I was not aware of any name given to me, but I felt their 'dreaming' and their stories of my origins.

I must admit, they looked after me. I didn't like being burnt but couldn't help but feel admiration the way native animals were being corralled by fire to make for easy pickings. I could burn as well - as I erupted over vast areas and absorbed fire and ash within myself. These dark-coloured people used me - but were not greedy. They respected my power and my ability to provide for them. They used my resources wisely and carefully, never taking more than they needed. They made their homes in harmony with my landscape, never disrupting my delicate balance. They believed in me, and I became part of their dreams. As I say, we were getting along fine.

I've already said I don't know 'time'. It's like a dot. Everything that has taken place over millions of years feels as though it has just happened.

But then, something changed. I felt the pain when ghostly strangers of another species landed on me and took over the land. They started taking more than they needed, destroying my forests and polluting my rivers. I felt the weight of stone being piled up on top of me as towering skyscrapers blocked out my sun and polluted the air. The water that flowed over me and surrounded me attracted piles of concrete in buildings that reached up to the sky. I felt the enormous pressure of roads, bridges and the traffic that raced over them. They gave me a name – 'Australia'.

I felt the pain and loss of the dark people that I had come to regard as 'my own'. I felt the changes - strange animals and huge stretches of fences that kept the animals in but locked out my original inhabitants.

Some of my native animals dig into me - but that is just a tickle. However, I still bear the scars of huge holes being dug into me by these ghostly figures as they sought to find - what they regarded - my hidden 'treasures'.

I don't know these people, but I can feel their emotions, their intensity, their ... spirit.

I know that water is my most precious possession. I felt the water in my rivers being polluted or channelled to distant places. I felt every change and they were piling up so that my landscape was altered. I became morose and out of sorts. I wanted to bust the concrete - and at times - I did just that. I tremored from within and caused havoc above me.

I've got stories many of millions of years old – but that would take too long. I could write a book about my new altered condition - but I won't.

I don't know about other lands. As I said, I separated and enjoyed my isolation. And then I felt another change. Like the first landing of pale people, it was subtle and silent but caused havoc all the same. I can feel the distress – oh no, not again – history is repeating itself!

# The Invasion

The North Koreans called it 'Kim' – a fault tolerant quantum computer, a one million quantum-bit machine that could solve problems many millions of times faster than conventional computers. A unique technology in which single photons (particles of light) are manipulated using photonic circuits that are patterned on to a silicon chip. This invention allowed previously impossible problems confronting climate, energy, healthcare, finance agriculture, transportation, material design, and many more to be quickly and efficiently overcome.

The North Koreans knew that they had reached the mountain but had not conquered it. They needed help to unlock the full potential of what they had stumbled upon. They turned to their Chinese friends for help. Chinese IT specialists immediately grasped what the ramifications of this new silicon chip meant and how it could be used to cripple other countries' economies and infrastructure. Using their complex system of computer spies, they could physically insert 'Kim' to a targeted country. Transport, military, finance, and governments could be rendered useless almost overnight. The North Koreans who unearthed this incredible advancement in computer technology, and the Chinese, had a unified grievance against America and, unfortunately as Australia was to find out, it too was high on the agenda to be taught a lesson. Together, they would harness their new superpower to teach their rivals round the world that they were in sole possession of a superior tool. The new regime of North Korea and China, now universally called the 'Power House' had allowed the rest of the world to witness exactly what 'Kim'—their simple new chip—was actually capable of. They dismantled the American defence by effortlessly taking over their systems. All infrastructure, transportation and the entire corporate American system was now hamstrung—their computers redundant. The world watched on in horror.

The Power Houses turned their attention to a large land mass, rich in minerals and with a small population. The Australians were all vaguely aware that China had been buying up large tracts of land, piece by piece, state by state, for years but, perhaps it was because of the vast distances, they turned a blind eye. Even the barrage of trade restrictions and inexplicable tariffs did little to wake up the nation. It seemed that no one wanted to put two and two together.

Although the media predicted a threat, most Australians were unaware of the intentions of the Power Houses. They went about their daily lives with the knowledge that they had survived the pandemic relatively unscathed and now this pending dilemma would simply disappear. Despite the horror of the dismantling of the American internet and satellite systems, they criticised the media for ramping up and sensationalising the current situation. The people believed that they had a strong government with stronger allies. 'She'll be right' was the mantra of the day. This cannot happen to us! However, the threat was ever present, like a big black shadow that follows every move.

It happened overnight. The Australians woke up to find their televisions broadcasting in another language. They ran to their mobile phones to find out the problem—but they were dead—the server no longer existed. They tried to get their money out of the banks, but the machines were rejecting them. They tried going to the bank—an institution they hadn't set foot in for years—but they were closed due to an 'internet malfunction'.

Overnight, the monetary system changed. The Australian dollar was obsolete and replaced with 'Kims' and 'Rams'. Australia had been invaded silently as if the whole population had been anesthetised and woke up to find they were in another world. A new government, a new language and a new name, swiftly spread over the land. Signs were dismantled and new signs in another language erected. A methodical dismantling of the English language took place.

Parents hid their fears from their children, but the older kids gleefully shared and embellished their anxieties with the younger ones. Blood thirsty predictions of a new life quickly spread through the schools. The children were quicker than the adults to pick up the scent of pending danger. Fear was coursing its way through society, creating restlessness and sleep deprivation.

The takeover was lightning fast and silent. People looked for leadership and direction, but the government was mute. Australia was no longer 'the lucky country', it was part of an alliance called the 'The Power House'. The rules had changed—permanently.

On reflection, the Australians should have realised that it was inevitable. The world was in turmoil. Despite the vaccinations, globally most people were still wary of symptoms and fearful that a new variant of Covid would engulf them again. The pandemic had left every country in survival mode, and this was the perfect time for the powerful to show their new weapon that could cripple an economy as quickly as pressing a button. The world could only watch on as they hastened to develop their own silicon chip to nullify this weapon of mass destruction.

Political correctness went out the window—the Aussies became bitter as their vulnerability became obvious. They were a small population adrift from the world. A new wave of people, ships and aircraft was breaching their shores. The rules changed rapidly, and the Australians were angry and confused about their plight. The Power Houses declared the new name for their annexed continent. They called it 'Nan Tudi'.

*I felt a shift in lifestyle as the pale people rejected the onslaught of the new invading force. I could feel their bitterness and their useless determination to continue living as they had in the past. Their once proud feelings of superiority turned into fear of the future. I can't talk for the future, but I will tell you that I will let you know how they fared.*

The court orders came. The Australian government was sentenced to crimes against humanity, dating back to 1778. They argued that it was a peaceful 'takeover' that gave the original inhabitants a superior way of life. The new 'Power House' Government showed pictures of First Nations people in chains and tethered to trees. They showed evidence of mass deaths caused by poisoned water holes. They showed current living conditions of over-crowded humpies of corrugated iron and tarpaulin on the fringes of outback towns. They showed lack of sanitary conditions and running water. The Australian government was accused of a long list of injustices spreading over more than two centuries that the outside world could not ignore,

*Yes, I felt these injustices. I think the life of 'the one who could disappear' sums up their plight. He was a leader of these dark people and greatly admired by his clan. I felt his feelings of pride as he established himself to his pale invaders as an excellent tracker and helped them traverse the land and survive. Many an occasion, he could have left them to die. I felt his pain when he was asked to help in the arrest and kill his own people, and I felt proud that he refused. Yes, he killed a policeman to protect his people and had no other alternative but to 'disappear'. I could feel the footsteps of the animals as he was hunted down. I felt incredibly sad when he was located and killed. He was called 'Jandamarra'.*

*But the court was wrong. These pale people did not come to my shores as conquerors. They came to use me as a human rubbish dump. They shackled their own! There was no elation, but the misery that followed their arrival, seeped down through me.*

The Australian government was asked to produce evidence of the respect shown towards the First Nations peoples in the Constitution and, of course, they could not. They were asked to play the national anthem and the new Power Houses laughed themselves hoarse when they heard the words, 'we are young and free'. The oldest culture on the plant is described 'young'? These people seem to think that the country just plopped itself into the ocean in 1778—ha ha. The newly established 'Power House' Government left the courtroom with a new set of rules. The old government was in disgrace.

*I could feel the confusion of the pale people. Now it is their turn to suffer the loss of their country, their freedom and their way of life. They could not understand what was going on. They could not communicate with the new regime. I felt their pride of their previous way of life which they thought (perhaps erroneously) was the envy of the world. They are now disorientated—aliens in their own country. I heard their laments: 'Who are we now?'—'Where do we belong?' I felt their seething anger and frustration. Most of all, I felt their fear.*

# The Rules

The Aussies had limited access to the new rules, which was mainly hearsay or embellished gossip. They knew that they could not get access to their bank accounts but had to fill in convoluted forms that only contained 'BSB' and the word 'Account' that they could understand. The Power House rounded up citizens of their own ilk for re-education. The internet was not accessible in English.

The Aussies did not have to travel far to see wave after wave of defence personnel driving their armoured cars. A few did take a stand and ran out in front of them—they were mown down.

The new Power Houses set up a citizen hierarchy with itself at the top. This meant that all urbane properties that had previously belonged to the rich, were appropriated for their highest officials—the most powerful ranks that had direct links back to their mainlands.

The First Nations people were second on the list and received substantial housing as they were considered a conduit to the management of the huge tracts of inland country. They were respected for their fire and water management. The conquering Power House citizens were the third on the list to receive housing. Next came all existing residents with The Power House heritage after a substantial re-education program was completed (this could take many years for the older citizens as the Power Houses recognised the difficulty of older people adapting).

The remaining population had no rights to land and would be moved to allocated settlements in due course. It took the Australians varying times to work this out. Firstly, it was the wealthy in hot spot areas such as, what they had previously called

'Sydney Harbour', who were affected. Then the ripple effect drifted down. The news spread about the big homes in prime locations with water and sea views being taken over. The original occupants quickly vanished, leaving the rest of neighbouring residents fearful for their futures. The less wealthy were glad that they only had small holdings that may not be wanted and hoped that they could cling on. However, gradually the Power Houses were handing out eviction notices to landowners in every city. As more Power House citizens flocked in, the cities were shrinking for the former owners and it was only the country dwellers who could now occupy their own property. This didn't last long, as all the land, whether it had rich soil or was arid, was considered an asset and no former Australian was entitled to claim any part of it. Of course, there were various ranks of officialdom within the new Power House government, but even their lowest ranks were given a new and very comfortable lifestyle.

It didn't take long for the 'Australians' to be displaced.

It also didn't take long for the conquerors to give them the derogatory tag: 'Big Feet and Long Noses'.

No official referred to a person as 'Australian' because that country no longer existed. It was only within their own communities that they called themselves 'Aussies'.

Their social lives ceased. If they went to the pub and managed to get a seat, they could be part way through a meal and a Power House official was entitled to tap the chairs. This signalled that the Aussies had to vacate their seats and leave the premises. The same happened on public transport. If they stood at a bar, unless there was no one else in proximity, they would not be served. They quickly became accustomed to being invisible. The only restaurants they had access to and just scraped in the 'affordable' category, were fast food outlets, but the same rules applied there—they had to give up seats to the hierarchy—which basically, was everyone who was not Australian.

*I felt the degradation of the conquered people. I felt the power of the new force. I felt the change and wondered about my future.*

Strangely, the Power Houses were not concerned about church services. People could congregate there with no restrictions. The clergy enjoyed their expanded numbers, but the coffers continued much the same as the working wage was synchronised and well below what had previously been 'the basic wage'.

The sports grounds were transformed—some into car parks. The huge ovals that held thousands of spectators were dismantled. The new Power House Government took over Parliament House in what was previously called 'Canberra'. The War Memorial was stripped of its memorabilia and used as public servant offices.

Contraception was free. The Power Houses obviously discouraged increasing numbers of 'big feet and long noses'. Access to medical centres was very limited. The queues to these buildings attached to the main hospitals were long and tedious. Student doctors and nurses were in attendance whereby they could get 'hands on' experience. The stories of operations where a person of childbearing age was sterilized were too frequent to ignore. The queues soon diminished.

Schools, particularly the large private ones, were the first to be taken over. Children were schooled collectively and at a distance from the Power Houses and the First Nations children. The conquered could only go to school up to the age of thirteen and then they were deemed eligible to work in factories or do manual labour. The Power Houses saw no reason for higher education for 'big feet and long noses' as they would not be eligible for any career of their choice.

Parents would not allow their children to go to a park or socialise with other children out of school hours, as they heard about families that were split and sent to different locations when property appropriation orders came into force. They spent their time on high alert.

*I feel the concern of parents for their children. I've already felt the pain of children being removed from their families and know the misery.*

The Aussies didn't know it, but the international press was full of it. Headlines, such as 'PLUNDER DOWN UNDER' captivated huge attention. The new Power Houses knew that the eyes of the world were on them and had a strict policy of their people fraternising with 'big feet and long noses'. If there was any suspicion of any alliance to anyone of European background, the culprit would immediately be sent back to their Mainlands in disgrace. In other words, they would lose their new and very comfortable lifestyle. The 'no fraternising' policy was strictly adhered to. There was pillage but no rape—they wanted to keep their race 'pure'.

Every household, during this initial stage of invasion, tried to continue life as normal, although now they all had to work, which was not necessarily the case during the pandemic. It took quite a while for the Aussies to wake up to the fact that their pay was coming out of their own bank accounts, thanks to the original convoluted forms that they had been forced to sign. The Power Houses controlled the tokens, with colours suspiciously akin to casino chips, which were deducted from the frozen bank accounts to pay a pittance for hard labour. The Power Houses looked down upon this new form of payment as 'dirty money'. The Aussies learned that to criticise the Power Houses was an immediate jail sentence, so they seethed beneath muted lips. Naturally, there were anti-Power House hushed nicknames behind closed doors—'Fried Rice' and 'Chop Suey' were jocular, almost friendly terms, but the most common usage, was GRAP (Greedy Ruthless, Asian Puppets). This new name for their archenemy was the mother of all insults and never spoken to an official face.

The Aussies were totally discouraged from speaking any words of the new languages, but snatches were learned from watching television. However, it was only the advertisements that were repetitive, so that they learned the name of popular drinks and food outlets that they could not afford.

Television news, beamed from the conquering Power House mainlands, now showed chaotic scenes of demonstrations, riots and shootings in Western countries, wars in the Middle East, and the occasional extreme weather conditions. However, the headlines always depicted joyful scenes from their own home fronts.

Registration for work was mandatory. The young and fit were sent to building sites, roadworks, landscaping, or refurbishing existing buildings. This was considered a far better option as the majority worked in the factories that had swung into action in old manufacturing buildings. Many of these buildings had been vacant for years. Work instructions were shown with hand signals and then strictly supervised as every factory had to produce a quota that increased steadily over time. The goal of the Power Houses was to make the workforce more productive and they had the power to control wages.

*When the pale people came to my shores, they brought in a powerful force that I could not understand. In the past, I felt the trade between the dark people, but this new species brought in paper and round metal shapes that ruled their lives. I was puzzled by the importance of this new trading system but well aware of its impact.*

Neighbours started disappearing and new Power House neighbours settled in. Nobody knew what was going to happen until officials came with the appropriation order and the occupants given twenty-four hours to pack their bags and head to the destination on the form. Armed military police manned the front and back doors of the residence and scrutinised all packed items as the occupants saw their homes for the last time. The tears flowed as they looked back on their forced abandonment of their former lifestyle. They knew that they could never return. Their only memories were the photos and memorabilia that they packed with their clothes into a travel bag, which was limited to one per person. Even a handkerchief from a distant holiday was now a prized possession. No one was allowed to take pets, vehicles, computers, mobile phones, cords, or battery charges of any description—they stayed with the property. Storage facilities were locked.

*Behind locked doors, I felt the fear from those people huddling together for comfort. I can remember my dark people running away and being cornered, not knowing what was to come. I've come to believe that people are their own worst enemies. Speaking for my land, and everything it provides—it's NOT a cruel world.*

The Aussies lived every second of their lives fearful of that bang on the door, as they knew that evacuation orders ensued and they would be out on the street, heading for an unknown destination that was their fate. Their house, gardens, furniture, and all possessions disappeared with a knock. They waited for it and, although it was no surprise, when it did come, it was a shock.

Yes, there were a few who tried to defend their properties. Perhaps, if they were armed, they may have inflicted some damage, although there was never any evidence of this. However, they did know from the neighbours that the response was a series of rapid machine gun fire and the quick arrival of a delivery truck from which drivers and their guards re-emerged carrying out body bags. The news quickly spread.

They didn't know that satellite images of long queues, crowded buses and large housing blocks were being shown regularly on international media. There were captions depicting their plight:

### Down Under and Out – Where have they Gone?

**Australians have been ousted from their homes and relocated to unknown regions in Nan Tudi (formerly 'Australia'). The cities are becoming empty of the Australian faces that made up a diverse multicultural society. The Power House Government denies that extended families are being split as thousands of people are being evacuated from their homes. The conquering Power Houses say that they are providing shelter and employment in ideal conditions to benefit the European squatters on this land.**

**They refuse to recognise the name 'Australia' or any derivatives thereof.**

An area was allocated to the occupants of the Fleurieu Peninsula, south of Adelaide, that had been known as 'KI'—Kangaroo Island. This large island could be seen from the southern coastline.

*I felt the split of my island that used to be attached and broke away. My original dark people called it 'Kartu'—Island of the Dead. I know it well and will let you know if the new evacuees fare any better.*

# Daishiu Dao – Kangaroo Island (KI)

This island became a settlement for the neighbouring mainland Aussies. Extended families were often geographically split. Even former friendships struggled to survive as the evacuees focused on their own survival. The new influx of residents from the mainland envied the original KI residents, who were allowed to stay on their home soil, but subject to the same living conditions as their fellow countrymen. However, the Islanders lamented that 'yes, they were on home soil, but the island is now alien'. The landscape for the new arrivals, as well as the original Kangaroo Islanders, was unrecognisable to their previous lifestyle.

Of course, mobile phones were banned. All communication was severed.

They started out with forced optimism: 'This is our new way of life and we may as well make the most of it.' There was no other option. Somewhere along the long journey that sapped their energy, their anger shrivelled. Eight large factories were earmarked for the island. Three were modified after being commandeered from existing buildings and now were operational. The rest were in various stages of completion. There was a large contingency of Power House officials to oversee, not only the working hours, but round the clock living of the internees. The Aussies knew that they either towed the line or were sent away—and it wouldn't be to Utopia.

The new arrivals were flung into the construction of huge blocks of apartments for housing or set to work on refurbishing existing buildings for Power House use. The housing blocks had no balconies or any outdoor living areas. The grounds were limited to cement paths. Older residents and couples were allocated a one-bedroom unit on the top floors. As the buildings had no lifts, this was a well contrived recipe for heart attacks. Funnily enough, the opposite happened—many became very fit and had stair racing competitions. No one knew what had become of the aged and infirm. Life became a set of rules and regulations with no room for individuality. What seemed like a blink of an eye, life had tipped itself on its head.

Large families got two large bedrooms and a family of four got two smaller bedrooms. No one had their own bathrooms—the ablution blocks were at the end of every corridor. The miniscule kitchens had a cook top, sink and a couple of cupboards that were situated in the corner of a room that the Power Houses described as a 'family room' but the occupants called 'the dog kennel'. There was a table and enough metal chairs for every family member. The futon served as a couch. If a small television was packed into the luggage, it was useless, as there were no antennae. Wire coat hangers didn't stop the picture rolling. The communal fridges were in the corridors, and everyone had to name and date any food items that were stored. The fridges were cleaned out weekly by the older residents, who also had to keep all the ablution blocks in tip-top order. Communal laundries were on the ground floor with washing machines that chewed up coins. They were constantly overloaded, breaking down and 'out of order' indefinitely.

Single people were housed on the lower levels in army style dormitories, which the guys called 'bull rooms' and the girls called 'the brain bank' as they reckoned they knew which part of the anatomy was used for thinking. These large rooms were furnished with a row of wooden slat-based beds with the most basic innerspring mattress. Every spring could be felt under the thin covering material, providing involuntary acupuncture. Communal wardrobes were at the end of the room. There were enough drawers under the hanging space for one per person, providing the only semblance of privacy. The communal kitchen was attached to the laundry and had wooden tables with attached wood plank seating. Each kitchen had one oven, four hotplates, a sink, and a couple of cupboards with some aluminium saucepans and plastic plates, bowls, glasses, and cutlery. There were cutting boards and two paring knives to share between all the residents. There was always a queue for the hotplates. There was a television on the wall, which was set to one channel that showed non-stop documentaries of the Power Houses mainlands. It showed military and air force might, and grand parades appreciated by crowded fans. It flicked over to beautiful gardens, giant pandas, monuments, clean rivers flowing from mountain ranges, and outdoor eateries with happy customers. The volume was usually muted as no one could understand the dialogue.

The rent was deducted from wages. The wages decreased as the rent increased and was non-negotiable.

Did the vanquished miss their old life? Of course they did. They talked ad nauseam about the houses that they were forced to surrender. The more they talked, the more the land, house and possessions that were once owned, grew in size as well as monetary value. A fly on the wall would have presumed that every Aussie owned a yacht and drove expensive European cars. They stopped short at describing private helipads. They talked fondly about barbeques, al fresco dining, parties, music, restaurants, concerts, TV programs having 'the news' on tap, riding, films, the pub, watching the footy, cricket—all sports on television. It wasn't so much the material possessions they missed, it was their pets, neighbours, going to the shops whenever they felt like it. They missed their trips into the country—hiking, bike riding, travelling to the snow, or visiting distant islands. They missed their lifestyle … their freedom.

*At last—they are forgetting about their possessions and missing me. Now that it's no longer accessible, I can feel the intensity of their love of my surrounding sea, my mountain ranges, my cliffs, lakes, forests, spectacular rock formations, and waterfalls. My list goes on and on. Oh, how they now yearn.*

There was occasional talk about their future—'we are all in this together, one big family'! Talk was cheap. The reality was that the island became split into factions as the internees became tired and disillusioned. There were those who ingratiated themselves with the Power House officials and were looked upon as a scourge by those who regarded themselves as 'true-blue dinky-di Aussies'. There was name calling for the Power Houses sympathisers who were regarded as traitors. There was no more derogatory name than to be labelled a 'GRAP'—it was the king-hit of all insults.

Recent immigrants, pre-invasion, extended their ethnic groups to include other immigrants and refugees. They didn't really care who was in government and were the most cheerful as they settled into a life that resembled the one from which they had fled. The Aussies wanted to embrace them as they had been through similar regimes and found it easier to cope, but birds of a feather tend to flock together.

Children were allowed to go to school up to Grade 8 and then dispatched to work on their thirteenth birthday. The younger children became fluent in the new language and managed to shut out their annoyed parents with their conversations. Those children with only a year or less of schooling struggled as they had limited knowledge of the official language. They were all very aware that they had been born with 'big feet and long noses' and therefore had no future.

The Aussie diet changed. Their stomachs shrank. Access to beef, lamb and pork was non-existent. However, kangaroo meat was relatively cheap and was the only meat that just scraped in the 'affordable treat' category. It was considered a 'special occasion' food. Pretty much every dish came with rice or noodles. In fact, 'noodles' became the new word for the evening meal.

*I felt the toil of the workers. I felt the control of the supervisors who could adjust the pay at a whim. I felt the demise of the queue of workers who had to cup their hands, like a begging bowl, to receive their tokens for their labour. These people who, until recently, had pride in their culture, their learning and their lifestyle, were now reduced to relying on their overlords and were beholden to their children for knowledge of the new system.*

Supermarket shopping was a nightmare as all the labels were in the new official language and no one knew if they were buying shampoo or olive oil. The sign above the supermarket was illegible to the Aussies, so it was dubbed 'Foodies'. There was only one checkout with a sign in English—'Big Feet'. They got used to the fact that there were many times when the checkout was not manned. They just had to stay in the queue and wait until someone sauntered over to the till. Because they didn't know the value of the coloured tokens, they had to spread them out while the checkout official selected the ones he or she wanted—the only time they saw the official smile. They suspected that they were getting ripped off and when they became more conversant, via the school children, of the value of their tokens, they knew that they were being robbed, which made it worse as complaining was counterproductive. The more the checkout officials smiled, the more they pocketed. If anyone argued, they were sent to the end of the queue, minus the groceries. Many a time on getting to the checkout, a sign would be placed on the counter and the queue would be waved off to another one to start the process all over again. It seemed it was a game that the officials enjoyed but the customers couldn't win.

There was no checkout for other goods as it was rare that anyone could afford to buy clothes or household items. However, if the tokens were pooled to buy a communal bath mat, the customer was treated with suspicion and asked to show the tokens before entering the shop. Of course, they had to wait for all The Power House officials to be served first.

Being searched regularly by security upon leaving Foodies became normal. Most of the smaller shops, such as hairdressers, had signs on the door—'No big feet and long noses'. That was not a worry, as no one could afford to enter.

*I now had two camps of people—the conquering newcomers— elated, enthusiastic and looking forward to the future.*

*I could feel the weariness of the other camp as their lives became a repetitive drudge of work.*

*It seems that one camp has to ensure that the other camp recognises their status as lesser beings.*

Lives became very mundane. They were tired and dispirited from long hours of tedious work with only one day off a week—Sunday—which was used to do domestic chores, stand in shopping queues and rest weary bones. Alcohol was banned and a punishable offence. The Power Houses did not want alcohol-infused labourers in the workforce. A person's background no longer mattered. The previously rich, famous or high-profile identities were treated with suspicion by the Power Houses officials as they may try to use their notoriety to influence others. They were only allowed the most manual of factory work where they could be under constant observation.

The Power Houses strictly administered the 'no fraternising with Big Feet and Long Noses policy' for their own people. Huge fines applied or even worse—being sent back to their mainland home in disgrace.

*I've felt the power of money in the past. This new system of special tokens felt a very effective way of putting my pale people in their place. They were beholden.*

Of course, for the Aussies, bribery was out of the question, they were all piss pot poor. They grappled with the value of the tokens that were their only source of income and had to rely on their school-aged children to learn the new system of payment. They now felt their erosion of status in the workforce and on the home front. Of course, all Power House officials disdained tokens. If they had to handle them, it was always with rubber gloves.

*I feel the plight of all of these newly vanquished people as they were flung to their destinations. There are too many stories to tell, but I can tell you what happened on Kangaroo Island.*

*I don't know why, but I felt their angst so strongly, those people exiled to Kangaroo Island. I followed their emotions, but there was one person who I felt most of all.*

# Gibbo

Gibbo couldn't have been more Aussie. He was an older bloke, married to Kaitlyn, who he called 'Kats'. He played Aussie Rules football for the Southern Districts, which gave him a bit of star status in his area. Being part of a team and enjoying the camaraderie of his mates was all Gibbo wanted. He hated the new conquering regime with a passion—part of the reason being that they don't play Australian Rules Football.

Gibbo's father was a paver and landscaper, with a retail outlet in the industrial area of a country town from which Kangaroo Island could be seen on a clear day. His English father had come to Australia for a holiday, met his Australian mum, married and stayed. There were three children—Jack, Jamie and Lexie. But from the very first day of school to the last, Jack was called 'Gibbo'. Also, from the very first day to the last, he loved to show off in the classroom. The teachers quickly learned that to banish him outside would invoke a series of physical antics and facial expressions that kept the rest of the class amused as they watched through the window. Hence, he was frequently seen outside the headmaster's door. The teachers knew that he did not have one academic bone in his body, but his cheeky grin and sense of humour made him popular with students and, to a degree, teachers alike. His report cards were always the same—if he only TRIED.

The family saved, and when Gibbo was ten years of age, they went on their first holiday to London and stayed with his Aunty Bev. Gibbo was her favourite nephew. Perhaps it was because she was a headmistress in a large school that she loved his cheek.

He could still remember looking out his aunt's window at Christmas time and seeing snow fall for the first time. He could also remember being curled up near the fireplace and listening to her stories. He could see in his mind's eye, the look on his aunt's face when she returned from the shops on a particularly drizzly day to find the furniture overturned and the youngsters—Gibbo at the helm—waging war with pretend weapons. Although she was a bit prim and proper, she could not help but laugh at his antics.

As he grew up, Gibbo knew what he wanted to do in life—play football and work in his father's paving business. He couldn't wait to leave school to be his father's apprentice. He learned the hard way that his father was a stickler for precision. If the path was a millimetre out of alignment, every paver had to be taken up, restacked in exactly the same position, and the job done again. He whinged to a mate one night, 'My old man is so pedantic that when mum asked him to hang the sheets on the line, I'll swear he measured the sheets, then the line, worked it out on the calculator, then hung them exactly in half'. However, he did concede that his father's work ethics earned the business a very good reputation.

Gibbo's mum loved organics. She refused to have a coffee at a café until the staff could prove that the coffee beans were organic. Of course, she drank it with almond milk. She tried the same trick on the pizza delivery outlet, but they were too busy to discuss the origins of every mushroom, capsicum, onion, and pumpkin topping and they hung up. She absolutely refused to have her children vaccinated. She was not going to have her children injected with any substance that she herself had not administered.

Gibbo's relationship with the police force began the night of the Year 10 formal. He convinced one of the school nerds, who they called 'Einstein', to hand over the keys to his mum's car. At the end of the night, Gibbo grabbed handfuls of decorations, streamers and balloons and tied them to the windscreen. His mates and Einstein jumped in, and he gave a burnout demo, much to the amusement of the kids pouring out of the building. The windows were down, the boys in the car were shouting their heads off, and Gibbo was screaming round in circles burning as much rubber off Einstein's mum's car as possible. It was the most exciting thing Einstein had ever done. Everyone was enjoying the show until the decorations covered the windscreen and Gibbo lost sight. He inadvertently steered the car into a parked car, which hit the one next to it and caused a five-car chain reaction. He didn't have a driver's licence to lose and, because it was not on a public road, he only incurred a hefty fine and court order to pay for repairs to the damaged vehicles. He was charged with dangerous driving and putting the lives of pedestrians at risk. It also made obtaining a licence that much harder when Gibbo reached the eligible age.

His parents were gutted when the police knocked on their door, but his mum told her friends that her boy had been egged on by his mates. 'He's too easily led and trusting for his own good'. To her mind, the fact that he was the driver was not relevant. His father secretly disagreed but went along with this edict.

Gibbo played Australian Rules football for the 'Panthers' Southern District side and got into their 'A' grade at the age of seventeen. He was well known in the area, and enjoyed the recognition. He was earning a good income from footy but there were times when it got him into trouble. He eventually got his licence, bought a car and loved hooning round with his friends late at night after a bout of heavy drinking. The police watched the roads for the tell-tale tyre marks, and he was arrested. His licence was confiscated, much to the delight of his parents, and he was put on a good behaviour bond.

Gibbo's team didn't make the grand final one year, so he and his mates decided to 'frock up' and head for the pub to watch the match. Gibbo wore a long, pink strappy dress with pink glittery thongs. The pub was packed and the televisions on. They were having a good time tossing the beers down and swallowing the odd pie. At half time, he decided to provide some entertainment. He didn't have much hair on his chest, but he did have long hairs circling his nipples. What better way to show them off, but to set light to them? His mates decided it was a great idea and joined in. The smell of burning hair permeated the pub, much to the astonishment of the bemused customers. That night they decided to have 'one for the road' at another pub. The security guard told them to go home and sleep it off. He wasn't impressed with a mob of frocked up, boozy customers. Gibbo saw red and took a swing at the guard. Fortunately, he missed and his mates stepped in and guided him home. However, there was another visit from the police the next day. His luck held as he only got a hefty fine and an extended good behaviour bond. His parents despaired. Gibbo spent his teenage years dodging trouble. He knew that if he got riled up, he had a fiery temper that his mates could usually curb.

He didn't become a saint, but when he met Kaitlyn, the police visits ceased, and his parents could once again sleep at night. He told her: 'Kats, from the moment I laid eyes on you, I was a gonner. I found it so easy to find trouble—didn't even have to go out of my way, but now all I want is to be with you.'

Kaitlyn, who came from a house that valued the virtue of seriousness and regarded humour as mindless garbage, loved him for his free spirit and his sense of fun. Gibbo could get on a train and have the whole carriage laughing and joining in with his repartee. Of course, Kaitlyn's parents did not share the same enthusiasm. They had sent her to one of the best schools in Adelaide and they socialised with people like themselves from academic backgrounds. This person that their daughter was besotted with was alien to their way of life, but they loved their daughter and decided that they had to love her choice of a partner. Although they had made that decision, they found the reality extremely difficult. For starters, Gibbo and subsequently his mates, calling their daughter 'Kats' grated on their nerves. To think that the name they had chosen, after much deliberation, for their beautiful baby girl, was mutilated to their faces, made them inwardly wince. The only thing that really pleased them was that Kaitlyn kept her maiden name after they were married. To Kaitlyn's parents, humour was a crutch for people who did not have the intellectual capacity to sustain a meaningful conversation. This, of course, included Gibbo. They abhorred 'small' talk. They found Gibbo's ready grin and flippant speech irritating. They had never used, and could not understand, slang. They also could not understand why anyone of any intelligence would kick, or run after, a ball. However, they did put on a brave, tolerant face in his presence.

When they were awoken one night to see their married daughter at the end of the bed with a suitcase in hand, they were overjoyed.

Gibbo himself could not believe that Kats happily agreed to get married. He always felt 'not quite good enough' and knew her parents shared the same sentiment. Kats had done very well in a private school. She had been a school prefect and was looked up to by teachers and students alike. She also had a business management degree, which Gibbo knew she could use far more effectively than working in a small paving business reception area. He loved her to bits and knew that she reciprocated—but for how long? He felt as though he had hit the jackpot—but could he keep it? Beneath his carefree persona lurked a very fragile self-esteem. His worst nightmare was that Kats would meet someone who would measure up to her achievements.

Gibbo and Kaitlyn were married when his parents decided to retire to a seaside town. Jamie and Lexie were working in Adelaide and Gibbo took over the paving business and the family home. There were no babies, but they had three border collie dogs that they idolised. However, life wasn't all beer and skittles. Kaitlyn knew that Gibbo got jealous at times. But he was always contrite the next morning. However, he went too far one night after she danced with an old school friend. Gibbo was beside himself with jealousy and raved on and on when they got home that night. He called the guy every name he could think of and asked Kaitlyn how she could bear being in the same room with that fucking prick, let alone dance with the bastard. 'I know why you fancy him, it's because he's got an arty farty degree!' Kaitlyn stared at Gibbo, which did the opposite to silencing him. He went on to accuse her of secretly having an affair. When he was in the shower, she threw some clothes into the car and spent the next few days at her parent's house. Gibbo had to do a lot of sweet talking to cajole her back home again. Kaitlyn told him that he was trying to control her. 'Gibbo, I love you for your free spirit, but you are robbing me of mine. I'm not an extension of yourself and if you treat me as such, we will have to part ways.' The thought of losing his Kats sent him into a spiral and he became an expert at hiding the jealousy that coursed through his body at times.

Her parents were quietly depressed at the reunion.

Business wise, they survived the pandemic better than some, and then came the invasion. The paving business continued, but the profits immediately went into a Power Houses fund. Their bank account was null and void. The money they had in their wallets was worthless, as the country to which it belonged no longer existed. Gibbo and Kaitlyn were now on less than basic wages. They knew what would happen next. They had heard about it loud and clear and had no idea how much time they had left in their home with their dogs. Every time they heard a loud noise, they jumped, thinking 'this is it'. They were angry but subdued and extremely frightened. Gibbo's flippancy continued, but only at half-mast.

They came home from work one evening, tired and dejected. Gibbo decided that they would spend a large portion of their weekly allowance on a dinner at what was previously thought of as a fast food outlet. Kaitlyn was too tired to object. They walked to the café as their car had run out of fuel weeks ago and they could not afford to even partially fill the tank. The car stayed in the driveway as a remembrance of their formal life. When they got to the café, they looked at the pictures on the wall and decided on a type of hamburger. The picture showed flat bread, toasted or grilled, stuffed with meat and salad. It looked delicious. There was no one in the café and they heaved a sigh of relief as there was a chance that they could finish their meal without being ordered to leave. They waited at the counter to order but were ignored. Eventually, a severely cross looking lady took their order. They went to sit down, and she came hurtling round the counter waving them off every table until they got to one next to the toilet door. As they waited with eager anticipation for their hamburgers, a group of Power House officials came in. After being seated, they were immediately served drinks and a large tray of assorted appetizer snacks by a beaming waitress. These were followed by their meals, which looked delicious. The officials were happily chatting and eating their dinner, giving Gibbo and Kaitlyn plenty of opportunity to watch and drool. The officials finished with cups of tea into which some of them poured a liquid from a pocket flask. This was accompanied by a selection of small custard tarts, mooncakes and sesame balls. They left the café with lots of chatter and laughter. Kaitlyn and Gibbo were given their meals. The hamburger looked nothing like the picture. The flat bread was not toasted or grilled, there was no meat in the centre, and the few bits and pieces of mainly lettuce looked as though it had been scraped off the floor. Gibbo looked at his plate, then up at Kaitlyn. 'What have we done wrong?'

'Nothing. We're an alien race'. They left dejected.

A part of them dreaded the day that they would get a knock on the door, but there were times when they thought, 'It's going to happen. Make it soon. We want to know our fate.' The knock came one morning, and they lost their home, the business and their three precious dogs, and were given their marching orders to board the bus. They still did not know where that bus was taking them. Gibbo was quiet and Kaitlyn cried the whole way. They disembarked at a ferry terminal and knew that their new home would be on an island.

# Sonia

**I can feel her strength. I can feel her grit**

Brought up in a country town in the Northern Territory, Sonia and her siblings became expert at hiding—even at night. Unfortunately, her mum couldn't hide. The kids begged their mother to leave, but she hung on inside that abusive relationship for a long time—possibly for a lack of an alternative.

Sonia was a teenager when the family quickly packed and departed before her father came home from the pub after work. Although her mother originally came from Sydney, they caught the bus to Adelaide. Sydney housing prices were way too high, so they took the more affordable option. They knew no one in Adelaide, but their mother ran straight into the welcoming arms of a cult in the Adelaide Hills. It was run by a chap called 'Salerno' and he aspired to create the 'ideal human environment'. Much like when she first met her husband, it was all fun in the beginning, and she became energised. She was surrounded by supporting friends. She had to sign the rental agreement form for her children, but she rarely visited and, as time went on, it became never. She wasn't allowed.

Sonia and her siblings knew nothing about the cult that was surrounded in secrecy, except that on the rare occasions they saw their mother, she was lifeless. All their hopes of her finding a pleasant lifestyle were dashed, and they worried. However, there was nothing they could say or do to extricate her from this strange lifestyle. No one knows why. Perhaps the police were getting too close to him—or the taxation office or angry family members who were not involved—but Salerno relocated to Queensland and their mother managed to come home. However, she wasn't the mother that they knew. Initially, she remained silent about the cult, but seemed to be permanently high wired, watchful and frightened. As time went by, she didn't say much, but the kids gleaned that Salerno lived like a prince and the women and children were his servants. Of course, the women had bedroom duties thrown in. It was a closed shop and anyone attempting to leave was immediately hunted down. Salerno seemed to have tentacles that covered a vast area. Even from a distance such as Queensland, her mother felt that she was under surveillance twenty-four hours a day.

When she returned to the rental property, Sonia's mother got a job stacking supermarket shelves at night and everyone contributed to the rent. Their mother was happy to pay it each fortnight and the kids were pleased with that decision as they thought it would help to improve her self-esteem and bolster her confidence. However, they got a shock when the real estate lady knocked on the door one evening to say that the rent was two months overdue. They could not believe it. Their mother was sending money to Salerno! She called it 'peace' money, but it created anything but in the household as they all had to work twice as hard to pay back the rent and, once again, get ahead. The kids were torn between resentment and love for the personable mother they once knew.

As far as the kids were concerned, there was only one person in that cult who achieved 'the ideal human environment'.

Sonia worked her way through UniSA and got her degree in graphic design. She worked for an Adelaide company and quickly gained the respect of her colleagues and customers. After four years, she was offered the chance to promote the Southern Vales wines and she jumped at the opportunity. During the pandemic, tourist numbers decreased, and it took many months for it to recover to a level well below pre-pandemic. Much like the Barossa Valley to the north, the wineries wanted to increase their tourist trade and formed a collective to advertise the region. Sonia was provided a self-contained cottage and was working on the promotional material when the invasion hit. She did not know where her city colleagues or family were relocated. The only people she had met were representatives from the wineries that were scattered over the Fleurieu Peninsula. After the invasion, she decided to drive into Adelaide to find her family. She knew that the fuel gauge was very low, and she did not have the money to refill, but it was worth a chance. It was a small car with good fuel economy, and she only had to travel forty-five kilometres. She got on to the main road and within five kilometres, met a roadblock. She was signalled over. She turned off the engine to save on fuel and waited for an official to come to her. She was asked for her work papers and the official seemed to be asking a question that she could not understand. He finally waved her through. She started up the engine and the fuel indicator had reached the end of the line. She knew there would be a little in reserve, but enough to get to Adelaide? She was determined to kick on. Another five kilometres went by, and she was pulled over again. Once again, she handed in her work papers but this time the official made it very clear that she had to turn around and go back from whence she came. He held his hand up to the traffic as she did a U-turn, dripping tears and with a fuel gauge showing empty. She limped back home. She was on her own.

# Hamish

*I'm not sure why I have feelings for this guy. He was born with a smile and, perhaps, a misguided optimism. He sees the good in the people around him. Perhaps it's because he enjoys my ocean so much, that I enjoy him.*

Following the invasion, Hamish McIntyre decided that he would not get involved in politics. He loved his country but recognised that the new Power Houses were already entrenched and nothing he could say or do would alter the situation. He would go with the flow.

He had given up trying to meet his friends after work or having a meal at the pub as the service was non-existent and you didn't know how long you had before an official tap on the chair said it was time to vacate. Added to the fact, no one could afford to dine out. He also knew that the clock was ticking down to stay in his small but beautifully positioned seaside unit.

Hamish knew from word of mouth that, when he got his eviction order, he would be allowed one travel bag. Unfortunately, he didn't have a large bag on wheels. He was saving for an overseas trip, which would necessitate a large bag, when the invasion struck. He had spent some of his reserves setting up his own physiotherapy practice and, although he was allowed to continue, the profits were immediately directed to a Power House account and he received the same wage allowance as everyone else. He rode his bicycle to work as the car had long run out of fuel. The only fuel stations that serviced the Aussies had a completely different colour system than the one they had known, and indecipherable instructions. No one knew whether they were putting in unleaded petrol or diesel. When the price rose substantially, many cars were abandoned to be collected by Power House trucks and hauled away.

With his bank account frozen, Hamish was trying to save for a travel bag, and he did not know how long he had to purchase one. The Aussies were allocated one 'Kmart' type shop and they had no way of knowing if the prices were commensurate with the other stores, but they had their doubts. Hamish joined the queue, but when he got into the store, the scant stock had the original price crossed out and the new the price with an increase of fifty per cent written in. He could not afford it. His 'hand luggage' sized bag would have to do. He packed his bag every day, adding and subtracting. He agonised over every article. How do you pack a hand luggage sized bag for an indeterminable length of time? He wanted to take as many books as possible and decided to put them into a small sports bag and tie them to the travel bag. He knew this did not conform to the 'one piece of luggage per person' but he would have a go. He decided that he would take his boots but string them together and wear then round his neck. He would have to tie his winter jacket round his waist. He didn't know if he would need sheets and if so, what size? He decided not to include them but put in the best towel he owned. He left space for his bathers as he was going to use as much free time in the sea as possible before his eviction orders. He knew he would have to forego the goggles and flippers. He took one family photo out of the frame and put it into a 'lock-it' bag. The travel bag bulged and threatened to split the seams. The sports bag was weighted with books.

The weekdays were busy. Word of mouth spread quickly, and he had officials walking in and, by their very presence, had to take priority. They had the right to order out any Aussies sitting in the waiting room. After treatment, they departed with a curt nod to him and without paying. His former customers had to wait until the end of the day. Pre-invasion, he had loved his evening swim after work, but now he was getting home late at night and had to be content with listening to the waves.

The knock came early one morning. He was greeted by two armed guards. One handed him a piece of paper with an 'X' on the map, marking the bus stop where he was to present himself. He had four hours to vacate. He had no idea where he was being sent. Hamish wandered around the unit, soaking up the layout so he could revisit it in his mind. He gazed out to sea for the last time, put his bathers into the bag, strapped them together, donned a cap, and walked out the door.

Although it was still morning, the sun quickly latched onto his body. He had a five kilometre walk but had countless stops to readjust the boot straps that were cutting the back of his neck, feeling more like razor blades as time went on. He also had to realign the sports bag that frequently threatened to topple over. There was plenty of company as men, women and children with eyes only on the road, slowly snaked their possessions along the way. Some adults had babies strapped to their bodies while dragging two suitcases that were too big for the toddlers trundling behind. Whether intentionally or not, there was plenty of debris, particularly children's shoes, scattered along the way. Some people, including Hamish, picked them up and wore them round their wrists to hopefully reunite them with their owners later. There were queues for the buses, which had been stripped of seats but had rows of straps, hanging like nooses from the ceiling. Crying children had to hold onto parents as they were jostled the one-hundred-and-twenty-kilometre journey to the seaport that was previously called 'Jervis Bay'. At long last, they all knew their destination—Kangaroo Island—or as it's now called, 'Daishiu Dao'.

Upon arrival, Hamish joined another long queue in what used to be the ferry car park. He stayed there for two days and wished that he had brought just one packet of biscuits. The Power House officials handed out bottles of water that had to be shared down the line. Hamish couldn't see the point of joining in the conversations protesting the treatment. 'We treated our animals better than this', 'wouldn't wish this on my worst enemy', 'this is worse than watching my footy team lose', 'having the mother-in-law stay for a year is a romp in the park compared to this', and so on infinitum.

*I could feel the anger that was prolific in those early days rapidly dissipating. These people were too tired and mentally beaten by what they thought was such a long period of time waiting for their fate. No matter what they said, there was not one person who was not scared of the future.*

Hamish did not hear a voice calling for a mass uprising. He did hear a quiet voice behind him. 'Whinging isn't going to help. I think the First Nations people would see our treatment as 'normal.' He turned round, nodded and introduced himself. A young guy shook his hand and said, 'Silo.' Hamish couldn't conceal his puzzlement and asked where the name originated. 'Well, I was a bit of a smart arse at school and always had my hand up to either answer the teachers' questions or to ask them to qualify the correctness of what came out of their mouths. I think it was my Grade 3 teacher who dubbed me 'Silo' as he reckoned my brain was a storehouse of information—mostly flawed. As I hated my real name, I refused to be known as anything else. (Hamish never did find out Silo's real name – it was Theodore). After the invasion, the Power Houses didn't have a problem listing me as 'Silo'—less paperwork for them – so now it's official.'

Hamish was happy to have company as it had been a harrowing past few days. They shared their experiences of being evicted. Silo showed Hamish a digital camera, one of the first to come on to the market, that he had brought with him. 'Yes. I know it's useless, as I cannot load any photos on to a computer or even get hard copy. Being almost vintage, I thought it may be of little interest to the Power House officials. So far so good. I just hope my luck holds when we get to our destination.' He told Hamish that he had been keen on photography for as long as he could remember and was rapt when he snagged a position as a photojournalist for a South Australian newspaper.

'I loved the work out in the field and then firing back to head office the most newsworthy images. Of course, there were some heartbreaking scenes that play on your mind for a long time, but there were also many events that were pure joy.' As they inched their way in the queue, Silo recalled in detail the shark attack that almost cost a young surfer his life. He told Hamish how one of four young surfers had paddled back to catch one more wave. His mates headed back to shore, but one turned round to watch his mate and screamed for help. All of the surfers turned round and headed back to try to help their friend and watched the great white shark circling the sea water that had turned red. One of the lads headed straight for the shark, then paddled as hard as he could for shore in an attempt to divert it away from its prey. He raced to his mobile phone, dialled triple zero and screamed for help. The media was always prowling the emergency calls and Silo was immediately despatched to the scene, arriving within minutes of the ambulance. As he was parking his car on top of the cliff, he watched as the youngsters tied their T-shirts round the top of their mate's arm, which had been severely mauled. The ambulance medicos were racing down the rickety wooden steps with a stretcher. It seemed as though the lads instinctively knew that they had to stop the flow of blood. They also knew from the mangled mess that, if the young surfer survived, he would only ever have one arm. Silo was in awe of the actions that these young guys had just carried out. At the age of fourteen, they had saved a life.

Hamish could remember the photo of the young surfer on the front page of the newspaper and the videos that flashed across the screen on every television news service that evening. As it captured a great deal of attention, the media followed the progress of the young lad's recovery. His friends received bravery awards. He loved the sea, and Silo's story not only made the media coverage come to life, but helped for a short time to settle his wariness of his future. Thinking of others overcoming adversity helped him to feel more optimistic of his own future.

They finally got to the head of the queue to board the ferry. Power House officials went through every item in their bags and both were waved on with a barking order that they didn't understand. The official handled the camera with a perplexed look on his face and after what seemed minutes, handed it back.

Silo heaved a sigh of relief. Hamish couldn't believe that his baggage passed muster.

Any thoughts of sitting in a chair for the forty-five-minute journey of the sixteen-kilometre boat crossing were quickly dispelled. The lower decks where the cars, caravans and motorhomes used to go were used to shunt the packed-in human occupants. For all anyone knew, the upper decks with chairs were empty. The ferry was crossing in the morning, but the occupants had had a sleepless night lying on the tarmac with their baggage for a pillow. The atmosphere was filled with the wails of children of varying ages who were not only hungry and thirsty, but extremely tired.

Silo and Hamish were jammed together. Hamish told him that the only time he had been newsworthy, was at the tender age of four. 'My sister, Felix, who was six at the time, and I wandered off to play in a partly built house but got lost returning home. I can remember wandering the streets with leaden legs and being frightened of being lost forever. And now, from hindsight, I know Felix must have felt the same despite putting on an older sister's brave face. A search party found us but there were repercussions. Mum's imagination had me drowned in a channel of water, so she enrolled us in swimming classes, which I loved. The flip side was that Dad built a high fence with a gate across the back yard to keep us in. Looking back, it didn't take long before we could open the gate. Although, back then, it must have seemed forever'. Silo grinned. 'I'm with you. I've never liked being hemmed in. My fear is that when we get to the island, I'll be given a job in a factory. The thought totally wrecks my brain.' Hamish agreed.

When the ferry arrived at its destination, the departure was slow and arduous. Once again, in a tunnel shed, all luggage was thoroughly searched. The reason for this was beyond anyone's imagination. Once again, Silo had to watch on as his belongings were scrutinised. He saw the Power House official handle the camera as if it was a foreign object. The puzzled official finally put it back in the pile of possessions and waved Silo on. He could breathe again.

Hamish had to remove the strap and his luggage became two. The official looked darkly up at him before removing the books. He threw the sports bag under a trestle table. He removed every item from the travel bag and Hamish had serious doubts that he could repack again. The official waved his arm to say, 'repack' then he pointed to the sports bag with the same gesture. Hamish fetched the bag and crammed his books into it as quickly as he could. It took three goes to get everything back into his travel bag and he was handed a dated card:

Hamish McIntyre
Block D
Building Site 232 – 7.00 am

Silo was waiting outside the tunnel. His card directed him to Block C. The blocks were set five hundred metres apart, the first being ten kilometres from the ferry terminal. Hamish felt sorry for the folks allocated the end blocks as the two of them wheeled their luggage down the road. They passed families juggling travel bags and carrying crying children and knew that everyone on the road was not only tired but extremely dispirited and anxious about the future that awaited them. Even the youngest child seemed in a state of alarm.

When he got to Block D, Hamish was confronted by a large room with beds in rows along two walls with a passage down the middle. Either side of the doorway to the kitchen area, laundry and communal bathroom was a line of wardrobes. He hung his few clothes up and found an empty drawer in which to put the few possessions that he had brought. There was no one in the room as they had not come home from work. He went through to the kitchen and laundry. My new home, he thought with resignation.

On the building site, Hamish was quickly accepted for his quiet manner, quick retorts and infectious laugh. He was disappointed that Silo was not working on the same site and didn't know until later that day that he was being employed as a painter on a building, which the Power Houses were refurbishing for their own use. That night Silo told him, 'I have no idea why I got that job as I have never touched a paint brush in my life'. Hamish could sympathise as he had not been near a building site since the age of four. However, they both knew that it was a better option as neither of them wanted to work in a factory.

Hamish gravitated to larrikin company–the likes of Gibbo, who collected people with his down-to-earth manner and irreverent humour. Hamish didn't know it at the time but they were on the same ferry going over.

On the building site, Hamish introduced himself and Gibbo immediately shouted out, 'Hey Beags, Tabasco, Tarantula, Presto, and Watsy–meet Macca.' He found out that Gibbo was married to Kaitlyn, who he called 'Kats'. Hamish asked if he had kids, 'No mate, we had dogs. You can train dogs,' Gibbo replied with a grin. Although they were all new to each other, it didn't take long for Hamish to make friends, and Gibbo escalated the process. The island was large, but it was a quick transition for everyone to get to know each other from the blocks. Gibbo did not always remember everyone's names, but he chatted to people in his block on the way to work, queuing up for shopping, in the laundry, hanging clothes on the line, and at work. The population would expand in the future when more blocks would be ready for occupation. Gibbo quickly amassed a group of friends and Hamish was welcomed to join them. Even though they were all new to the island, Gibbo quickly became an old hand. He despised the 'GRAPS' with a passion as well as perceived sympathisers. But then he wasn't the only one. Hamish stayed out of that one.

# Jia Chen

For many years, home for Jia was in the city of Chengdu. His parents deeply believed in the ethics of Taoism, which advocated compassion, loyalty and honesty. Being the only child of parents who believed that the earth and human beings were bonded in a mutual understanding of preservation, gave Jia a background of simple living in harmony with nature. Jia's father was a policeman who was known for his compassion for the victim and his dogged persistence of tracking the perpetrator. Jia's mother worked for a British clothing factory. She packaged and sent off internet orders. Her employers gave her the opportunity to learn English from a private tutor and all three in the family attended. There was competition in the household and 'English homework' was often extended as Jia competed with his parents to learn and advance. He was not yet at school before he decided to think in English. His neighbourhood friends were perplexed at these strange words coming from their friend. When the year's tuition finished, Jia's father paid for another private tutor so that they could retain and extend their vocabulary.

Jia's world of school, friendships, favourite spicy food, and a comfortable knowledge of his surroundings was tipped upside down when, nearing his final years of school, his father was sent to England to work in the embassy. He never found out why this transfer to another country took place but was aware that his father would often stop talking when he came into the room and remained tight lipped about his day at work. Adjusting to life in England was a completely new world for the whole family and Jia would never forget his first day at high school, mainly due to a string of highly embarrassing moments. He was surprised at the diverse ethnicity and the different speech patterns of the students despite the fact that they were speaking the same language. He was shocked that the highly praised English he spoke in Chengdu took a battering as the students chatted among themselves or directly to him. They spoke so fast! He was not surprised to be sent to a special class to improve his grammar and resolved to work hard at home to get to classroom standard. He found the school lunch difficult, eating a pasta dish with a fork while trying to understand the chatter around him. He floundered on the sports field, dressed in his classroom uniform while everyone else was in sports gear. He felt so obvious and foolish among his peers. A long list of embarrassments became a blur and at the end of the day he consoled himself with the one good thing that had happened—he had met Bridie. He was walking along the corridor for the last lesson of the day, looking for his classroom and obviously looking lost, when this girl came beside him and asked what class he was looking for. He showed her the textbook and she said she was going to the same class. She sat next to him, which gave him reassurance, and after the class she showed him where the library was located. Bridie was born in Ireland, and she told him as much as she could about her country as they made their way out of the school gates. He realised later when he heard her chatting to a group of friends, that initially Bridie slowed her speech down and Jia felt more relaxed being able to understand and converse. Jia loved looking at Bridie's eyes. They were so expressive. They lit up and seemed to smile at him. At home in Chengdu, he mixed with his schoolboy friends and was amazed that he could feel so comfortable with this Irish lass. She didn't hesitate to introduce him to her large group of friends. His parents were astonished at how quickly the phone rang for Jia on weekends and he was asked to join in on outings. Jia worked hard during the week and was thrilled when he got into one of the top English classes after a few months. He felt more relaxed understanding the repartee that flowed around him. He was even able to, fairly tidily, eat pasta at lunch time and converse at the same time! He was blending and over time, his memories of his home in Chengdu began to fade. Jia often wondered what his life would have been like if he had not had the luck of meeting Bridie. He guessed—lonely.

One night at the dinner table, his father simply said, 'We're going home.' Worse was to follow—they were not going back to Chengdu but were being transferred to Shanghai. Jia's world once again was tipped upside down. He was in a state of utter confusion. It would not be so bad if he could go back to his hometown, but to completely start again in a strange city was overwhelmingly horrifying. The next day at school he was wracked with worry and did not hear any of the conversations around him. Bridie noticed and suggested that they meet in the library after school. It was rare for Jia to be with Bridie by himself and he was grateful for the opportunity. Bridie tried to reassure him. 'You will be able to find a career in your own country, perhaps teaching English, and return one day to England. With your sharp brain, who knows Jia, you may become the prime minister. That's one thing about this country—they will take anyone!,' she teased. She took his hand and looked him in the eye. 'My Irish intuition says that you will be back.'

The end of the year was rapidly approaching, and Jia was honoured to accompany Bridie to the class formal dinner/dance. He was taken aback when he entered the hall to see a large banner over the top of the stage:

## GOODBYE JIA AND GOOD LUCK

# The Ferry

*Although they didn't know it at the time, it was on that ferry crossing to Kangaroo Island that was the start of people coming together. Despite their anxieties, I could feel a tiny grain of optimism.*

It was on the ferry trip that Gibbo started a friendship group. In typical style, in that hull, he called out, 'Shit, isn't this fun. I've always wanted to sail the seas in an upright position and now, at last, I can fulfill my dreams.' He went on to talk about the delights of going to an exotic island. The guards were too far away to shut him up. Other people started to chat around him. One guy introduced himself as Ken Truscott and retorted, 'Yeah, I reckon there will be luxury hotels and hot and cold running topless barmaids delivering cocktails at all times of the day and night by the resort pool. Can't wait.' 'Now with a hot sarcastic sense of humour like that, we can't fucking call you "Ken"–that's Barbie doll's boyfriend. Hey, everyone. Meet 'Tabasco'. The name stuck. A roar of laughter came from behind and Gibbo turned around to look up to a tall, gangly guy. 'So, what's your nickname?' he asked. 'Well ...' came the reply ... '... when I got to high school, I had a huge growth spurt and the kids reckoned I was all legs, so they called me "Spider"'. 'You look more like a tarantula to me,' Gibbo responded. 'Hey guys ...' he shouted to no one in particular ... 'Meet Tarantula.' Another name that stuck.

Kaitlyn was jammed up against Sonia and they talked about what they had packed, which was a hot topic. They had heard about people trying to pack bags with armed soldiers watching their every move. 'It's so hard to think when someone is pointing a machine gun at you.' They had also heard about parents having to shush their youngsters as the soldiers could get heavy handed when agitated by crying children. They both agreed that putting enough items into one bag to last four seasons for an indeterminable length of time, was extremely onerous. Sonia described the aqua leather jacket that she had bought after months of saving, that reluctantly had to be left behind. The girls agreed that shoes, being so bulky, had to be multi-purpose. Even though it was a hot day, they both wore boots but had sneakers tied together and wrapped round their necks. Everything from sheets, towels, toiletries, clothes, memorabilia had to be jam packed into that one suitcase.

Kaitlyn, much to Sonia's amusement, described Gibbo's attempt at packing. Most of the suitcase space was taken up with football trophies, medals, footy guernsey, footy photos, footy stats, and footy boots. When Kaitlyn queried his rationale, the response was, 'Kats, we won't be getting Pro Harts on the wall, we'll need these to uplift the décor.' 'You can't dry yourself with a footy trophy,' she retorted.

'I was hard pressed to convince him to be a tad more practical and he doesn't know it but will soon find out—I repacked his bag,' Sonia laughed.

Sonia had a ready laugh and Kaitlyn often mused about this first meeting when she said, 'You must have had a very happy childhood, Sonia.' She never did work out why she made that comment when she had just met this lady. Sonia looked at her hard and replied, 'My childhood was fraught with anxiety due to my father's alcoholism and violence. When I was fifteen, he came home and went for me. I backed off and was jammed against a low cupboard. Dad was unsteady on his feet, and I pushed myself up onto the cupboard. As he got close enough to grab me, I kicked as hard as I could. I kicked him where it really, really hurts. He backed off and he never touched me again. I realised then that he was a coward. Us kids put so much pressure on Mum to leave and take us with her. She did eventually and we headed for Adelaide. I didn't see my dad again. He missed out on seeing his kids reach adulthood.

He became a grandfather by my other siblings, but he never knew it. The bottle was his only friend, and he died a lonely old man.

Anyway, that's enough of me and my dodgy background. Where did you meet Gibbo?'

Kaitlyn told her that one of her uni mates suggested going to a footy match. 'The idea appealed as it was cheap to get in and I'd only ever seen it played on TV. I was looking for a break as I'd just finished a lengthy assignment. The girls joked about all those testosterone-filled guys in their tight shorts and put up their hands to join in. Kaitlyn's parents had bought her a car, so they piled in and went to see the 'Panthers' play 'The Eagles'. They got there early so that they could get close to the action. It was halfway into the first quarter that Gibbo spied the girls, particularly the one with long, dark hair. He played to impress and at the end of the day won 'Man of the Match'. He told her later that he was chomping at the bit to talk to her, but had no opportunity to make contact as the coach was busy giving his motivational spiel at half time. As soon as the match finished, he rushed over just as the girls were leaving. 'We're having a few beers at the Port Noarlunga pub to celebrate our win and would sure like some company. If you would like to join us, you'd be more than welcome.' Without waiting for a reply, he gave a huge smile and said, 'See you at the pub.' He waved and then rushed into the change room.

'We got close to not making it as we thought he said the 'Noarlunga pub' and went round in circles before deciding to give up. One of the girls suggested to clock 'Port Noarlunga' into Google Maps and we were finally on our way.

Gibbo told me he nearly died of disappointment when we were not there as the team had to chant their winning song, listen to another spiel from the coach, shower, dress, and then rush off. He was standing with his group of mates at the bar, watching the door and vaguely listening to the team congratulating him and recalling the win, when the girls walked in. He waited for me to walk through the door. However, I went back to the car to make sure it was locked. Not knowing that I was the driver, he later told me he thought he was going to die of disappointment. When I walked through the door, he reckons he took off so fast that he almost tore a hammy. I think I fell in love with his carefree manner and sense of humour in the pub that evening. I had never met anyone like him before. That was the start of our relationship.

'Did your parents fall in love with him too?'

Kaitlyn laughed and explained why her parents and Gibbo were poles apart. 'They couldn't understand him,' she said. 'Mum and Dad took life very seriously. They could not understand how I could fall in love with someone who had left school at the first opportunity as they valued higher education above everything else. They mixed with academics. They had very formal dinner parties where they drank a limited amount of top-notch wine and discussed world affairs, scientific theories, classical music, opera, and literature among a whole range of other topics. There was never any banter, and I cannot remember anyone ever telling a joke. They probably did, but it would have taken them out of their comfort zone.

I'll never forget one New Year's Eve. I was about fourteen years old when they hosted a dinner party. They hired a string quartet to perform upon their guests' arrival. They put all their energies into making it a fun night and thought it would be a hoot to have a quiz with the theme of 'Shakespearean Plays'. I don't think the party lasted until midnight.'

Sonia laughed and asked, 'You were going to uni when you met Gibbo. What were you studying?'

'Business Management.' My reasoning was that I didn't know anything about a business, either large or small, and it sounded "exotic". My parents put up with this choice thinking that once I had that degree under my belt, I would branch out to a higher level. I can remember the words, 'Bachelor's degree in international finance' being mooted. Poor Mum and Dad, they didn't envisage me being in reception at a small landscape and paving company.' Kaitlyn paused and looked at Sonia with misty eyes. 'Now I cannot imagine my parents labouring for foreign Power Houses.'

Sonia commiserated as she also did not know where her mum was sent or how she was managing her life under a new regime.

She didn't know Gibbo, but the little that she had seen, she could understand that his in-laws must have thought he was from another planet. Kaitlyn confirmed this suspicion.

'Gibbo could have been talking Japanese as far as my parents were concerned as they didn't understand landscape paving, pubs, cars, footy, or his jocular bullshit manner. After a match, particularly if they had won, Gibbo would be enthusiastically describing his ball skills and would say something like, 'I grabbed a high screamer off the enemy's back on to my pecs from outside the fifty-metre mark and absolutely smoked it.' I had to explain that he had kicked a goal, but of course my parents had 'why didn't he say so?' written all over their faces. They often used to look at me with blank expressions as though I was an interpreter. Poor Gibbo tried so hard at times to be formal, but it sounded so false and that made everyone feel more uncomfortable.

Kaitlin told her all about the business where she and Gibbo worked but didn't mention the border collies as that was too painful. Even before the ferry docked, Kaitlin called her 'Sunny - just like your personality', and the friendship flourished.

*I felt the weight of people on that ferry. Through all the anxieties, I could feel the beginnings of friendship. I also felt the youngsters—they were not wracked with the same pain—they had their parents for support. Like all young ones, they were a mixture of fear and adventure. I particularly felt two young girls.*

Lucy's grandparents came from Cambodia and were placed in a detention centre in Sydney in the mid-1980s. They did not know whether they would be allowed to stay in Australia or how long they would be held in detention. The invasion brought home to Lucy all the stories her mother had told her. She felt as though she was walking in their footsteps and felt that if they could survive and come out the other side full of life's wonders, then she could too. She was only twelve years old.

Maddie was the same age, and on that packed ferry, the two girls recognised each other from the Power House school that they had attended prior to their eviction. They traded stories of the schools that they had attended prior to the invasion. They swapped stories of the sports that they had loved playing and the ones that had been forced upon them. Lucy asked Maddie if that was her real name and was told that it was short for Madeline. 'I don't know why they bothered to write 'Madeline' on a piece of paper, as they called me Maddie before I even popped out.' Lucy laughed and told Maddie that when her grandparents were in a detention centre, the television constantly showed an old American comedy called, I love Lucy, and they loved it. They would call out, 'Here's Lucy' and laugh their heads off. It was probably the only fun they had. When I was born, Mum and Dad named me so that when my grandparents came to visit, they would say '…and here's Lucy.' It always put a smile on their faces. I reckon I'm the favourite.'

They ran through the television programs they enjoyed the most, the games that they had played on their electronic devices, the bikes that they had to leave behind. Maddie told Lucy that she didn't have a bike, but a 'Trek', and went on to explain, 'I got my first bike from Father Christmas when I was five and it was Dad who said, "Oh look, it's a Trek." I think he said that before I had ripped off the wrapping paper.' Lucy laughed. Every bike I had after that, it didn't matter what brand, I called 'Trek'. They both loved skateboarding but had gone to different parks in the Fleurieu. Lucas, her younger brother, was cranky, as he didn't have a companion, but Lucy shrugged him off. They talked about teachers that they liked and the ones that they didn't. Maddie asked Lucy what her parents did for a living and was told rather sheepishly, 'They were both teachers.'

'Oh, you poor thing,' was the response, but Lucy just shrugged, 'They were okay.'

Maddie told Lucy that she really wanted to be an actress, which was something that she would never have admitted in the past for fear of being ridiculed. Lucy didn't have any long-term ambitions. She was happy to take each day as it comes and disregarded the future as something that would not affect her. They both knew that they had limited time left at school before they would be out in the workforce. They also knew that they had limited time to learn the official language.

When they got to Kangaroo Island and settled into school life, Lucy, with her optimistic outlook, became a mentor for Maddie, who had become quiet and withdrawn—the very opposite of the kid who had previously loved to entertain and tell jokes. Lucy told Maddie about her grandparents, often exaggerating the perils that they had faced fleeing a brutal regime and surviving the over-crowded leaking tub of a boat. 'Gee, man,' she would often quip. 'If they could survive, then we can too.' It did help to anchor Maddie.

# Jia Chen

The feeling of his life spiralling out of control continued when Jia left London for Shanghai. He assumed that he would go to university and major in languages. He also assumed that he would be teaching English. Instead, his father organised a career for him in the police force. This was not alien to Jia's code of ethics but was not his first choice.

As he progressed through the ranks, he became aware of corruption within the force. Some officers were living beyond their means and one, Liu Li Jun, had a reputation as an addicted gambler, but still managed to maintain a high standard of living. His counterparts viewed his actions with suspicion.

When Jia woke up to the news that his country and their ally had disabled the Australian government and were claiming the land as their own, he was thrilled and disturbed. He knew the benefits—more land for his people and rich resources. However, he could not erase the thought that his government was guilty. He conceded that they did not take the land by force but stole it. His fond memories of England—an ally to this southern land—also made it difficult to justify. The papers were full of the news. They described how the people of the Southern Land lacked morals, honour and history. They pledged to respect the First Nations people as the true inhabitants of this land and that they would 're-educate the 18th century invaders.' They declared the land be called 'Nan Tudi' and the word 'Australia' never appeared in any form of media. 'This part of the world belongs to Asia,' screamed the media headlines. 'And it is our rightful duty to ensure that it remains among our Asian friends.'

'Nan Tudi' was discussed at length in the police force as many officers had already been given their orders that they would be sent over to this land to retain law and order. They were also told to act with honour and integrity. It was a surprise to all when Liu Li Jun received his notice of transfer, which caused an undertone of mirth in the ranks–'law, order, honour, and integrity–Lui Li Jun? –definitely not!

During Covid, Jia had had a hard time working to enforce the rules of confinement as well as doing his job of criminal investigations. He was regarded by his peers as someone who would rapidly advance in the ranks and having his father as mentor aided his career.

No one was surprised when Jia was asked to go to the south of Nan Tudi to oversee operations. He arrived by plane, was taken to a hotel for rest and was debriefed the next day. Jai spent time touring the streets in an armoured car. He came to know the system. He knew huge numbers of people were being evicted from their homes for re-education. He witnessed the long queues for buses, and he knew that these people did not know their fate. Some of the heavy handedness that he witnessed made him feel uncomfortable. He was told, under no circumstances to speak English or fraternise with anyone deemed a candidate for re-education. That way, he was able to understand if there was any talk of retaliation and report back. His job–law and order at any cost.

Jia had not long settled into his new home when he got his orders from the mainland that he was to head an investigation into a heinous crime committed on an island, called 'Daishiu Dao'. Jia selected Yi-Jun to join him, as he was not only good company, but they could practice their English speaking in private. They quickly delved into their pasts, and both felt as though they had known each other a lifetime.

# The Big Bash

The Power Houses declared a public holiday for some significant imperial historical mainland event. It wasn't until one of the smarter kids found out at school that the rest of the island knew about it. Gibbo and Kaitlyn swung into action to organise a community cricket match. Gibbo's first thought was footy, but Kaitlyn talked him out of that one. It simply wasn't practical. At first it looked like a bit of a fizzer as everyone was too tired to get excited about a game of cricket, but Gibbo and Kaitlin revved up the old juices and the anticipation accelerated. Gibbo enlisted the aid of the wrinklies, who worked in Power Houses' kitchens as kitchen hands and tended Power Houses' gardens, to keep everyone informed and delegate tasks. Within a few days, a program had been set up and pretty much everyone wanted to get involved. Along with everyone else in the group, Hamish had an after-hours job. He put up notices advertising the 'Big Bash Cricket' on all the corridor fridges in every block. The Power House officials tore them down–but not quickly enough. The kids at school passed on the message of a pending cricket match. For the first time since arriving on the island, there was a buzz in the air. Collectively, everyone contributed a little kangaroo mince and flour, which the wrinklies turned into mini pies. Buying tomato sauce from Foodies was impossible, so a BBQ sauce made from tomato purée and soy sauce was a good alternative. A version of 'Lamington' was made using stale cake and packets of jelly and coconut, so they were various colours. Drinks comprised of cordial and water.

The day of the cricket match saw a huge gathering at the building site car park for The Power House Officials. Of course, this was out of bounds for the Aussies but the Power House officials were busy enjoying their public holiday at one of the island's many beaches (also out of bounds for 'big feet'). The Gibbo team had put out bins painted with stumps and bails. Although Silo had not met Gibbo, he heard that paint was needed and managed to commandeer some to pass on via Hamish. Silo knew that punishment would be swift if he was caught with pilfered paint but decided it was worth the risk. Anything to break up the monotony of the working week to provide a molecule of fun for one day was worth the anticipation of a day of relaxation.

A pitch had been measured out and painted. Everyone came carrying the Power House issued iron backed chair. The rules were simple. Every player—man, woman or child—was part of either a 'Gibbo' or 'Bagsy' team. If a bowler got a wicket, he handed over the ball to the next person. If a player got more than ten runs, he was declared 'out'. A catch could be taken from a ball that had bounced once. This meant that up to fifty people from each side could take part. The kids loved it. For the first time since the pandemic and invasion, people could relax and forget about the daily grind. Hamish introduced Silo to his working group, who accepted his name without raising an eyebrow. Gibbo was more interested in what he was carrying. 'I know what it looks like, as my old man had one, but what the fuck did you bring that for?' Silo explained his previous job and that he couldn't cope without a camera, no matter how useless. 'Well ...' replied Gibbo, '... that makes you the official photographer.'

Gibbo's mob was in full flight, slinging off at the opposition. The umpires were copping a lot of flak, and the scorers were accused of not being able to count. Hamish went in to bat and made a duck. One bounce and into the hands of one of the thirty fielders that kept the batter walking back to his or her chair. As he was walking back to his seat, Hamish thought about his childhood friend, Freddie, who never walked without a ball in his hand, and swung his arm to imitate a bowler. He couldn't help but wonder what happened to Freddie after the invasion. There was a round of applause for his effort when he returned to his seat, particularly from the opposition. Gibbo shook his hand. 'Well done, Macca!' And he swung a friendly arm around his shoulder. Hamish was part of the 'Bagsy' team. Silo took a photo of the two of them in this pose with huge smiles on their faces. Kaitlyn, who he had met beforehand, came up to Hamish, threw her arms around his shoulders, tousled his hair, and also congratulated him on his efforts.

**Oh, oh—I can feel negative emotions. I feel friendship from her, but I feel that old jealousy bubbling from him.**

Although his team was fielding, the car park was covered with eager players. Hamish took the opportunity to sit with Tabasco, Watsy and Silo and they reminisced about their former lives. They asked why he was called 'Tabasco' as they were not aware of the conversation with Gibbo on the ferry going over. He replied that with a name like Trescott, he was known at school as 'Scotty'. Now he was the only one with a lengthened nickname and didn't mind being called Tabasco. 'It sounds hot,' he told them.

Silo looked thoughtful. 'Trescott. Wasn't that the name of the newsreader on TV? Any relation?' Tabasco got a sheepish look on his face. 'Yeah, that was my old man.' Silence filled the air as they sat there in thought. 'Yeah, I know. If you didn't read about it, you would have seen it on TV. I was only twelve at the time when my life, as I knew it, went up in smoke. When Dad was not at the television station, he did a lot of emceeing at social functions. He was often out at night. He would get out of bed late in the morning, so that when we were school age, we only glimpsed him on the weekend. In the early days, Mum would go with him to these night-time social events, but after us kids were born, she only occasionally accompanied him. I think Mum was always aware of Dad doing 'extra-curricular' duties, but when it got too blatant and the media showed pictures of Dad and 'Hannah' in various romantic embraces, Mum went ballistic and Dad promised that he would never so much as look at another woman. And he kept his promise–for a short while. Dad went back to his old tricks that once again got the media attention and Mum ordered him out of the house. At the time, us kids were caught right in the middle of a very bitter wrangle, but the worse part of it was, everyone knew about their separation because of Dad's profile. I copped a lot of flak at school and became very quiet and sullen. The teachers were sympathetic, but I couldn't spend recess, lunch and the walk home with them.'

'Yeah, that's the trouble with high profile jobs,' Silo sympathised. 'I knew a lot of television personalities through my work in the media and they could easily come into the firing line by just making a flippant comment at the wrong time or in the wrong place. Although, your dad does sound a bit of a pants man. How did you cope with that?'

'Well, although I really didn't know my father, I could understand his behaviour to a point. He was part of a huge social network and was out and about day and night. He reckons he had the women coming on strong–that he fought them off. We know from what happened in court that that was not always the case. In fact, a whole bunch of them said the opposite.'

'What about your mum? How did she survive the public attention?' asked Hamish.

'Mum was a journalist with a newspaper. That's how she met Dad in the early days. She enjoyed the social life and recognition that went with being 'Mrs Truscott'. She was 'famous' among her friends, acquaintances and the people she met along the way. It was incredible in one way what happened, as my parents always got on so well, teasing each other in a playful way. She had always endured his infidelities stoically. But when the media continued flaunting Dad and now Tania's (the latest) intimate embraces on several occasions, and accompanied it with articles and photographs, Mum could no longer ignore. She took him to court. The media also went there for the ride so that all the dirt and name calling became public. I don't know how long it went on for but as a kid, it seemed like forever.'

'Gees, Tabasco, I reckon it would be tough to have your parents split up but for it to be on show for everybody to see and cast an opinion, must have been a living hell,' chipped in Silo and everyone agreed. I can remember all the media cover but can't remember the outcome. What happened? Was it resolved in court?

'Well,' continued Tabasco, 'public opinion was with Dad, probably because people felt they knew him, seeing him on TV five nights a week. Poor Mum felt discarded like an old toy. Then she pulled out the big guns. Looking back, I think it was to ensure that she got custody of us kids. She accused Dad of molesting Lindy, my younger sister. Can you imagine what that was like spread over the paper and TV? Like me, Lindy had already withdrawn into her shell, but now she was clearly suffering. She was only ten years old. Lindy was interviewed by the police and had to have a medical examination. The latter was inconclusive. I still to this day do not know the truth of the matter, as Lindy, through love, fear, bribery or erased memory, remained tight lipped. Her mental health has always been fragile, and I think about her heaps. Dad was taken off the newsreader desk and given behind-the-scenes work, which he hated. Without the fun of the social life, Tania (and all the others) quickly disappeared. So, to answer your question, my family remained fractured.'

After a long silence, Tabasco went on to say that one of the reasons he was drawn to Gibbo was his new name–far removed from Trescott. Added to the fact that Gibbo couldn't give a toss about anyone's background. He takes you as you are. They all agreed, and the subject drifted to Gibbo. They discussed his kind nature, lack of inhibitions and seemingly carefree spirit. But they worried about him. 'Gibbo's not one for rules and this island has more rules than ... than ... what's that golf course in England that made up all those rules?'

'St Andrew's. But it's in Scotland,' replied Silo.

'Yep, that's the one. Reckon this island has more rules than that book.'

'Unless of course the word 'rule' is between Aussie and Football,' chipped in Watsy. He went on: 'If anyone comes foul of the authorities, it's going to be Gibbo. He doesn't like rules and this island is coming up with more every day.'

Gibbo wandered over with his chair and slouched next to Watsy. 'What are you guys on about?' he asked.

'We were talking about you, Gibbo, and how you don't care much for rules. Gibbo grinned. 'No.' Then, after a pause, '...unless they are about Aussie Rules Footy' and wondered why they all cracked up.

'Hey Gibbo, you haven't had a bat, and we need a captain's knock,' a voice called from the field. Gibbo laughed and told his friends that he was probably the worst player on the field. 'This game's too bloody slow for my liking.' But he went off with a wave and a cheer from the spectators.

Kaitlyn, Patsy and Sonia walked past. 'Come and join us,' called Tabasco. They were on the building site all day and in the bullroom at night. They were hanging out for some female company. Kaitlyn introduced Sonia and she sat on the chair vacated by Gibbo. Watsy found chairs for the girls and for the first time since arriving on the island, they could sit in the sun together, watch a very haphazard cricket match, and chat.

**I've felt their constant fear but now I feel the breath of their tongues. They haven't forgotten the future—it is always with them. Today they are talking of the past and I can feel camaraderie.**

They traded previous occupations. Sonia explained why she was working in the Fleurieu Peninsula at the time of the invasion. She did not know where her city colleagues or family were relocated. 'Perhaps, on reflection, I should have headed straight back to Adelaide at the beginning of the invasion ... but then I would probably not be here now and wouldn't have met you guys,' she said with a smile. Hamish thought she was talking directly to him, but then, so did everyone else. Sonia had a knack of making everyone feel special.

They looked at Watsy. 'What were your parents like?' they asked. 'Well ... they were pretty regular, but they loved to spend. Whatever money came into the household, was spent ... some prematurely. I'll never forget when Dad heard he had got a midyear bonus. I can't remember the sum, but they figured it would well and truly cover a forty-foot boat with two outboard motors. It had a cabin downstairs with a shower and toilet, small kitchen and outdoor dining. Dad was as proud as punch. He tied boogey boards to the boat and us kids had a whale of a time on our tummies riding the waves. It was terrific. However, the pandemic hit, and the company privately told management that the media and shareholders would be onto them if they handed out bonuses at a time when people were being laid off work in large numbers. The bonus was cancelled to a future date that, as far as I know, never eventuated. Despite two healthy incomes, money was always the root of every argument. I decided at a pretty young age that I would never live like this, so I grew up with a 'mean button' very close to my heart.

I was a saver and whenever the opportunity arose to spend, I declined. I worked two jobs—one as a computer technician and the other as a celebrant—mainly weddings, but a few funerals thrown in. I was really quick to press the mean button, which was in the same vicinity as my belly button—ZZZZ—no—to the overseas working holiday—I can make more here. ZZZZ—even interstate holidays went off the radar. ZZZZ—no to expensive restaurants. I saved and bought a couple of rental properties and invested a bit on the stock market. On reflection, I squandered my youth to shore up my old age. Guess where all those savings went when the invasion hit?'

'Oh, crickey Watsy,' said Tabasco. Next time I get my pay tokens, it's probably your hard-earned money I'll be spending as I had more debts than savings.'

'Talking of tokens,' retorted Watsy, '... if I had won the amount I get in my pay packet at the casino, pre-invasion, I don't think I would have bothered to collect and I was the King of Misers!'

Gibbo came off the field, grabbed a chair and joined them with his back turned to the cricket match. 'I've never batted for so long. I was trying to give lollypop catches to the kids, but all my hits found empty spaces. What are you guys on about now?'

'We were talking about parents and their foibles,' came the answer.

Gibbo looked serious. 'I miss my old man even though he could be a pain in the arse. When I first started working for him it was always "not good enough, Jack. Do it again." Looking back though, it was what I needed as I would have stuffed up every path and driveway I laid. My dad loved tape measures. He would take me to the barber and say, 'Just 125 millimetres off. Thanks, mate.' Of course, the barber was a nervous wreck.

The only thing that Dad couldn't measure accurately, or anywhere near accurately, was the width of his old truck. He would drive down the surrounding streets to our house and clip just about every car parked along the way. We lost track of the original colour of the old truck. He backed into a shop's car park one day and didn't realise that he had hit the fence. He came home dribbling a sheet of corrugated iron. He couldn't understand where it came from. 'Someone must have put it there.' Until Mum went to the same shop and photographed a gaping hole in the fence.

When I got into trouble, and you won't believe this, it was on a regular basis.'

'Shit, Gibbo. We thought you would be next on the list to be canonised!' chipped in Watsy.

Gibbo grinned. 'Yeah, well, my old man wasn't nearly as gullible as Mum.' She was something else again. She was into organics. When we were in primary school, we would be taken to a restaurant or hotel for family birthdays and special occasions but the only thing 'special' was that they were especially embarrassing, as Mum took it upon herself to ensure that there were no hidden ingredients on our plates. There were times when all the staff would surround our table. We were not game enough to take a mouthful until the ingredients and their origins were explained. We jacked up in high school and wouldn't go near a restaurant with our parents.

A voice called out from the field, 'Hey, Gibbo, young Freckles here won't give up his bat even though two umpires agreed it was plum LBW. He wants it "reviewed" by the third umpire, and you're the captain.'

Gibbo turned round, put his hand in the air and shouted, 'OUT!' The kid walked. Gibbo laughed and said, 'I know I've seen it on TV, but I haven't taken much notice and wouldn't have a clue how an umpire can accurately send a batsman off the field with an LBW call. I'm not even sure what it means.'. 'Leg before wicket,' answered Silo and tried to explain the intricacies of where the ball can hit on the batsman's pad in relation to the wickets behind. 'Yeah well, with my limited concentration span, any game that takes five days to play and can end in a draw was never on my radar. I've always gravitated to action and plenty of it.'

Kaitlyn reminded Gibbo, 'You were telling us about your mum.' She always enjoyed Gibbo's version of his mum's antics. Kaitlyn's relationship with her mother-in-law was fairly easy going. His mum welcomed the change that took place when Kaitlyn hit the scene and Kaitlyn ignored the food fetish and anti-vaxxing extolments. She enjoyed the fact that his mum was naively convinced that her son could do no wrong, but only got into trouble due to the rather dubious company he kept. Kaitlyn didn't have to feel on edge as she did when Gibbo was in the presence of her parents. Gibbo and Kaitlyn became experts at listening to his mum extolling his virtues while keeping straight faces. They would sit in the car later with Gibbo imitating his mum and Kaitlyn laughing herself hoarse. Kaitlyn looked expectantly at Gibbo.

'Yeah, as I've said, Mum was heavily into "organics" and she was an ardent anti-vaxxer. When Jamie, my younger brother, married Claudia Vetolli, the shit really hit the fan. Claudia's dad had a cellar and made his own salamis and pepperonis. When the two mothers got together to discuss the menu for the wedding reception, they were really talking different languages. Mum knew as much about antipasto as Claudia's mum knew about a lentil casserole in a soybean sauce.'

'I needn't have worried about Claudia and how she would handle Mum. She really had the smarts. Years later, when they got the kids vaccinated, mum cried so hard, she burst blood vessels in one eye and ended up with a black eye and wearing sunglasses for a couple of weeks. Claudia ignored the theatricals. She sent my brother, Jamie, into the boxing ring to cop all the flak!'

The cricket match was nearing an end, particularly for the adults. The kids were happy to keep going until called in for tea. They set about to light the small piles of wood interspersed with paper that they had laid between cement building blocks. They waited for some coals and then covered them with sheets of iron they had scavenged from old properties. There was a plentiful supply that littered the landscape due to the bushfires that had swept through the island. They heated the mini pies, covered them with BBQ sauce and savoured the memories. The adults swirled their red cordial round the plastic glasses, sniffing and talking of 'bouquet' and which side of the hill this little drop came from. They sat in groups and talked about their former lives. Gibbo talked about playing for the Panthers and some of the antics they got up to, particularly on those interstate trips immediately after the season had finished. They celebrated, no matter where they finished on the ladder. He had to water it down a bit in front of Kaitlyn.

Hamish told them about his love of the sea, getting his first surfboard and joining the volunteer surf lifesavers. 'I really miss the sea. It's so close here that when the wind is blowing in the right direction, I can hear it at night. It's a pity that it's been declared out of bounds.'

Bagsy came up to Hamish. 'We've been declared the cricket winning champions. I don't know how they worked that one out as the scorers quit their jobs ages ago. I won't prepare my speech until I see the silver plated, engraved cup.'

Like Gibbo, Bagsy drove a cement truck, not always to the same building site, but they knew each other. Bagsy introduced his partner, Nat, and Hamish introduced Sonia. 'How long have you two been together?' asked Bagsy and they cracked up. They both looked at their wrists, which once sported watches, and said, 'About three hours! '

Inevitably, the conversation went back to their former lives. 'We told the GRAPS we were married as we didn't want separate accommodation, but they didn't care one way or another,' Bagsy told them. He went on to say that he had met Nat in a London airport as they both worked for a tour company over there. The pay wasn't crash hot, but they were seeing a lot of countries and had very few expenses as all meals and accommodation were provided. It was in the winter season, when the touring buses out of London stopped, that they met for the first time when they were assigned to a ski resort in Austria. 'I grew up fairly close to Falls Creek and went skiing and snowboarding with my parents every winter so was able to snag a job as a ski instructor. Loved it! Nat was the ski rep, organising nightly activities and all guest services, like lift passes, ski lessons, etc. We were working pretty much together, and it suited us just fine. We did this for a couple more years, touring during the summer and ski resorts in winter but we couldn't be together on every tour, so decided to head home and get married.

The group were a bit incredulous. 'You gave up a PAYING job, touring round the world, to return to Adelaide? You either must have been in love or temporarily deranged!'

'Yeah, I know it sounds crazy, but we had been doing it for a few years. Don't forget, we were catering for under thirties, mostly their first trip overseas and they were in party mode-big time! For some of them it was the first time away from parents and they were cutting loose. The exact moment they stepped onto the tour bus was when they lost any molecule of rational thinking that they had ever previously possessed. We got sick of putting drunks to bed and listening to people repeating themselves with swollen tongues. Half the time we didn't even know what language they were speaking.'

'Nat came from Adelaide, so I headed there and got work. We both had degrees, so we picked up work pretty quickly. I worked for a financial institution and Nat for a pathology company as a radiographer-a far cry from our former lives touring the European countryside.'

'We had everything organised for the wedding-invitations sent out and the honeymoon trip to Hawaii (one of the few places we had not been with the tour company) pre-paid when the pandemic hit. We didn't want an extravagant wedding, but we did want more than ten people-particularly as my side of the family was coming over from Victoria. We had to cancel. I know that it doesn't really matter, as it's only a piece of paper, but to tell you the truth, we were looking forward to a slap-up party and an overseas trip as we knew that we would be busy saving for a house-one last fling. When the pandemic restrictions started to ease, we were too wary of a second wave to go through all that organising again, so it never happened. On reflection, we should have started the ball rolling as soon as we hit the Australian shore.'

That took them to the topic of what they would do on hindsight. Sonia looked at Hamish and said, 'I tried to get back to Adelaide, but it didn't work.'

'What happened?' asked Hamish. 'Well, I got past the first official block, but I couldn't get past the second-a very severe looking official made it very clear that I had to turn around and go back. However, I don't think I would have made it as the fuel gauge was showing almost empty and I had another thirty kilometres to go. I think that official did me a favour, as I don't think I'd change anything.' 'Neither would I,' he replied. Nat looked from one to the other. 'Are you sure you've only just met?'

The 'Big Bash' was an event that was talked about for days and Gibbo's mob was soaking up the success and enjoying the memories of the new friendships that had been forged. They knew that there would be very limited opportunities to be together again, but they vowed to make the most of them. For Hamish it was a day he would never forget for many reasons.

# GRAP

Within days, it all went horribly wrong for Hamish on the building site and on hindsight he didn't know whether he would have acted any differently. Communication at work was reduced to barking orders with a background of machinery noise. It was 11.00 am when commotion broke out on the site. Hamish had just come down from the scaffolding to get more cement, when one of the GRAP supervisors yelped in pain, holding on to his shoulder. Hamish couldn't believe the kerfuffle over one dislocated shoulder. He quickly put the shoulder back into position and made hand signals to strap the arm. The GRAP, by this time, was yabbering away to his mates and they all nodded to Hamish, who turned to head back to the scaffolding. He ran straight into Gibbo, who had just delivered cement from the small truck he drove and whose mute face looked like granite and eyes that stared with total hatred. This episode took minutes, but the repercussions were lengthy.

That night in the bullroom, Gibbo, who lived in Block B, came bursting in, stood centimetres in front of Hamish, and shouted, 'You lot, meet a fucking GRAP. This motherfucker couldn't fucking wait to put his fellow fucking GRAP out of his fucking misery and give him a fucking happy ending. I want you all to know that he's the worst kind of fucking GRAP that ever trod this fucking earth.'

'Gees, mate,' said Johnno Vallorani. '...you need a few more swear words, you're getting a bit repetitive. Learn Italian, they've got heaps!' Gibbo turned on Johnno. 'Are you siding with this fucking arsehole?'

'No way, mate.' And Gibbo turned on his heel and left the building. Hamish knew in the pit of his stomach that he had just made enemies with pretty much the whole population of the island. He was no longer 'Macca', he was 'GRAP'.

There was very little communication on the building site, but the bullroom was a different story. It was near on impossible to get any quiet time and Hamish learned to absorb himself in a book despite the background noise. For the first time in his life, he became a loner. He ignored the petty menacing, starting from pages being ripped from his book to a red 'X' being painted on the floor in front of his bed. He could not store food items in the corridor fridge, so had to join the queue each night after work at Foodies.

It didn't take long for the supervisors to work out that Hamish was on the outer from his work mates. Recognising the symptoms, they felt sorry for him, making the situation even worse. There were many eyes on Hamish's outstretched hands receiving extra tokens at the end of the working week. Hamish knew that this 'reward' would do him no favours. Except for Silo, Gibbo's Bluey gang sniffed the slight change in Power Houses attitude towards Hamish and escalated their threats. He now had to check his clothing and bed for sharp objects that were readily to hand from the site. Then Gibbo decided to up the ante. One of his mates was off a farm and, not only had plenty of practice in snake handling, but loved to bag, release and observe them. Gibbo thought it would be a hoot to put a copperhead into Hamish's bed.

'I just want to scare the bastard, but if it happens to kill the fucker, that would be a bonus,' he told the cockie, who bagged the snake and placed it under the doona. 'Reckon it will enjoy a nice, comfy snooze until it's rudely awakened by a slimy GRAP,' he told his mates, who were suspicious of sharing space with a copperhead but didn't want to look like wimps. The snake didn't settle comfortably. It wriggled out and started investigating the surrounds. When Hamish got home with a few ingredients from Foodies, there were men running and shouting in all directions. The copperhead was climbing above on one of the rafters. The cockie was shouting for a broom and shovel. It took hours before the snake was bagged and removed. Johnno told Hamish later that they were scared shitless of the snake but didn't want to appear wussy as they thought it was a prank that was a bit over the top. He also said that everyone in the bullroom thought it would stop Gibbo from continuing his vitriol. Everyone was sleep deprived that night and didn't want to blame anyone except Hamish.

# Shark Bait

The building site gangs were rotated to drive the small cement trucks. They had to sign in and pick up the keys from the GRAP supervisor. Gibbo used his mates to distract the office GRAP. They had stuck a nail into one of the trucks tyres and it was going flat. They gestured to the GRAP, who went to investigate. Gibbo was able to sign the keys in and used another key on the board to fill the slot. When the office was shut, locked and vacated, Gibbo and Tabasco snuck back in and drove to Block D. Tabasco was astounded when Gibbo suggested that they take Macca for a swim. Gibbo had come across a tin boat with an outboard motor on one of his trips to different building sites. He told Tabasco that one of the workers was originally from Kangaroo Island and he knew the owner of the boat. He also said that, not far out to sea, there was a reef and the wreck of an old coastal trading boat. Tabasco was delighted when Gibbo said he was going to invite Macca for a swim. To Tabasco's mind, helping a GRAP is a serious community offence–aiding and abetting the enemy–but Macca had acted instinctively and enough is enough. Tabasco found Hamish in the kitchen and excitedly told him that Gibbo has organised a truck and they were going for a swim off a reef. Hamish was worried on two fronts–the sea is out of bounds and therefore an offence, and secondly, Gibbo. 'Come on, Macca. A once-in-a-lifetime chance, but daylight is running out, we've got to be quick.' The thought of being in the sea again, perhaps for the last time in his life, was very enticing. Hamish tossed off his boots and headed for the truck. Gibbo gave him a big grin and said, 'Come on in, Macca, we're going to find a reef and I know you love the sea.'

***I know the sea on top of me and I know that there is no old
coastal trading boat wreck along that coastline of water. I also
know that there is no reef.***

Hamish got in to hear Gibbo cheerfully talking about the boat
that he found, the petrol that he had milked from the cement
truck, and the source of his information as they drove along. The
windows were down and with the smell of the sea getting stronger,
Hamish started to relax and settle his worries. They came down a
hill, round the bend, and there was the most delightful sight–waves,
with the sun dancing on top, were lapping at the sand. Just for a
moment, Hamish was able to recapture the joys of the sea prior to
his eviction. When they got to the boat, Gibbo poured the fuel into
the tank. The engine took a while to rev, but finally they were off
with Gibbo shouting, 'Sea Ho me hearties!'

Gibbo was going far out to sea, and they were all intent on
finding the reef. Hamish suggested that they head back to shore,
but Gibbo said he was determined to find the reef and the trawler
wreck. 'What do you want to do back at shore, dog paddle?' The
sun was getting low when Tabasco called for Gibbo to stop the boat.
'Let's forget about the reef. I want to go for a swim.' There was no
anchor in the boat, so Gibbo said he would stay aboard. Hamish
and Tabasco jumped into the sea. The feel of the water on his body
again was delicious and Hamish turned on his back and floated
in the sun before a strong swim. After a while, Gibbo turned the
boat round and picked up Tabasco. He then gunned the motor
and headed away. Hamish put his hand up out of the water so that
Gibbo could locate him. Perhaps he had swum too far, but the boat
was heading away from him.

Tabasco was yelling in the boat. 'Get Macca! Get Macca!' but
Gibbo responded, 'Let's give our GRAP mate a little overseas
holiday.' Gibbo shouted over the sound of the boat motor and
the slapping waves, 'Reckon "Shark Bait" might like a little swim.
He loves the water.' Tabasco shouted, 'Gees, Gibbo, don't get too
carried away, mate. This is far enough.' Gibbo had a steely look on
his face and replied, 'Who's driving this fucking boat?'

'Get Macca. He's too far out,' Tabasco continually yelled, but Gibbo was heading back to shore. Tabasco had been sitting on an old polystyrene esky and upended it, throwing the lid out to sea.

Hamish was now alone in the water. He felt sure that Gibbo would leave him there for a short period before returning. It wasn't until he could no long hear the boat motor that he realised Gibbo had no intention of returning. He was on his own. He was stranded, alone and abandoned—like a piece of flotsam tossed into the sea from a vessel. The feeling of helplessness engulfed him, and he felt like a child again, adrift from support. He couldn't see the coastline and night was rapidly approaching. He shook with fear. He had never felt intense hatred before, but he felt it now.

*I could feel the emotions in the waves. I felt his sense of helplessness and his loathing of one of their parties.*

Hamish knew that he could easily swim or float further out to sea when it got dark. He also knew that his chance of survival was slim. He saw something white in the distance, bobbing away. A shark was the first thing that came to mind. He was going to swim away from it, but it seemed to be floating rather than moving through the water. He decided to swim towards it and as he got closer, he recognised it as polystyrene. He presumed it was some flotsam from an old oil tanker. Hamish instinctively knew that getting to it would be his only chance of survival. The more he swam, the further away it seemed to get. He tried floating with the waves as the sun rapidly sunk into the horizon. Hamish had felt alone on Kangaroo Island, but now he was not only alone, but stranded. He decided that he would either swim or sink, so the chase was on. The esky lid was not always visible as it bobbed and dipped with the waves. Hamish had to rely on his strength of powerful arms, strong legs and staying power. He felt as though he was motoring, but every time he caught sight of the lid, it seemed further away. The next time he sighted it, he could make out some indentations. At last, he was getting closer. The sun had disappeared, and the sky was a soft glow. Night was closing in.

The lid disappeared and Hamish thought for a moment that it had either sunk or was a figment of his imagination. It bobbed up again and this time he could almost touch it. He lunged and got a fingertip to it, but the lid swivelled around and caught another wave. Hamish pushed his body to the limit and lunged again. This time he was able to grasp it in his hands. He grabbed hold of it and threw his body over the top. He lay there catching his breath.

Night was rapidly approaching, and Hamish knew that if he fell asleep, he could easily slip off the lid. The chance of finding it in the night, was nil. He was glad he had not taken off his belt, which, in his enthusiasm to see the sea again, was a complete oversight. He managed to unbuckle it with one hand while holding onto the lid with the other. He had to get the belt round his body and the lid so that they could become one. The sunset on the horizon only shed a dim light, and he had made several attempts to hold onto the lid while trying to thread the belt under it, over his body, and do up the buckle on the side. The movement of the waves was not helping, but he managed to buckle the belt before the night sky blackened.

*I could feel this lone swimmer in the sea. I could feel him floating on top of my waves. Stay floating. Don't give up. Don't go further out to sea. I feel danger in the air.*

Hamish was now in the dark with the star-studded sky and a slim sliver of moon overhead. He decided that he had to trust the lid to make its way to shore. He couldn't help thinking of being circled and attacked by a shark. He could almost feel it biting into his leg or arm. The vivid description that Silo had painted while they were walking to the ferry was in his uppermost thoughts. A fourteen-year-old surfer was attacked by a shark and lost an arm, but also nearly lost his life. In his mind's eye, Hamish could see the ring of red sea water surrounding the lad. He could feel the hopelessness that would have engulfed the youngster as a huge predator circled him. Hamish could feel the same panic inside that boy. He used his arms and legs to escape perceived danger.

Although the day was warm, with temperatures in the low thirties, the night air chilled Hamish's body. The water was warm by comparison. He knew he would have to move constantly to keep his body as warm as possible. But in which direction? He thought that if he found the Southern Cross he would have a chance of finding north and south. He had never taken much notice of the night sky and regretted not being more attentive. At first, the sky looked like a mass of stars, but he thought he could make out the Southern Cross. He could clearly see the two 'tail stars' and, looking up, he could see four stars in the shape of a square, the top one barely visible. He could remember a teacher on a school camp showing the class on an outside whiteboard how to use the stars to find 'south'. You draw a line between the two longest points of the cross, go to the pointer stars below the cross, then draw a line between them and another at 90 degrees. He tried to draw imaginary lines, not knowing whether he had remembered correctly or not. He knew the sun set in the west and he would have to move his body eastwards. However, he didn't know whether he had swum in circles and lost the direction of the setting sun. He had to take a punt that, yes, he'd located the Southern Cross, and he had successfully located south. He would now have a 50/50 chance of moving to the east. Hamish had no confidence in his navigational skills, and he didn't want to swim in the wrong direction, so he had to steer himself, with the guide of what he hoped was the correct identification and reading of the Southern Cross, and his trusty piece of polystyrene beneath him.

*You have located my stars. I feel tiredness in the water. Stay awake!*

Hamish knew that staying awake would be his only priority and he also knew that if he started to feel drowsy, particularly with the movement of the waves, that he would have to get the adrenalin flowing. The quickest way to do that would be to put himself into more danger. From time to time, he did feel fish movement brush against his body and his heart would start racing again. As the minutes ticked on, Hamish had plenty of time to reflect on his life.

He thought about his parents. Where were they? They lived in a different area, and he had no idea where they were relocated. He knew they would worry about him and wonder where he was. They had loved to travel, tripping around Australia, terrorising road traffic as 'Grey Nomads' with their caravan behind them. His dad with his camera, taking photos and identifying birds. His mum with a pair of binoculars round her neck, but not at all keen. They would probably now be working in some sort of factory. They didn't deserve that. Hamish thought about his older sister, Felicity (Felix); her husband, Hayden; and their little boy, Tommy. He had loved visiting their place and playing with Tommy. Where were they now? Tommy would have been reaching school age and wouldn't know that he had limited opportunities in life. He felt so sad at the thought of bright, happy little Tommy being discarded by the system.

Hamish had no idea of time and knew that the minutes would seem like hours. It only took a few minutes to think, and he had to see out the night. He let his mind drift back to his childhood. He could picture his dad, an electrician and a very good handyman. His mind 'watched' his mum at her desk doing all the bookkeeping for the electrical business while also handling reception. He felt their encouragement in all his sporting attempts, which he enjoyed but never excelled in. He pictured himself following Felix into ball sports, mainly to be part of the team, and he knew that unlike her, he would never be an 'A' grader. He could remember those first swimming lessons and how comfortable he felt, even as a beginner, to be in the water. He thought about those early days when he went to 'Little Nippers' at the surf club. The Christmas when he got his first surfboard—was he five or six? The first time he stood on the board and 'rode a wave'—memory says he rode it for ten minutes, but it was probably less than one.

He felt something brush against his leg and he started swimming again, legs kicking. His heart was racing, and the vast emptiness engulfed him. He thought swimming was not an option, as he could be going in the wrong direction. His movement could also attract the attention of a shark. He settled and let his mind drift back to his childhood home conveniently situated halfway between the beach and the city.

Although he made light of it to Silo on the ferry crossing to the island, Hamish remembered, or perhaps remembered what he had been told over the years, how he and Felix had become 'missing children' and a search party was hastily assembled to find them. He could picture the two of them playing in the cubby house that his parents had built at the end of the yard. As he floated in the water, he could visualise the small table, chairs, a wooden 'stove', and some miniature cups and saucers. According to Felix, who was six years of age at the time, and two years older than Hamish, after a while they got a bit bored, and Felix decided that she knew where there was a real house being built and they could watch the workmen. She said she knew the way and Hamish, who idolised his older sister, knew he would have been more than happy to follow. He could picture his mother working in the kitchen, content in the knowledge that the children were in the cubby house. She had no idea they had left the premises.

He was getting cold. Time to move.

As he was swimming, Hamish could also picture the panic on his mother's face when she came down the yard to find the cubby house empty. She rang his dad, who came home immediately, and they searched the house before calling the police. His dad raced over to all the neighbours in the surrounding streets to see if they had wandered their way, while his mum stayed home waiting for the police car. When they did arrive, his mother had it in her mind that the two of them had wandered down to the tram line, which had a deep concrete channel running beside it and because of the recent rains, the water would be flowing. She was convinced that her children would wander that way as she knew they were both fascinated by water, and she could see Hamish, being the youngest, falling in. His parents headed for the tram line.

Felix did find the partially build house eventually, but there were no workmen (he heard later that it was a Sunday). Hamish thought about the pile of sand that they played in and imagined walking through the house with no walls, but timber frames. There were wires dangling down and he captured the feeling of importance playing in this real cubby house. The problem was, Felix was not sure of the route home. They wandered streets that seemed to go in circles and came across 'their' house once again. By this time, Hamish was tired and whinging, so Felix decided that they would rest in the pile of sand. Apparently, they slept until 5.30 pm.

Time to move again to stay alert. He looked up to the stars for reassurance that he was moving in the right direction. However, he was not confident that his navigational skills were working and imagined himself heading further and further out to sea. However, he had chosen a course and had to stick to it.

He read the cutouts from the paper many times over the years as the media had latched on to the police response and their call to the community for a back-up search party for two missing young children. Felix woke first to hear people calling out. It was not only the police involved, but also many neighbours and a contingency of Rotarians. Felix was convinced they would get into big trouble if they were spotted, added to the fact that they had been told to be wary of strangers. They saw some men walking round the house and, even though they were calling out their names, Felix convinced her little brother to keep very quiet as they cowered behind the sand. The men went away. Now they could move and go home, which Felix confidently announced she could find. They went down a couple of streets and a group of people came towards them. One lady called out, 'There they are' so they took off but were quickly chased down. By this time, the two of them were bawling. Someone phoned their parents, who caught up to them before they reached home. They kept on bawling, thinking they were in big trouble, but to their amazement they were smothered with hugs and kisses. Their mother told them many times over the years that Felix was most incensed when she heard that they imagined the children running beside the concrete channel parallel to the tramline. 'I would never take Hamish there,' she declared. 'What do you think—I want to kill him?'

It was due to this episode that Hamish's mother decided they would both immediately be enrolled in swimming classes–which he loved. The flip side was that his dad had a fence built across the driveway with a security gate, so now when they were playing in the back yard, they were locked in.

Hamish loved the freedom of his childhood. Riding his bike with mates down to the beach. Of course, he didn't wear his hat or smother himself with block out. That would be wussy. He remembered loud and clear the agony of sunburn. Getting into a warm shower that, when the water hit his skin, stung all over. The peeling of flakes of skin. His mum couldn't believe that he could get so burnt and would buy a more potent block out. Memory told him that this happened every summer.

He thought about his teachers at school and felt immensely sorry for giving his physics teacher such a hard time. He had always been a happy kid at school and couldn't believe that his cheeky teenage backchat could get under his teacher's skin. Mr Major (the kids called him 'disaster' behind his back). However, with the encouragement of his classmates, Hamish made a habit of some smart arse replies to Mr Major's questions. This came undone when his mum went to the school one evening for parent/teacher interview night. He was grounded every weekend for three weeks, which included surfing. Hamish kept his lips zipped from there on in. His mum told him years later that it nearly killed her as well—as she was grounded too!

Hamish thought of his childhood mate, Freddie, who lived across the road. He was called Freddie because he spent all his free time emulating Freddie Flintoff, the English fast bowler and batsman—a true all-rounder in Freddie's eyes. It was only his mum and dad who called him by his real name—'Jonathon'. Freddie would walk along the footpath to school, swinging over arm with a pretend ball in his hand. Even at preschool, Freddie would be rubbing a plastic ball down his shorts. 'I'm Freddie Flintoff,' he would say as he ran up to bowl under arm. He had posters of Flintoff on his bedroom walls. Hamish shared Freddie's enthusiasm after Freddie had had a good day with the ball. He commiserated when the wickets didn't fall and agreed when the umpires couldn't see an LBW—even when it was plum, and Freddie's LBWs were always plum.

Freddie was not academic, but he wasn't dumb. He could see no reason to store knowledge that he had no interest in. However, when it came to cricket, he was a powerhouse of information. He could not only tell you the final scores of every cricket match dating back to the year dot, but he knew how many runs or wickets each player made in every series. His favourite, of course, was the Holy Grail—'The Ashes'—when his hero was in action. Hamish was proud to be Freddie's mate and didn't worry that he couldn't match his cricketing prowess as Freddie was not a pretty sight on a surfboard.

Where was Freddie now? Probably on a construction site somewhere as he did an apprenticeship as a chippie so would be in high demand. However, the new Power Houses did not seem interested in past knowledge or skills, so he could be in a factory. How could Freddie survive without his cricket?

He cringed at the thought of aiding and abetting Thommo in his uni days. Thommo funded his way through law school by writing off cars for anyone wanting to cash in on the insurance. He always felt guilty about this, but Thommo was a charismatic character and it all seemed a bit of a lark, but the insurance companies were loaded so what was the problem? Hamish squirmed at the thought.

He thought of Gibbo, who had been so friendly when they first met on the building site, but who now hated him. Surely his 'crime' was not that serious. If it wasn't just the incidence of helping a GRAP with a dislocated shoulder, then what could it be?

**I know the answer to that. I feel jealousy.**

He went over and over in his mind what he could have said or done to get Gibbo so offside, but he came up with a blank.

Time to think of other things. His mind wandered to Year 7— the 'snogging' year when he had his first kiss with Mandy with the blue eyes and long, blonde hair. Mandy's skin erupted in early teenage years and, of course, she was known as 'Pizza Face'. Years later, he said yes to Mandy when she asked him to escort her to the Year 10 'formal', but Marivon, who was the most confident and, in his eyes, the best looking girl in all his classes, also asked him to escort her! He couldn't believe his luck as he really wasn't part of her mix. He made a wishy-washy excuse to Mandy, who surprised him by not being overly concerned. The night didn't work. He thought he was the coolest dude to have Marivon on his arm walking into the huge school gym, complete with hanging helium balloons bunched up on the rafters. Marivon scooted off pretty much straight away and he went over to Mandy for consolation, who also gave him short shift. Another embarrassing moment—and he had a long list.

*I can feel emotions dissipating in the sea, replaced by acceptance. Keep alert. Don't give up!*

He thought about survival. Did he want it? Everything from his past was gone. There was not a shred left. Perhaps, unwittingly, Gibbo had done him a favour. If he had to choose any way of dying, in the sea would be at the top of the list. What's the point of continuing this life on Kangaroo Island with no future? But then he got a flash of Sonia with her ready laugh and big brown eyes that seemed to light up. He relived the moment when someone asked if they were sure they had only just met and the laughter that ensued. He had only known her for a short time that one afternoon, but somehow, he managed to get a picture of her in his mind. He memorised the words she spoke, which seemed to be in sync with the movement of the ocean.

It was the thought of seeing the look on Gibbo's face that also made him want to stay afloat. He was not going to let the bastard beat him. He had been a fool to get conned. Keep going. He was getting very cold. Time to check the Southern Cross and keep moving. He felt as though he had been in the water for hours, but it was probably not more than two. Dawn was a long way off and sleeping was not an option. He was getting cold again. Time to get the arms and legs moving. Where was the Southern Cross? Yep, he located the shining stars and was moving in the right direction—maybe.

The waves were churning. All night they had been rhythmical and now they were alive. He had company.

*I felt a lot of movement behind the lone swimmer on top of the waves. I hope it's friendly.*

He felt a surge behind him and movement on both sides. He had company. No point moving as he couldn't outswim the forces surrounding him. He laid still and tucked his arms in but he knew his legs were dangling. A pod of dolphins enveloped him. They were curious. What is this thing floating? 'Hey guys,' called Hamish. 'Which way to shore?' The dolphins chattered and swam around him and then went on their way. It was at this time that Hamish felt overcome with loneliness. Oh, to be a dolphin and be able to join them. He thought about the life of a dolphin riding the waves. But then their lives were not without danger either.

Perhaps this is what happens before you die—you go back to the past. Way back to watching Play School on TV, sitting on a bean bag while Felix was jumping up and down doing all the actions that the adult presenters were doing. He could even sing the song—'There's a bear in there and a chair as well, there are people with games and stories to tell. Open wide, come inside—it's Play School.' It was still going until the invasion. His mind snapped back to the recent past—the invasion. He 'walked' around his small unit, picturing the table, chairs, cupboards, and the small verandah looking out to sea. He recaptured the feeling of walking out of his unit for the last time. His mind wandered back in history. How did the First Nations people feel when European ships arrived at their shore?

*I can answer that as I felt all their feelings: They thought they were seeing aliens with blanched faces, white arms, some with legs with red stripes and feet that had no toes. Some of the male ones didn't even have facial hair and some just had hair above their lips. The ladies had no legs or toes but managed to move regardless. They carried sticks that made a very loud sound that could kill an animal. The sight of these aliens was both mesmerising and frightening at the same time.*

Perhaps they must have felt like we do. We are in our own country, but we are not home.

I wonder what the time is—midnight? Six hours before dawn. He had to stay awake. He was paddling to try to warm his body when he spotted a light in the distance—an oil tanker? His first reaction was to frantically wave, but common sense kicked in. It was a long way off and he was a miniscule dot on the ocean. However, it had to be sailing out to sea, and he was moving away from it—hopefully to shore. For the first time that night, he felt like he was going in the right direction—unless he was moving in circles!

**I feel heavy with tiredness. Keep going. Don't sleep!**

Somewhere between feeling pleased with himself and drowning, Hamish realised he had slept. He woke up to find himself on his side with the esky lid down by his leg. It must have slipped through the belt. He had swallowed water as his mouth was open. He felt nauseous. His most pressing problem was, 'had he changed direction?' He had to find the Southern Cross again, and somehow it seemed to have retreated into the night sky. He was wet through to his bones and very, very cold. He had to get back onto the lid before it slipped away. He dived under, located the side of the lid and pushed it up with both hands until he got it up to his waist. He then felt for the buckle to do it up a notch so that it could not slip again. It meant undoing the buckle and chancing that he would lose his lifeline in the process. His fingers felt numb with the cold, but he managed to do up the buckle. Was it tighter, the same, or looser? He wasn't sure. Every bone in his body said 'move', but not before locating the Southern Cross. He felt like his brain had frozen. Think!

Hamish was not confident that he was paddling in the right direction. The night sky seemed to have a film over it, when he thought he saw a glimmer of light. His heart pounded. No, he must be hallucinating. The very first rays of dawn appeared, and he couldn't believe that the longest night of his life was nearing an end. The light was a long way off and way over to his right-hand side. Land was not in sight. He paddled, watching the dim rays brighten on the horizon. For the first time that night, he felt a glimmer of hope that he could make it to land. He paddled as the sun rose from the sky and, if he was seeing correctly, foliage appeared in the distance. It could be a mirage. He wasn't going to get his hopes up. The waves churned as another pod of dolphins engulfed him. This time he was happy to be part of their scene, even for a short time. The dolphins circled him and surfed the waves. They were enjoying themselves and Hamish laughed along with them. He had been so preoccupied with the dolphins that he hadn't looked to the horizon, and this time it was definite—he was heading for shore.

He was now in water shallow enough to be able to stand. Now was the time to unleash the esky lid—his lifesaver. He would keep it as a memento. Walking through the shallow water onto sand was not easy. His legs were still numb from the cold, and they felt like jelly. He staggered up the embankment and onto the road like a drunk.

He could see the apartment blocks in the distance and was heading down the road towards them when a Power House car pulled up beside him. The officials jumped out, shouting at him. Hamish didn't have a clue what was being said. They bundled him into the car and took him to a police station, where he was interrogated by two policemen who had a translator with limited English. 'Name! Address! What were you doing outside of your precinct?' The fact that Hamish was still shivering from cold was not a problem for them. He answered their questions: 'Hamish McIntyre, Block D20, single men's quarters. I was going for a swim and got caught in a rip and was swept out to sea.' He showed them the esky lid. 'I used this to get back to shore.'

*I feel relieved - you've made it, son, but the hatred has left your body. I can only feel tiredness washing over you - you're spent.*

Eventually, the police bundled him back in the car and took him straight to the building site. He knew that, somehow, he needed to be particularly vigilant as the building site was a high-risk area with no regard for work safety measures. He didn't know where the power tools came from, but the equipment was very dated. Of course, no one ever inspected any of it. There were no boots, hard hats, earplugs, goggles, gloves, high-vis clothing, facemasks, safety harnesses, or sunscreen. What you rocked up in was what you wore all day—even if it was shorts, thongs and T-shirts. Hamish thought it would be ironic that he could survive a night in the sea only to die falling off rickety scaffolding during the day. He had to stay super alert.

# Best Mates

Tabasco was in distress. He returned home from what Gibbo had called 'a prank', leaving Hamish overboard, and he couldn't stop thinking about Macca out at sea. Okay, he threw him an esky lid, whoopy do! He liked Macca. He didn't like GRAP sympathisers, but he thought that Gibbo had overreacted when Macca helped a GRAP with a dislocated shoulder. He was caught between a rock and a hard place as he regarded Gibbo as his best mate and he valued the friendship. He told his friend, Patsy, what they had done. She was horrified and told Kaitlin, who in turn tore a strip off Gibbo.

'Gees, Kats, it was just a lark. He was a surf fucking lifesaver. If he can't save his own life, then there's something wrong. He's spent a lot of time in the water, and I bet he had a cupboard full of medals. He knows how to survive at sea. We didn't go far out. He'll be okay,' he lied.

'He'd better be,' replied Kaitlin, '...and you have to forget this ridiculous vendetta against him.'

'I will love,' replied Gibbo.

Gibbo was in the cement truck pulling into the building site when he saw the police car from which Hamish emerged. He jumped out and raced up to him, throwing his arms around his shoulders. He called out, 'Hey guys, Macca's back.'

*I feel words of joy, but I also feel underlying animosity.*

'Where's he been?' asked a work mate. 'Judging from arriving in a police car, I'd say in trouble,' responded Gibbo.

'I thought I was 'GRAP,' said Hamish.

'No, mate. I can forgive and forget.'

Hamish was too tired to think about it. He had to put in a day's work on the site and the physicality of it kept him awake and on his feet. That was probably the longest day he had ever experienced and when he got back to the bullroom that evening, he flopped into bed, not noticing that the red cross that had been painted on the floor, had been scraped off.

For the following weeks, Gibbo was at his friendliest best. 'Hey, Macca. Come and join us,' he said when they had their ten-minute lunch break. As there was nowhere else to sit, Hamish complied. Gibbo, particularly in Kaitlin's company, told all and sundry what a great mate Macca was and always would be. Tabasco found it hard to look Hamish in the eye, but Gibbo didn't have a problem. Hamish went along with it as there was no alternative.

Gibbo took it upon himself to organise activities in the evenings as television in a language they didn't understand was painfully boring. If the summer skies were drizzling rain, they played cards or had putting competitions inside. Gibbo pulled the tables together that were used to sort clothes from the laundry and made a barrier out of the bits of wood he had collected. This became a table tennis table. At first, they had to use old tennis balls, but he found some aerated practise golf balls that did the job. The bats were made out of wood. He was a scavenger and found some old golf clubs on what was probably a golf course before the invasion. Was someone having a bad round? There was a golf course on the island, but of course, Big Feet and Long Noses were excluded. He organised a footy match in the space between apartment blocks. However, tackling was not an option as the ground was cement.

What he couldn't scrounge, Gibbo shoplifted. In his words, when he confided to his mates, but definitely not to Kats, it wasn't stealing as the bastards had stolen the whole lot from them. He was just retrieving what he was rightfully entitled to. He knew that if he got caught the penalty would be harsh, but he was very good at it. He used his cheeky grin and yabbered away and gesticulated to the security guards about anything that came to mind. They were so busy trying to work out what he was on about, they forgot about checking what he was carrying. He had it down to a tee.

Sundays, being a day off work, were the most popular for community activities. They had a game of 'footy' with a round ball that Gibbo had found among a whole heap of rubble. It was flat but he stuffed it and tried to fashion it into an oval shape. One of the guys forgot the 'no tackling' rule, which resulted in a pile of bodies on the cement. Except for the one on the bottom, there were mainly cuts, scrapes and a great deal of whinging.

'Tarantula', who was all legs and often told stories of his previous escapades as an alcoholic—some screamingly funny, but a lot very sad—was on the bottom and couldn't get up. He had hurt his back on landing.

'Macca,' Gibbo called, '...you were a physio. Help this poor sod.'

Macca looked at his hands. They were calloused and as rough as sandpaper.

'Help me Macca,' said Tarantula, '...I have to get back onto the building site as I'm dead set not going into a factory.' Macca worked on his back on and off for the rest of the afternoon, and Tarantula was full of praise for his quick recovery. 'I know his hands were as rough as a bag of broken glass, but I reckon my back feels better after the fall than before it,' he told anyone who would listen. Thereafter, Macca was pronounced the official physio.

Gibbo found some old tennis balls and they used a lump of wood that he whittled down to resemble a baseball bat. He made a small baseball pitch in between the apartment blocks, which became popular for those participating and spectators alike. The building site car park was now fenced, locked and out of bounds. The cricket pitch was a narrow laneway between the buildings. It resembled the old practise nets that used to be part of many ovals. He made two basketball rings—one to put up on an inside rafter and the other on the outside of the building. There was no doubt about it, Gibbo was lifting the spirits of the island's Aussies. Sunday afternoons were the highlight of the week as this was a time when they could all get together. The domestic chores had been done and everyone looked forward to their 'Sunday arvos'. Monday morning was the most dreaded as the time in between often passed painfully slowly. Hamish particularly looked forward to being able to see Sonia again.

# The Wedding

They had finished the day's work on site and were walking through the gate when Bagsy (famous for his team's cricket win a few weeks prior) was lamenting the fact that he and Nat had finalised their wedding plans and had sent out their wedding invitations at the time of the invasion. Nat had bought the wedding dress. The bridesmaids all had their dresses. The men had picked out their outfits that matched the wedding party and they had paid a deposit to the hire company. The marriage celebrant had prepared the spiel. They had paid a deposit to the winery that was catering. Everything was done and dusted—and then the invasion.

That got Gibbo thinking.

'Shit, Bagsy, you don't have to be dead to be stiff. Why can't we have a wedding?'

'No reason,' replied Bagsy, '…except we haven't got a venue, music, outfits, catering company, or grog and there's no way on Earth that any of those things are going to appear out of thin air.'

'Leave it to me,' said Gibbo.

It was at this time that Gibbo started his hooch distillery. He knew he was breaking the rules, but he didn't lose sleep over it. He kept it entirely under wraps—even from Kats. On his rounds in the cement truck, he had come across a disused shed in a paddock. He had busted the lock and looked inside. There was an old table, a couple of broken chairs and a weather-beaten cupboard. There had been major fires on Kangaroo Island just before the pandemic and this was probably the only building on the property that had managed to survive. The previous owners would not have had the time to rebuild. It was his!

Gibbo's only knowledge from his teenage years of trying to grow marijuana and dabbling in beer brewing was that, to make hooch, he would need yeast, sugar, fruit or vegetables, water, and an airtight container to keep contaminates out. The airtight container was a problem, and then he remembered old Mr Whitford from up the road's shed. It was filled with balloons and when he asked what they were for, Mr Whitford had a crooked smile on his face and replied, 'They're party balloons.' Gibbo had a pretty good idea what was in those 'party balloons'. However, he had no idea of quantities and knew that he just had to experiment. He didn't know how long it would take to ferment. He also knew that he 'couldn't go missing' as he only had himself to blame for organising all those activities. He needed time by himself, and Kats provided the perfect opportunity when she got sick. She didn't know whether it was the flu or tonsilitis. She did know, however, that she wasn't going to the medical centre doctor. The next day when the factory supervisor called, she was running a fever. She made hand signals to say that she was very ill and contagious. It hadn't been that long since the pandemic. The official fled.

Gibbo was able to keep up his communal activities in the evenings and disappear at night. He did not allow himself torch light until he got well away from the apartment block and was well out into the open land. He did the walk so many times, he could almost get the whole way in the dark. Shoplifting the yeast and balloons was easy. He had to buy the sugar as it was too bulky. The rotten fruit was readily available in the bins, particularly from the Power House premises. For some reason, the GRAPS ignored his scavenging and seemed to enjoy the sight. He carted the water to the shed in buckets. His first attempt was abysmal—the balloons burst and there was a mess and smell that he had to get rid of. He realised that he would have to let some air out without letting air in, so with the next batch, he pin pricked the balloons. He checked them each night and, so far only one balloon had burst. After five days, Gibbo could smell the fermentation and had no idea of the strength of it. However, he told Bagsy that he was ready to swing into action to make a memorable wedding day. Bagsy was doubtful but went along with it.

Kaitlyn's health was improving when Gibbo told her of his plans to hold the wedding for Bagsy and Nat. Her enthusiasm grew each day as she got better. The venue was easy—one of the block's bullrooms. The decorations were not a problem—Gibbo was able to shoplift a pile of old streamers and add them to his stock of balloons. He didn't know until he was told that Watsy was a marriage celebrant in his previous life as he did this mainly on weekends for an extra income. Music was the problem. There were plenty of musos but no instruments. A few people brought their guitars strapped to bodies, but that wouldn't be enough to provide music. However, there were some who brought the old 'ghetto blasters' and a stockpile of CDs. They were so antiquated as pre-pandemic and invasion, the party music was provided with the aid of a mobile phone and a speaker stick. There was not one mobile phone on the island that didn't belong to a GRAP. It was Silo who had the strongest sound system, but crap CDs. However, when Gibbo sent out a call, the collective CDs were narrowed down to dance music from the 80s and 90s. Of course, Sonia was asked to do the invitations and, in conjunction with Watsy, to prepare the marriage certificate.

Gibbo and Kaitlyn swept into enthusiastic action taking Bagsy and Nat with them. They decided on an 'adults only 'evening'—the wrinklies could mind the kids. Catering? We could all contribute. It would be a veritable feast and not one grain of rice was allowed. Music, venue and celebrant chosen. 'Drinks?' asked Bagsy. 'Just you wait and see. I have it all organised,' said Gibbo, '… and it's not going to be just raspberry cordial. Your only job is to find the fanciest outfit possible and leave the rest up to us. Now, let's set a date as soon as possible and have a party.'

They chose 3.00 pm Sunday week. Sonia's handmade invitations were distributed among their friendship group which, collectively was now a large one. The invitations had time, date, venue, and dress code: 'Make an effort!' The venue was the bullroom in Bagsy's and Nat's block so that they could come down the stairs in style. They decided against the brain bank, as the girls had far more memorabilia cluttering up their large room. Some of the guys even had photos of their first car stuck onto their wardrobe drawer without a family member in sight.

Gibbo called for a pre-wedding meeting. He was unanimously voted emcee and best man. The furniture would have to be moved to make room. Everyone would take their food, plates and glasses to the venue at lunch time on the day. Silo would be the official photographer as he was the only one with a digital camera. The only problem was they couldn't get hard copies. Everyone else had relied on their mobile phones to take photos, but of course, they were all in a bin. Hamish was happy to help with the furniture removal, decorations and setting up of the tables for food and drinks. Even those who were not attending the wedding contributed. With a community contribution of tokens and scavenging from government bins, the wrinklies made batches of the kangaroo mince party pies and lamingtons that were so appreciated at the cricket match. The community anticipation hung in the air and gave everyone a much-needed lift. 'The wedding' was the major topic in the queues, the laundries and walking to work. Word had got around that 'Gibbo was doing something special', and there was much speculation.

Sonia was commissioned to make the wedding gift. Anyone who wished to participate in a 'draw Bagsy and Nat competition or anything associated with a wedding' submitted their efforts and Sonia built up a collage on a piece of cardboard. Gibbo offered to make the frame which, of course was scavenged. It was a ripper—a few burn marks here and there on the wood gave it a rustic look. They had to do it in secrecy, which made it even better. They couldn't wait to see Bagsy's and Nat's faces when they received it. The anticipation of the wedding and giving the gift gave everyone a new lease on life—something to look forward to.

*I felt the air of anticipation. I felt the friendship and love.*

That Sunday morning, Kaitlyn and Patsy did Nat's hair up with a few flowers added. The girls were busy with makeup and someone came up with some nail polish. 'Now, who in the fuck would pack that?' they laughed. Gibbo was busy. He had moved the hooch in buckets to the bullroom and made up some 'punch' with raspberry cordial. This time it was going to have a kick. Even Kaitlyn didn't know about it. Gibbo had a special white T-shirt, on which Sonia had painted a black bow tie.

Just before 3.00 pm, they all gathered in the bullroom. Bagsy and Nat made their appearance on the stairs, which had been decorated with streamers and balloons. They made a human aisle for the bridal couple to walk to Watsy the celebrant whilst chanting: 'Here comes the bride and groom, the classiest couple in the room. They want to put things right by getting married here tonight.' Gibbo and Kaitlyn were standing next to the celebrant. Natalie had borrowed an emerald green outfit. With her blonde hair swept up, and green eyes glowing, she looked radiant. Bagsy's outfit was put together by a combined effort. He beamed when he saw Nat all dressed up for the first time since their eviction and was obviously as proud as punch. The ceremony began and Watsy went into his spiel:

'We are gathered here today to witness the marriage of Natalie Jane Osborne to Andrew John Bagshaw.'

There were a few sniggers as nobody in the room knew their names other than Nat and Bagsy.

'According to the laws of Australia, (groan) this ceremony is a solemn commitment for life for Natalie and Andrew to pledge their love and support for each other. We may not have an Australian government, but we do still have Australian laws, which advocate decency and respect for each other. Natalie and Andrew have grown together with love, understanding, trust, and respect for each other. Andrew, do you choose Natalie to be your partner for life?'

'I do.'

'Natalie, do you choose Andrew as your partner for life?'

'I do.'

Gibbo produced the rings. The bridal couple repeated a pledge after Watsy, and exchanged rings.

'I give you this ring to celebrate my love for you and as a pledge to honour and grow with you for all of our lives together.'

Watsy beamed, 'I now pronounce you man and wife'. The cheer went up, and Gibbo took centre stage.

'I can't say I've known Bagsy and Nat all my life as it's only been a few months, but I feel like I've known you all my life. In fact, Bagsy, I don't even know what you used to do for a crust. 'I worked for a financial institution,' he replied. 'Hey everyone, we have a wanker banker in our mist. The party has to be called off.' He threw his arms around his mate's shoulder and added, 'But we'll forget about that as you have a proper job now.' They all laughed and Gibbo put on his solemn face and really did become serious. 'Sometimes, when the going gets tough, the friendships that are forged are stronger, and that is how Kats and I and—I think everyone in this room—feel for you as a couple. He went on to relate Bagsy's story of how the wedding was booked and deposits made before the invasion. 'I know this is not the way you had planned your wedding, but it's the next best thing and I hope everyone enjoys the party. Before I call upon Bagsy … oops, Andrew … to say a few words, I'd like them to accept a "little something" we have rustled up for this occasion.' Sonia went behind the food table and headed back to Gibbo with the 'painting' with the back facing outwards. In actual fact, no one had seen the finished product except Hamish. She handed it to Gibbo. 'We would like to give you this little gift that has been a contribution of many hands.' He turned the picture around and everyone gasped. Bagsy and Nat had tears in their eyes, as did pretty much everyone else. Now I'll hand you over to Bag … Andrew!'

'Good evening. I can't believe this … WE can't believe this. It's bloody terrific!' He looked at Nat. 'We're both stuck for words, but I do know that this gift will be treasured for a long time to come. I don't know what the wedding gifts would have been like had we got married before the world tipped itself upside down, but I don't think that anything could have been as good as this. I … we … would like to thank you from the bottom of our hearts, and rest assured it will be the most prized possession in our luxury apartment.' There was lots of laughter.

'I'd just like to share a little story of how Nat and I met. I'm very nervous, as you can hear in my voice, but I'll just talk slowly to overcome that.' The gathering laughed.

We met at Luton Airport, heading for a European ski resort. Nat was to be in charge of organising lift passes, administration and activities, and I was going as a ski instructor. We both worked for the same tour company during the summer months, and I had heard beforehand that she was pretty 'laid back' and I thought, 'That's cool, so am I.' We were on the skinny side of making our flight when Nat suggested a coffee would be a good idea and I thought, 'Yeah, sure' but I was kind of thinking that going to the gate might be a better one. But hey, I'd prefer to have a coffee with this beautiful lady. So, we sit down for coffee and they're calling the flight. I'm getting nervous, but Nat seemed relaxed, and we were having a lovely conversation about our past summer trips and all the strange things that can happen when you get thirty-odd young people on a bus to do their first European tour. They didn't think 'tour', they thought 'party'. Nat reckoned that they saw the bus and lost their capacity for rational thinking at exactly the same time. I did hear the call for our flight, but Nat seemed oblivious, so I thought she must know something that I didn't. Twenty minutes goes past and really, on the inside I'm ready to run for the gate, but I'm going to be working with this lady for the winter season and don't want to hear any stories that I'm all stressed out. She wasn't in a hurry, so neither was I. Eventually, Nat looked at her watch and said, 'Shall we head for the gate?' Whew – what a relief! We get up and meandered to customs, and Nat looks at me and says, 'Gees, Andy, I haven't got my passport. I must have left it back in the cafeteria!' I was kind of thinking, 'Well, one of us can catch this flight' but the moral of the story is that we had a moment in the airport where we had a slight panic. We weren't laid back anymore. We explained to the customs man what was going on and he wasn't impressed. I think he was more stressed than we were. So, we raced back to the cafeteria, dodging people ambling towards us. We find the passport and were running flat out with the customs man belting alongside us. It must have looked like we were practising the sprint for the Olympic Games, but with obstacles of people and luggage in our way. We could hear the final call in the distance and somehow tried to accelerate. We arrived at the gate just as the flight attendant was closing it. We must have looked a sight—red faces and puffing like steam trains. Fortunately, she smiled at us, opened the gate and said, 'Keep running, I'll try to stop them from closing the aircraft door.'

One person was not going to catch that flight. If one person missed it, both of us were going to miss it.'

There were sighs from the crowd.

'We decided there and then—that's it, we're in it as a team. That was our first obstacle. We made it—sweet, but from that point on we kinda decided we would stay as a team, and things developed pretty rapidly.' There were sniggers of laughter. 'As a friendship—for those of you thinking otherwise. As my grandmother would say, "That's your own mind."

Now, I would like to thank Gibbo for organising a special day for Nat and I, and for being the best man. Thanks, mate. Also, to Kaitlyn, who is a beautiful bridesmaid, Patsy for the decorations, and Sonia for the invitations. A special thank you to everyone who contributed with preparing this venue and providing the food. Ok, it's not the Hilton, but gees, at this particular time, it's going to taste even better!

Gibbo took centre stage again.

I would like to thank the wrinklies for preparing the food that is to follow. They were able to produce a feast as the community contributed the ingredients to make sure that this would be a memorable day—not only for the bride and groom, but to everyone in this room. There is a special 'drop' waiting for you. The punch is a wedding special with alcohol. Now I know it's banned, so not a word outside this room. If a GRAP gets wind of it, we didn't know it was alcoholic—we made some 'punch' out of old fruit in the laundry. However, we can't help ourselves and go ballistic, so Macca will be our barman.

A big cheer went up and Hamish covered his surprise with a big smile. 'Nat and Bagsy are going to sign the marriage certificate, Silo is going to take some photos, and we will need a few minutes to get the food ready. So, just mingle everyone.'

They cranked up the ghetto blaster to its max and played 'Laid Back' while everyone chatted. Tarantula went to Hamish. 'I've spent my teenage and adult life fighting alcohol, but when there's none available, I don't think about it anymore. You see Macca, I haven't got a stop button. Probably born without one. You guys have stop buttons that you may find hard to locate at times and, at the worst, don't find it till the next day. I keep going until I can get help in rehab. Macca, don't let me drink any of Gibbo's hooch. Hamish told him he would take him back to his block and stay with him, but Tarantula told him that was a dumb idea—'What, miss the party? No, I'll be smart enough to abstain'.

He wasn't.

**I've felt this guy in the past – he is not in control of his own actions. I don't know why.**

The evening was a resounding success. The punch went down a treat and the floor was packed with dancing bodies. Hamish delegated some of his bar duty time to dance with Sonia, who he had met only fleetingly since the cricket match. Sonia told Hamish that she had heard about Gibbo taking him out to sea on a boat and leaving him stranded. She had heard a very condensed version, where Hamish could see the land and had to swim for it. However, she was puzzled why he had taken so long to get back to work and assumed that he had spent the night at the police station. The music had stopped but they stood where they were. Hamish thought about it as he knew that Sonia and Kaitlyn were good friends, but decided to tell the truth as verbalising may help to get it out of his system.

He told her about being conned into getting into the cement truck. 'It was my own fault. I should have known better. Every instinct in my body told me not to get in that truck, but the lure of the sea was too great. I thought I may never get the opportunity again, so I grabbed it.'

He described the feeling when he realised that Gibbo was not going to come back. He described the feeling of loneliness with no land in sight, and night approaching. He relived the endless landscape of the sea, the vastness and the knowledge of death. He talked about finding the polystyrene, strapping it on and giving himself a slight chance of survival. He told her about the Southern Cross, the fish movement on his legs, and the fear of sharks. He told her about the dolphins, falling asleep and nearly losing his life raft. As he was talking, he didn't realise that Sonia had tears running down her cheeks. He also told her that thinking of her kept him going. When he got to the part of reaching land, Sonia threw her arms around him and sobbed.

'It's all over now, Sonia, and there's no sense in telling anyone else the truth. What happened that night is between us and it will serve no purpose to make it public. Somehow, I feel that talking about it has helped erase the memory.' They held each other tight.

It didn't – that night in the sea was etched in the memory – nothing could remove it.

At one stage, Gibbo came up to him, threw an arm around his shoulder and called out to Silo to take a photo. Hamish smiled because he felt so relaxed, and he was thoroughly enjoying Sonia's company. Everyone appreciated the good old 'Aussie style' food. The party had to wind up at 8.00 pm in order to get the bullroom back to rights again and let everyone in the block get some sleep, ready for work the next day.

This was another day to be remembered for many, many reasons.

# Hooch

The day before the wedding, an off-duty Power House policeman pulled up in sight of the old shed. He got out to relieve himself and, as he walked back to the car, he noticed the shed. He also noticed that the grass had been flattened near the doorway. He was curious. He walked across the paddock and went inside. He knew what was going on—he could smell it. He walked outside and followed the flattened grass a little while. He could see the apartment blocks in the distance. He smiled.

Everyone was talking about the wedding. 'Good onya, Gibbo,' they called. Silo was only too happy to show the wedding photos as the camera was handed round in communal laundries and kitchens.

For Hamish, it was a memorable day as he had been able to be with Sonia again and they planned to get together whenever possible. This was difficult for single people as there was absolutely no privacy, and free time was scarce.

On the building site during their lunch break, they surrounded Gibbo and asked how they could get more hooch. 'Nah,' said Gibbo, '...it was a one-off, mate. Too dangerous. I did it for Bagsy.' Gibbo couldn't go to the shops, play cards, have a game of baseball, throw a ball into a hoop, put some washing on the line, or put food into the fridge without someone asking how they could get more hooch. So much for telling the wedding guests to keep it under wraps. He had no intention of keeping the hooch going. The more he resisted, the more incessant the cry went up, and people were offering to pay. Gibbo couldn't believe his ears.

'Come on, guys, give it a break. We are all piss poor enough without an added expense,' he responded. 'It was a one-off,' he reiterated time and time again.

That night he went to the shed to dismantle. He was glad to do it as every time he went there, fear clutched inside him, and his heart pounded. He wanted to get it over and done with as quickly as possible. He got inside and got the shock of his life. Sitting on one of the old chairs that he had glued back together, was a GRAP policeman. Shit, I'm done for,' Gibbo thought. But the policeman smiled and made the international gesture with his fingers–tokens! Gibbo got the idea. This prick wants me to continue making hooch as a token-making operation. I can't report him as he's not 'fraternising'. Taking tokens from one of us would probably be applauded and I can't say no. Holy shit, I'm between a rock and a hard place. Gibbo smiled and nodded. Part of him recoiled at the thought of taking tokens off his mates but the other part knew that he now had police protection. He held up an empty packet of sugar and pointed to some leftover rotten fruit. The GRAP nodded and, pulling out his mobile phone, pointed to a day on the calendar. One week's time. Gibbo shook his head. 'Can't do, it takes longer,' he said, pointing to a date three more days on. The GRAP tapped on his mobile the '½' symbol on his calculator and pointed to the money sign on his mobile. The greedy prick wants half the proceeds. I'll be working for a GRAP and ripping my mates off. How am I going to get out of this one? Gibbo mused. He now had ten days to bottle the hooch, distribute and receive half the proceeds.

**Just as I feel storm clouds gathering, I feel trouble brewing. I have felt your impulsiveness in the past - don't go back to that shed!**

Gibbo told his mates that he had changed his mind. 'Shit, you guys really know how to lean on a fella. I've decided to play along with it and provide more hooch. However, you are going to have to provide me with jars, empty bottles and anything you can get your hands on and, yes you will have to pay because while you are tucked up in bed, I'll be working my butt off.' Not quite true, as really, the fermentation that he had pretty much perfected, worked by itself. He would have to find a funnel as he could not think of a way of gesticulating one with that cop prick. A week later, on the building site, he surprised Hamish by asking if he would help to distribute the hooch.

'It will be a piece of cake, Macca, and you have the smarts. We will use the bullroom at my apartment and punters will come to us. We will stagger the time, so we don't have too many people milling round. All you have to do is just hand out the bottles and I'll work out how much is in the container and take the tokens. We will have plenty of guards on the door. The thing is, the GRAPS don't like coming to the apartment blocks–haven't seen one for weeks. I just can't distribute it quickly by myself.'

Hamish was uncomfortable but felt compromised in front of his mates. They took it as an honour that Gibbo would ask Macca to be his right-hand man. They now assumed that Gibbo and Macca were best mates. On the Wednesday evening, it all went surprisingly well. Gibbo and Hamish sat at a table at the end of the bullroom, and (mainly guys) came with their tokens. Tarantula was one of the first and bought two bottles, which was his entire pay for the month. Hamish tried to discourage him, but it didn't work. It all went quickly and smoothly. Gibbo put the tokens into a plastic bag, and they disbanded. As Hamish left the building, Gibbo called out, 'Thanks Macca. Much appreciated.' Hamish just waved and left as quickly as he could.

Gibbo took the plastic bag to the shed that night and the GRAP cop was sitting in the same chair waiting for him. He seemed very relaxed and cheerful. His moon face was sweating from the heat of the shed. The buttons on his shirt were straining with patches of bare skin showing in the spaces in between. He was not in a hurry and started to chat using gestures. Gibbo got the impression that the GRAP was happy to work together as a team. Gibbo was puzzled as to how this policeman was going to exchange the tokens. Government officials looked upon them as something to be reviled and, if they did have to touch one, it was always with rubber gloves. He knew he would never find out. By gesturing to himself and

Gibbo and rubbing his fingers together to indicate tokens, he was saying, 'We will start a business venture together.' Gibbo put the tokens on the table and started to make two piles. The GRAP shook his head furiously and shovelled all the tokens back into the bag. Gibbo was seething. Fucking hell, he thought, he wants the whole fucking lot and I'm going to be working for this prick for the rest of my days, bleeding my community for what? Jack shit! He doesn't want a partner; he wants a puppet. I'm going to be sitting on this prick's lap like a ventriloquist's doll infinitum while he pulls the strings. He's going to happily watch me dance to his tune. What else is he going to get me to do? I'm sure he's not going to stop at a small batch of hooch and a handful of tokens. If … no … when I get caught, this piece of shit will be the first to see me swing in the breeze on a short piece of rope. Gibbo's blood was boiling inside his body. His stomach churned and he wanted to throw up as he watched with disgust the mute smiling figure in front of him. He watched his extended stomach pushing at the shirt buttons as the GRAP exhaled. He looked at the mouth liquid dripping onto his rubbery lips and his round sweating face with abhorrence. After what seemed like an eternity, the GRAP took out his mobile phone, showing Gibbo the next week for collection and, still smiling, turned to the door with his plastic bag.

*I feel the bitterness in your spirit. It's not that big a problem. Let him go on his way. There is no one to curb your anger and defuse the situation. I'm worried about you. Don't do anything rash.*

Gibbo's brain was racing - what could he do? He knew what Kat's would say – 'walk away'. But she would be wrong, this policeman could and would make his life *totally* miserable. Gibbo went over to the leftover fruit, grabbed the knife that he used for paring, took two quick steps, and lunged to the door just as the GRAP was opening it. He pushed the knife as hard as he could and the GRAP dropped. He was bleeding profusely but still breathing. Gibbo got the chair and banged it as hard as he could on the GRAP's head. He took out the knife, turned the GRAP over on to his back, and plunged it into what he hoped was his heart. The GRAP gurgled and lay still. Gibbo put his hand on his chest. He didn't think the GRAP was breathing, but he kept it there to make sure. His pent-up anger erupted. He had to wipe the smile off that ugly, lifeless face or it would come back to haunt him. He sliced his face from the top of the hairline, down the nose and through the mouth. Not good enough. He made another diagonal slice across the right eye down to the jawline. The smile was now looking more like shock. He finished it off with a slice down the left eye to make a star pattern. There was no smile left. He bundled up the body, removed the mobile phone and plastic bag, and stuffed it into the cupboard. He had to get rid of the body and leave no evidence. He had to give himself some thinking time. He had to remove all traces of hooch plus blood. He had to get the shed in pristine order, even if it took all night.

He went backwards and forwards to his unit, carrying back water and rags. Kaitlyn woke up a couple of times and he said, 'It's okay, love, just a bit of a mess to clean up in the shed as a couple of containers have burst and there's not only a mess, but a smell that could be detected for miles.' When he finally got to bed that night, he lay awake working out a plan to dispose of the body. He knew he was drop-dead tired but he had to get his brain into gear. He eventually got to sleep as the sun was rising and Kats was calling him to wake up.

The next day was a nightmare. Gibbo was in the cement truck, and he swung back to the shed. He had to move fast and leave no trace as the truck was on a time schedule. He grabbed the body and threw it into the passenger seat. He knew he couldn't put it into the cement as it could come out in one big lump. Gibbo headed for the boat. He would head out as far as he could and toss it overboard. He would disconnect some wires before arriving at the next building site and be stranded with a broken-down truck. He rounded the corner to the cove. 'Shit! The boat's gone. The bastards have found it.' He had to go back to the shed, put the body back in the cupboard and get back to the building site as quickly as possible. He now had to rethink and come up with Plan B.

**I feel trouble. Oh – what have you done?**

# The Fire

That night, Gibbo went back to the shed with a can of fuel he had milked from the cement truck, and a box of matches. He didn't want the shed to go up in a ball of fire as it would attract too much attention. He didn't want fire trucks or the police to investigate. He wanted it to burn and smoulder. He used the fuel sparingly, like stepping stones across the floor surface. He poured small amounts on the table and chair. He used more fuel to douse the body and the outside of the cupboard. He dropped a match, but it missed the fuel, and the flame went out. He had a couple more goes before the flame hit and the fire sparked. He had done it. He was on his way home in the dark with the torch in his pocket. He turned round and could see the glow.

**My rain clouds have been gathering.**

He was so busy thinking of last night that he didn't feel the rain. His foremost thoughts were what he should have done if he hadn't lost his cool. The rain's fine drizzle had turned into drops before Gibbo realised the consequences. He turned around and saw smoke, but the glow was minimal. Should he go back and have another go? The rain would be a battle. He decided not to. He had put enough fuel in the cupboard and had started the fire right next to it—the body should be cremated. By the time he got home, he was wet and cold. Kaitlyn woke up but once again, but he reassured her and said, 'It's all right, love, everything is back to rights.' He couldn't sleep, listening to the rain.

The next day, Gibbo had a problem: what to do with the mobile phone and the knife. He decided that the phone may come in handy. He turned it off and threw it into his pocket. He could smash it if it wasn't of any use and that could go in the cement truck. In the meantime, he would hide it in a fridge, packaged like a sandwich. He thought of the perfect place to hide the knife.

That day at the building site, Gibbo was tired and withdrawn. His mates immediately noticed but he told them that one of the containers had leaked and he had spent all night cleaning up. 'With the right wind, the smell could carry to the other side of the island. I can't continue like this. It's too bloody risky and it's doing my head in. I'm not going to make any more fucking hooch.' His mates sympathised, and the word spread. Gibbo was relieved that everyone had dropped the subject and life could get back to what it was. He deeply regretted making the hooch in the first place and decided that what had happened was now a community problem, not a personal one. He made the hooch in good faith and any consequences had to be shared. He didn't realise just how much the community would have to pay for this glitch that he had created. He returned to organising and participating in the evening activities. He found some old carpet and made a 'bocce' mat. He levelled a patch of dirt near one of the blocks and put in a putting hole. With the old golf sticks he had found, they would take it in turns to have chipping and putting competitions. He was back to his old self.

Gibbo was on his way back from the shops when one of the older schoolgirls, in bare feet, called, 'Hey Gibbo.' When he got adjacent, she said in a low voice, 'Thought you'd better know that the Chop Sueys are getting very serious at catching shoplifters. They're telling us at school that the stocktake numbers are not adding up. The token system makes it easy for them to detect any discrepancies.'

'They're probably using an abacus,' chirped in Gibbo. 'What's that?' 'Never mind. Why are you telling me this?' The kid looked up at him with a grin and said, 'No reason, just thought you might like to know. They think it's us kids and they're watching us like hawks. This is stupid, Gibbo. We're not game to even think about it. If we got caught, we may never see our parents again and the thought of that blows our brains away.' The kid looked down as if the thought had dragged her head down to her feet. 'Where are your shoes?' 'Can't afford them. Parents are handing down any shoes with some life in them to younger kids. But when your feet grow like mine to size 9, they are way too expensive for anyone to buy. The Power Houses reckon if you're going to have big feet, you will have to pay!' Gibbo asked her name and told her to come to his block the following Sunday and he would find her some shoes. Then, with a wry smile, he said, 'Thanks for the info, kiddo.' Gibbo did find a pair of size 9 sneakers and was very proud to hand them over. 'They have got some life left in them AND they're matching.' He didn't tell her that he traded some articles from Foodies that he forgot to pay for, to get the shoes.

This incident got Gibbo thinking. He told Kaitlyn, 'The families are doing it tough. We are finding it hard enough to subsist and we don't have dependants. If they are earning more than we are, it wouldn't be much. I reckon we should organise an op shop–the wrinklies like volunteering for that sort of thing. It could open on a Sunday arvo. If we pool our resources and use one of the laundries in the block, we can give the proceeds to the families. We can sell books–they're in demand.'

Kaitlyn was enthusiastic. 'And you can donate the hooch tokens to kick it off.'

'I forgot to tell you that I've already divvied it out, Kats, and given it to some families. I didn't have enough for every family on the island– just two blocks. I did it very quietly and you should have seen the look on the faces of those people. They were just so grateful. I was able to knock on doors in the evenings and pass the tokens on. I did keep a bit back to give to Tarantula, although he didn't deserve it, as he spent all of his pittance and would have gone hungry. However, I've made up my mind never to make another batch of hooch again.'

Kaitlyn gave him a hug. 'You are all heart and you'll always have mine.'

They decided to call it 'Gibbo's Op Shop' and Sonia did up some posters to put on the communal fridges. 'Bring your unwanted goods–anything at all–and we will sell them and help our struggling families clothe and feed their children. Any unwanted shoes, books, clothes, toys, household items, etc will be gratefully received.' She included the block number and date. The majority of Aussies thought it a great idea and looked carefully at their few possessions to see what they could cull. Hamish had brought as many books as he could pack and, even though most of them had pages ripped out, he knew they would be wanted. Sonia invested in some cardboard and made posters to decorate children's bedrooms. She did a series of Harry Potter scenes for the older children and Paddington Bear and Thomas the Tank for the younger ones. Some of the single folk bought Sonia's posters and then donated them back so they doubled in price. The wrinklies made cakes and biscuits, which were popular.

The opening of the op shop achieved a meeting ground as people came out of curiosity. Tabasco, Watsy, Bagsy, Nat, Patsy, Tarantula, Presto, and Beags all eagerly wanted to help but mainly got in the way as there was little to do. The wrinklies had it all under control and made it plain that they were in charge. It was easy to set up as it just needed a couple of tables, but it was chaotic.

Tabasco saw Sonia and went over. 'Where's Macca?' Then he answered his own question. 'Probably held up in a queue.' He looked serious. 'Sonia, there's something I should tell you. I was with Gibbo the night we left Macca out at sea. Has he told you?' She looked at him and nodded. 'I was sick with worry that night and had to tell Patsy. When he showed up to work, I was so relieved and vowed to make sure we will always be friends no matter what Gibbo says or does. I knew how far out we had taken him, and he would have had to spend the night at sea. I never had the nerve to talk to him about it, but I'm buggered if I know how he survived. He certainly showed a truck load of courage and I'm full of admiration of him. I didn't know that Gibbo would leave Macca floundering out at sea. I yelled for him to turn the boat around. But I should have done more. I should have taken control of the boat, but to tell you the truth, I was frightened of capsizing. I'm surprised that Macca can stand being in the same room as me, as he probably thought I was Gibbo's little helper. I never told Macca that I threw the esky lid overboard.' Sonia went to speak, but Tabasco put up his hand. 'What could he say—"Well, aren't you the generous one, thank you!"' I was thrilled to see Gibbo treat him as a long-lost friend when that police car brought him to work. I figured that Gibbo must have felt just as guilty as I was. We were talking about it the other night and Patsy told me she had told Kaitlyn. Now I'm wondering if Kaitlyn had given Gibbo a hard time because she's pretty good at that. When Kats has a beef, we all run for cover. Even Gibbo heads for the hills. Now I'm wondering if he wasn't contrite at all.' Sonia told Tabasco not to worry and said it was all in the past. 'Gibbo can be hot headed, but he does have a kind heart. Look around, he's organised this to help the kids. We have to forget the past—we have enough to worry about in the future.' She gave him a smile and said: 'But I admire Hamish ... oops, Macca ... just as much as you do.'

People came with their bits and pieces, which the wrinklies tagged. Some non-affordable grocery items turned up at budget prices and were snapped up. They had enough stock to trade for two hours. Bagsy, Nat and Kaitlyn counted the tokens and divided it into separate plastic bags ready for distribution. Like everyone else, Hamish was enjoying the camaraderie and being with Sonia. The word spread and the enthusiasm for 'Gibbo's Op Shop' grew.

Gibbo was determined to keep it going and, despite the warning, decided to up the ante with shoplifting. He wanted the GRAPS to contribute to his enterprise. However, he had to be more vigilant than in the past. He was familiar with the security guards—always stopping to chat and using gestures to get his message through. He got to know the serious 'no-nonsense' ones as well as the more jovial ones. However, it was the slack ones that he liked the best. He knew the ones who had a smattering of English and didn't call them

'Fried Rice' or 'Chop Sueys' to their face. There were times when he got past the checkout and the security guards had changed. He couldn't chance it, so he would leave his purchases on the ground near the checkout and put the items he had taken, compliments of the Power Houses, back on the shelves. He then had to purchase something small so as not to attract any attention to himself and start the checkout process all over again. He never stole expensive merchandise as this would immediately create suspicion if the fridges or shelves were inspected by the GRAPS. He hid his cache of chocolate, tinned fish and other small items in various communal fridges under fictitious names. He was able to slip in his goods anonymously, as the op shop was always a scene of chaos.

After the second opening, when the wrinklies declared the op shop closed, the group went to the kitchen to divvy up the tokens and discuss if they could keep it going in the future. They knew that the number of donated goods would dwindle as everyone had few possessions. However, the edible items were a winner, and the wrinklies could be relied on to make cakes and biscuits. They decided to enlist the help of single folk to retrieve old fruit from Power House bins, which could be used to stew or make into jam.

As they were sitting chatting, Gibbo asked Patsy about her life before the invasion. 'You seem to go pretty quiet when we talk about our old lives, Patsy. Where did your folk originate from and what were they like? Patsy replied, 'My real name is "Pacita", but my younger sisters and brother couldn't wrap their tongues round that one and it was only Mum and Dad who called me that. My Aussie father was much older than my mother, who came out from the Philippines when she was a teenager. I grew up with a retail background. My father had surf shops and I worked in one–but not Dad's. When I heard Watsy talk about his parents and upbringing at the "big bash", I couldn't help thinking that his folk and mine should have got together and evened things out a bit. Watsy, I know that you came from a family of big spenders, but mine–well, Dad, was the absolute opposite. You see, he was diagnosed with a dead quarter of a heart and no pacemaker or any medical intervention could help.

He was told to be "careful" and, trust me, he was. However, because of his weak heart, he always got the sympathy vote.

I was the oldest of five kids—three sisters and a brother. Mum and Dad rented a two-bedroom, ground level duplex with a makeshift bedroom that was once the front porch. It had no internal access for my brother, so even as a preschooler, he had a key to get into his bedroom.

'A latch-door toddler—reckon that would be a first,' mused Gibbo. 'My parents wouldn't trust me with an outside room and key when I was a teenager!' There were nods and laughter. 'Yeah … well, the duplexes were one behind the other on our block and we had the 'behind' one. You can imagine that seven people living in a two-and-a-bit bedroom home with one living area and one bathroom, was very crammed,' continued Patsy.

'Sounds luxurious,' chipped in Watsy.

'Yeah, I know. It sounds salubrious in comparison to the housing now, but back then it was considered extremely basic. During the weekdays, Dad had a sports wear/surf shop in Adelaide, and he would catch the train into work to open up at 9.00 am. However, because of his weak heart, he had a sleep every afternoon, so he had to have a hotel room as it was too far for him to come home. He changed hotels frequently, but I didn't know why.

On the weekends, us kids would have to play over at our friends' houses as Dad's weak heart could not take the presence of noisy, active children. So, he would sit in the lounge room, listening to his CD collection, while rolling his own Drum cigarettes. Dad believed that smoking was only related to lung disease and would benefit a weak heart by helping him to stay relaxed.'

They all choked on that one.

'I can never remember Dad doing anything round the house— like clearing blocked drains, or doing any repairs. Mum had to do all that. I never ever saw the landlord or a tradesperson. If the hotplate on the stove didn't work, it stayed that way.'

'If the stove didn't work in our house, it was quickly replaced with the most upmarket, expensive one on the market. No waiting for 'specials' in my family. Sorry, Patsy, tell us more about your background,' interjected Watsy.

Patsy smiled. 'Well, coming from a Philippine background, us kids all went to the local catholic school. I don't think I ever saw Grandma without a string of rosary beads in her hand. Mum spent a lot of time at the church, but Dad wasn't so committed— just Easter and Christmas. I'll never forget having to rock up at the church for my First Holy Communion in a dress that Mum made—I think—the night before. She put some lace on a white T-shirt and made a skinny tube out of a piece of white cotton material. She hemmed both ends and elasticised the top. She was so pleased with her efforts that I didn't want to tell her how awful the finished product looked. I was also so excited about my special holy day, particularly the party and games that followed. I got dressed, but the skirt was too long, so it had to be hoicked up around my chest. It looked terrible, so my sister found some ribbon to cover the elastic, and she made a bow. She also did my hair with fresh flowers adorning. Mum was beaming and I was miserable because I couldn't walk. My legs were jammed together by the material. We had over a kilometre to walk to the church, so my sisters, brother and mum all took turns to grab both of my arms and leap me along. I virtually jumped to the church. When I got there, my problems increased. The first thing we had to do was genuflect (which Patsy demonstrated by getting down on one knee and making the sign of the cross). Of course, this was impossible. All I could do was bow from the waist. All the kids were dressed to the nines, looking like miniature brides and grooms, and there I was in an outfit that I couldn't walk in. I managed to slink down in the pew by holding onto the seat in front with my arms and extending my legs under the seat—like a seesaw. It was painfully uncomfortable, but standing for an hour throughout the service was not an option.

'We didn't know you were religious, Patsy.'

'I'm not, Sonia. It's a boys' club and I'm not a boy,' she added with a smile and continued, 'When it came time to walk up the aisle to receive our first holy communion, the 'brides' were on one side, with the 'grooms' on the other. Well, the space between me and my 'groom', and the kids in front, was widening and he was whispering, "Walk faster." I was doing a running shuffle at this stage and when we got to the altar we had to kneel in front of the priest. This was impossible as I tried bending my knees and it just wasn't happening. The priest must have decided that I had a physical disability and solemnly gave me my communion. I then had to get back to my seat, minus the 'groom' as he disappeared as quickly as he could. The party food afterwards helped my mood but I couldn't join in any games. But then, neither could the other girls—the playground was not suited to mini brides. While the boys tore around, we had to glumly sit and look pretty.

I'm not sure why Dad wasn't there for my first communion, but I think it must have been at the start of winter. You see, the Adelaide winters were too harsh for Dad's weak heart and every year he would have to go to places like Italy or Spain. However, there were times that severe weather conditions prevented this trip, so he would head off to Queensland.

Well, one night after tea, Dad told us that before his heart gave its final beat, he would like one little indulgence. The next week, this little treat turned up in the form of a brand-new, shiny, silver Maserati. Of course, us kids went wild with excitement until we were told that we weren't allowed inside it as we might damage the leather seats. The Maserati was kept in a garage at the end of a long and narrow driveway. Dad only had centimetres each side when he backed it out.'

Silo was puzzled. 'Your dad sounds pretty wealthy. How come your mum didn't question his finances? She must have been surprised to see a new Maserati in the driveway.'

'She was absolutely IT ignorant. Dad was a whizz on the computer and all transactions were done electronically. Mum showed no interest at all—I think she was probably too busy with us kids and the church.'

They all looked at Patsy, who continued, 'Well, one day when Dad was still in Italy or Spain, and Mum was at the church arranging flowers; my older sister, Therese, and I went hunting in their bedroom for our Christmas presents in the hope that it wouldn't be the usual pair of brown school socks. Anyway, we found a packet of Drum with some papers and, of all things, the keys to the Maserati!'

Someone chipped in but Patsy retorted, 'What do you mean "oh no?" We couldn't believe our luck! We decided we would have our first cigarette sitting in Dad's car. We had rolled cigarettes for him in the past and were pretty good at it. Anyway, we lit up and I coughed so violently that the cigarette fell from my fingers onto the floor. As I picked it up, I saw a large, brown envelope on the floor of the car and pulled it out. Inside were pictures of Dad and what us kids regarded as lots of really old ladies. They would have been at least thirty years of age or even a bit more. In those days, although he was computer savvy, Dad believed in hard copy. The photos were taken in holiday locations such as Italy, Spain or Queensland. At the age of thirteen, I had no idea what was going on, and then Therese told me that the ladies must be nurses as it was too dangerous for Dad to travel on his own with his weak heart. So that explained that, although I always thought nurses wore some sort of uniform—not bikinis!'

Gibbo had a huge grin on his face. 'I don't know about everyone else, but I thought you and your sister were going to try to back the Maserati down the driveway.'

Patsy just laughed. 'No way, Gibbo. We valued our lives way too much to even think about it.'

So, what happened to your old man?

'Well, Dad's heart conked out not long before the pandemic. He was just a few months shy of his seventieth birthday. We all got a huge shock—but not from his death. It was his last will and testament that sent us into a spin. We found out that Dad had purchased both duplexes when my oldest sister was a baby. So, he was the landlord. We also found out that he had two other sportswear/ surf shops in Sydney as well as a pile of blue-chip shares that you couldn't jump over. Dad's will was a fairly messy affair and probate took ages. We didn't have much time to enjoy our new wealth when the invasion hit. I wonder what Dad would have thought had he known that his accumulated cache went to foreign hands.'

Silo shook his head in bewilderment. 'It's amazing. You didn't even know your Dad owned property. I'm not having a go at you, Patsy, but your dad sure had the smarts to keep his financial affairs hidden from the family. I can understand your mum having other priorities but as you got older, you kids would have asked questions and been very computer savvy.'

Patsy chuckled. 'You're right, Silo. Believe me, as we were growing up, we did ask questions about the family's financial status. However, Dad was very good at discouraging any conversation along those lines. He took the tack that talking about household money was not dignified and that we should come up with more intelligent questions about the world's economy, that would affect everybody. When Dad died, us kids collectively couldn't break into the myriad of passwords that he had set up for his financial affairs. Of course, his accountant and lawyer were in the know.'

They all thought about Patsy's childhood and pensively chatted about the naivety of childhood. The forbidden swear words that had no meaning but sounded delicious in the school playground. Nat told them that when she asked her older sister where babies came from, her sister wasn't sure, so Nat said she would ask Mum. Her sister thought for a moment and then responded decisively, 'That's a really dumb idea—she wouldn't know!'

# The Rules Change

It took a few weeks before the shed was investigated by the police, and the charred body discovered. Gibbo started to feel confident that it would never be discovered as this burnt out shed melded into the landscape. Due to the major bush fires on the island before the pandemic, that had caught the world's attention—burnt out properties, particularly outhouses, still dotted the island. However, Gibbo's optimism was short lived.

*I felt the body being removed. I felt the shock and horror of the discovery. I feel vengeance.*

The body was taken to the morgue, where it was identified. The autopsy revealed murder by stabbing. Initially, the police officer was not missed as the administration was in the embryo stage and massively overstaffed. Everyone assumed that he had been transferred back to mainland Nan Tudi (Australia) as the police force was sending personnel backwards and forwards. He had not been on the island long enough to forge friendships. He had also walked to his destination that night as the police car that he used during the day was a communal one with many drivers, and he only had the keys to that one vehicle. It had taken a relatively long time before anyone became suspicious of his absence and started to investigate. The Power Houses were incensed.

The Big Feet and Long Noses would have to pay.

The rules changed rapidly. Notices were placed on every block, inside and out:

# THERE BEEN STABBING AND YOU GUILTY OF MURDER
## ALL PERSON BE FOUND AND PUNISH
## ALL PERSON OVER 15 YEAR, NOW
## WORK SIX AND HALF DAY WEEK
## NIGHT CURFEW 8.00 pm
## NO TOGETHER HALF DAY OFF WORK
## YOU BE TOLD WHICH DAY OF WEEK HALF DAY BE
## YOU BE HUNT DOWN AND PUNIS

**I have felt the swift retaliation before. *The offence was enormous. Any person or persons under suspicion would be dealt with harshly. The brutality of the murder would be met with greater brutality. I have felt this before with my first people—the conquerors needed to flex their muscles. They had to show who was boss.***

The Power House officials poured over the housing blocks. Surveillance cameras and flood lights were immediately installed. They removed the basketball rings from inside and out, the old carpet that had been used as a pitch and the wicket painted bins. The ground used for chipping and putting was cemented. The old, scavenged golf clubs, the baseball bat whittled from a lump of wood, old tennis balls, and the home-made football that had also served as a basketball, was removed. The Power Houses did not want the Big Feet to congregate. They were useful only as labourers.

Yes, there were suicides, particularly among the wrinklies, who had decided that their miserable lives were now intolerable. The Power Houses certainly did not discourage this but quickly removed the bodies from the cement below the upper story units.

Gibbo was scared. He had been scared before—getting into trouble at school as a youngster (which was fairly frequent) and at times when he was playing footy. He was scared during the pandemic and, of course, during the invasion. But he had never felt scared like this. He didn't want to eat or talk but knew that he had to act as normally as possible. He also knew that, despite asking everyone at the wedding to keep it to themselves, just about everyone on the island knew about the hooch. How long would it be before the police linked the hooch with the shed? There were times when his hands shook so badly that he had to thrust them into his pockets. However, every person on the island over the age of twelve was a suspect in the eyes of the Power Houses.

At the building site the next day, Gibbo could see by the gaunt faces and lack of camaraderie that he was not the only one who was frightened. It was about 10.30 am when three police cars pulled into the building site. Police jumped out shouting and they all had to line up. Gibbo was certain that they had come for him and had to keep his hands in his pockets. The police shouted a name, 'And Rew Bag Shaw'. Police had raided the housing blocks and found a small bottle of hooch in his possession. 'Shit, they've got Bagsy,' someone whispered. The raid was ad hoc but three more bottles of hooch were found and the owners arrested. They must be linking the hooch with the shed. Gibbo's hands were going ballistic in his pockets and he was sure that everyone would notice. As soon as he saw the police car, his mouth instantly drained of all moisture and he could feel his face pulsate and redden. Oh, for a drink of water. If any official asked him a question, he knew his voice would be cracked and give him away. He tried to slow his racing heart-beat down by taking deep breaths and slowly exhaling. It didn't work. He could feel beads of moisture on his forehead – a dead give-away. He must look so OBVIOUS! His hands continued shaking in his pockets. Had they also found the phone? Apparently not as the police bundled Bagsy into a car and drove off. Any hooch that was left on that island was disposed of, and containers cleaned and thrown in bins that night.

They were all issued with a summons to a Power House building on their half day off work. Two days later, they found out that they all had to be fingerprinted and issued with a tracker. They heard about the long queues that they would have to join. 'Dog registration used to be easier than this,' Gibbo told Kaitlyn. Satellite images of people leaving the Power House buildings with their tracker anklets were beamed across the world. The information was the leading media news splashed across televisions and the press:

**'Australians Tracked in the Outback'.**

(Old allies did not recognise the new The Power House name of 'Nan Tudi').

**These photographs show internees on an island that we know as 'Kangaroo Island' off the coast of South Australia. This dictatorial new regime is making it compulsory for all ex-Aussies to wear a GPS device on their ankles. Their movements can now be traced. These images of queues of people include children, some possibly as young as twelve years of age. Why this sudden decision to track every internee is a mystery as this is not compatible with the Power House's persistent claim that their rule will provide a better lifestyle for all.**

The articles went on to describe to their readers the long hours and menial work forced upon the once proud Australians.

Beags was standing in the queue on his afternoon off when he was pulled aside by two GRAPS. No one knew why. He disappeared into the administration block.

Gibbo was convinced that they would query him about the hooch. They must be making a connection with the shed. At the very least, they will find out that I supplied the hooch. Time is running out.

It was Kaitlyn who was asking questions. 'Gibbo, has this murder got anything to do with the hooch you were making?'

'Of course not. Gees, Kats, give us a break.'

'Who else knows about it or helped you to make the hooch?'

'I swear. No one.'

When Kaitlyn stared at him with a raised eyebrow, he continued. 'To tell you the truth, Kats, I wanted to do it on my own.' He gave her a grin. 'I wanted to be the hero.'

Kaitlyn knew that last statement was definitely the truth.

Gibbo had to act fast to use the mobile phone to contact the outside world and get help. He had to get it out of the communal fridge where it was wrapped in an old singlet and covered in alfoil. It looked like a sandwich with Gibbo's name marked on the plastic bag. And no one ever touched anyone else's food. He would have to warm the phone before turning it on as the condensation could render it useless. He had an unmarried aunt in England, who was a headmistress of a large school. She was a very determined and feisty lady. Her favourite saying was that she had had plenty of suitors, but none that suited her. Gibbo, as a kid, loved dialling out to Aunty Bev, and he could remember her phone number. He was always the first one to talk to her when she answered, and she always made a big fuss of him. He hadn't seen her since he was ten years of age, but he sent a Christmas card each year. In the last one he had enclosed a photo of himself and Kats. He had to make a telephone call just before dark as the cameras and flood lights would prohibit any movement at night. He would have to make it before he was fitted with a tracker. He also needed privacy and the only place that had a slight chance of affording that luxury was at the clothes lines. He put the phone in the middle of the dirty clothes basket and placed it on the floor next to a washing machine. It had to stay there all day. He knew he was taking a risk but if the police were to get him—and the chances were very high—he wanted a fair trial. He wanted the world to know. In his mind, this was his only chance of survival.

Just before nightfall, Gibbo went to the laundry. No one there. He got the phone and took it outside to the empty, walled clothesline enclosure. The rain had slowed down to a drizzle. There were a couple of sheets, some towels and some children's clothing on the lines but they were wet. No one would want to take them inside. Windows were closed due to the rain, which helped Gibbo as he did not want his voice to carry. He dialled. The phone rang and rang. Come on, Aunty Bev—it's Saturday, about 9.00 am your time—you have to be home. Come on!

Gibbo was about to give up when he heard a voice. 'Hello'. Relief ran through his body.

'Aunty Bev, it's me, Jack Gibson,' he said in his loudest whisper. 'Ja ...' she started to say, but he chipped in. 'Please don't talk. Just listen.'

'I want you to go to your government and the media. I want you to tell them what is happening in our country that was called Australia. Someone killed a Power House policeman and we are all being treated as suspects. I am ringing from Kangaroo Island that was in the international media before the pandemic because of the large-scale bushfires. It's now called 'Daishiu Dao/Kartu'. I don't know where Mum and Dad, Jamie or Lexie are as we have all been split up and sent to different allocations. We have no way of communicating with the outside world. I have nicked this phone and will have to destroy it after I hang up. Our only use to the new Power Houses is labouring. We get one half day off a week. People have been taken away on suspicion and I doubt we will ever see them again. Aunty, I want the world to know what is happening because if I do get arrested along with other innocents, I want a fair trial. If your media can track down prisoners and you find out that I'm one of them, cut the photo of me out that I sent you at Christmas time. If I am arrested and we are all suspects, I want my photo splashed across the papers and TV. Our lives are hanging by a thread. I have to hang up now, but I'm begging you to inform your government. Will you do that?'

'Yes, Jack.' He hung up. The following Monday, his tenacious aunt took time off work and headed to Parliament House. She made it very clear that she wanted to see the prime minister's press secretary and would not leave the building until her request was granted. She wanted written assurance from the prime minister that her statement had been sighted. That week also saw her in the offices of every major newspaper and Scotland Yard. She was informed that, to date, satellite images showed no signs of any maltreatment, but further observation of conditions on Kangaroo Island would be closely monitored in the future. Scotland Yard requested the name of the informer on the island.

Before being fitted with a tracker, Gibbo had to find a new shed. He found a burnt-out ruin with a partial roof that was further away but, to a degree, feasibly accessible. He put his fingerprints over every surface. He decided against smashing the mobile phone and instead putting it in the cement mixer, as it may be useful in the future. He buried it in the dirt near the wall that had a rust mark from the home-made basketball ring. The following day, he was fingerprinted and one ankle adorned with a tracker. Because of the large-scale use, these GPS devices were rushed off the production line and had to be cut off to be unarmed. The removal of the device for the wearer would have caused a quicker police response as they were rarely monitored. It wasn't feasible for the Power Houses to track every person on the island every day and night. They were only scrutinised if the wearer's behaviour was a concern to any relevant authority. They were useless as no one had time to go anywhere outside of work hours, except to the shop and the clothesline. However, they were demeaning for the wearer. They felt they had been branded.

# Concerns

Nat was distraught when Bagsy was arrested and taken away. She went to Kaitlyn, sobbing. 'They have taken my Andy, Kats, and there's nothing I can do. I don't know if he will remain on the island. I don't even know if he is alive. This is like a terrible nightmare and it has all been over a bottle of hooch. I know Gibbo supplied the hooch to make our wedding memorable and had no idea of the consequences, but I wish we had not got married. Everything has gone pear shaped since our wedding and I blame myself for that. I should never have gone along with it. But Kats, that's being smart on hindsight.' The tears were flowing when she added: 'Kats, a part of me wants to know where Gibbo made that hooch. But, another part of me says it doesn't matter.' Kaitlin threw her arms around Nat's shoulders as they sobbed together.

Hamish shared his afternoon off with Kaitlyn and they were both summoned on the same day to be fingerprinted and fitted with a tracker. There were only five people between them in the queue and Kaitlyn said to each of them, 'Can I jump the queue as I really want to talk to Macca? I'll go back to my original place when we get close to the end.' 'No worries, love,' was the response.

Kaitlyn asked Macca how he was and then she turned to him very seriously and said, 'Macca, I want to talk to you about Gibbo. You see, what I love about him is his flair. He has a fair bit of larrikin in him and a great sense of humour. But, when he gets riled up, he really can't see the woods for the trees at times. He basically loves people—well, his sort of people. He gathers them up and they respond. He will go to great lengths to please people. He couldn't wait to get that cricket match, organised and basked in its success for days. He'd say "Did you see the kids, Kats? They were having such a good time." But he can be a bit black and white. I couldn't understand why he took such a disliking to you, Macca. I'm not sure what that was all about. All I know is that he ranted about you being a filthy, rotten rat. I thought he'd get over it quickly, but it seemed to fester inside him. Of course, I haven't known you long, Macca, but my impression is a normal, decent guy with a nice nature … (she smiled) … and good looking.' She gave him another impish grin and added: 'I couldn't wish a better person for my friend, Sunny.' They shuffled along in the queue.

'I couldn't understand the person I know as Gibbo wanting to harm another human being. You see, Tabasco told Patsy, who told me about the boat trip, and I went off my head. Gibbo was contrite and I was really pleased to hear about him putting out a hand of friendship to you at the building site. I felt that 'my Gibbo' was back. Macca, I'm really sorry for what he did to you.'

They continued shuffling along in the queue. 'It's okay, Kaitlyn …' said Hamish. '…it's all in the past. In fact, it now seems so long ago, I'd almost forgotten about it.' This wasn't true, but he downplayed what really happened to make her feel better. Telling the truth would be of no benefit. To change the subject, he said, 'Gibbo told me you had dogs. You must miss them.' Kaitlyn looked at Hamish and said, 'I know he told people we didn't want kids. He'd say, "Nah mate, we had dogs—you can train dogs." I heard it time and time again, but it wasn't quite true. We did want kids but it just didn't happen. We even had a pact that if we had boys, they would have 'Gibson' for a surname and the girls would have my surname 'Stewart'. He'd say, "We'll start a trend, Kats, and have a family tree with straight lines, no branches. Reckon that's fair play." Gibbo thought he had originated a brilliant idea; however, he got mumps in his early adult years and always blamed this for a low sperm count.' Kaitlyn paused. 'Yes, we did love our dogs.'

As they shuffled along, Kaitlyn told Hamish that she was really worried. 'You see, Macca, when I got the flu or whatever

117

it was, I was only vaguely aware that Gibbo was not always at home. I did wonder how he came up with the hooch. He was hell-bent on making Bagsy and Nat's wedding a hoot—and he did it. We all needed a bit of a lift at that time as life continued to be such hard work. Then, after the wedding, when everyone wanted more, Gibbo went out at night. I didn't know where to. One night, I woke up to see Gibbo with a heap of rags in a bucket and I asked him what was going on. He said something like, "It's okay, Kats. A container has burst and you can smell it for miles. I just have to clean up the ..." Macca, I'm not sure, but I think he said 'shed'.' Hamish sucked in his breath and was silent. They shuffled along in silence. 'Look, Kaitlyn, the thing is ... we are jumping to conclusions. Gibbo is just one person on this island. There are plenty more desperate, and probably mentally unbalanced, people who can't figure out the consequences and would like to kill a GRAP. I think Gibbo is too smart for that. We don't know where he made the hooch but the likelihood is that we are coming to the wrong conclusion.'

Kaitlyn wasn't the only one who was suspicious of the link between the hooch, the shed and the murder. At the building site that day, when Gibbo was off in the cement truck; Watsy, Presto, Tabasco, and Tarantula talked about their concerns and decided to confront Gibbo to hear his take on the matter. They decided they couldn't do it on site and also, they wanted Macca and the girls to be in on it. They decided to go to Gibbo's unit that evening.

Gibbo's back was to the wall. 'I'll tell you where the hooch was—and it wasn't in a fucking shed. In fact, now that I know, along with everyone else, the whereabouts of the shed where the murder took place, it's in an ideal position. I just wasn't smart enough to find it in the first place. There is an old burnt ruin with an undercover lean-to. Reckon you've all been past it going to the shop. To my eye, all structures with a tin roof look the same. I may have even mentioned a 'shed' to Kats. However, to make myself absolutely clear, I used a three-sided lean-to—think it was part of an old verandah that was left standing after the main building was annihilated by the bushfire. While you guys were busy sleeping, I was working for a cause—to make Bagsy and Nat's wedding a bloody good one. Now you miserable lot of clever dick detectives are turning on me and accusing me of fucking murder. Shit, you guys really know how to deliver a killer punch. You're not wrong that I hate the bastards, and if I could have got my hands on one of them, I would have done exactly the same. If the killer was one of us, he's a bloody hero. No ... take that back ... he's a war hero and should be awarded a Victoria Cross. It could have been, and probably was, one of their own for any number of reasons we don't know about. Guys, if I was involved, I would be crowing from the top of the roof, and bugger the consequences. I'm just sorry it wasn't me. I never went to any fucking shed.'

***Oh, oh ... I feel someone is all fired up and fighting for peer acceptance, but he puts another meaning on the look that passes between a man and a woman.***

Gibbo misread the look of surprise that passed between Hamish and Kaitlyn. 'And now, unless you are all going to shout me a beer ... ha ha ... you can all fuck off!' Everyone except Tabasco felt that they had been barking up the wrong tree and left feeling relieved. They would leave Gibbo alone.

# Tarantula

Hamish, Watsy and Tarantula shared the same bullroom with eight others. The mornings were always the same and had to start before sun up. It was a case of first up, all up. Hamish would dress and queue up at the ablution block. Pity help the poor sod who had diarrhoea that spread through the community at breakneck speed. He would then head to the kitchen to queue up for the toaster and the kettle for a cup of tea. Breakfast consisted of a piece of toast and, with luck, jam or peanut paste. The three of them would take off for the five-kilometre walk to the building site with last night's leftovers (usually noodles) in a container for lunch, and a bottle of water. They sometimes met others along the way, who joined them. Tarantula had talked about his adult life and described some of his party antics, but it was mostly fairly jocular. This particular morning, as they were walking along, Hamish asked Tarantula where he went to school. Tarantula looked at him with a big smile and said, 'St. Lukes College.' He then added in a posh voice, 'I know, one of the most expensive private schools in Adelaide, and before you say what everyone else says—"Your parents must have been very rich"—the answer is no, they were most certainly not.'

'So, you got a scholarship, Tarantula. You must have been a genius,' retorted Watsy.

'Wrong again. No scholarship, and I was a very average student. Not like you, Macca.' They walked along in silence and then Tarantula told Hamish and Watsy how it all came about.

'My parents had a farm in The Mallee area, known for its poor soil and endless seasons of drought. I went to school at the local primary school and did all the things that country boys love—played footy in the winter and cricket in the summer. Because of my long legs, I got the name 'Spider'. I wasn't a star like Gibbo on the footy field, but I did okay and had plenty of friends. I was tall for my age and always did well in track and field events. They were probably the best years of my life. Mum and Dad were deadset that my younger sister, Raylee, and I would go to a top boarding school in Adelaide for our high school education. The theory was that we would hob-nob with elite society, eventually join them in a highly paid profession, and keep our parents in a life of luxury in their retirement years. Their aspirations may have come about because Dad inherited a struggling farm and, I think, felt trapped and wanted a far better life for us kids. The words 'politician' and 'barrister' were dropped fairly frequently. I think they enrolled me at St. Lukes College and Bugs at St. Hilary's when we were born. It wasn't a problem when I was in lower primary school, but as I edged towards Year 7, the kids gave me a really hard time—calling me a snob and saying I was 'up my bum'. I hated the idea of going off to a boarding school where I didn't know one person. In our small town, we knew everybody. I was not aware until later on what sacrifices Mum and Dad had to endure for me to go to this salubrious school until they pointed it out in no uncertain terms.

The first day of boarding school was unbelievable. There I was decked out to the nines in a St. Lukes College uniform facing a huge, stone, 19th century building with arches, set among a vast expanse of manicured lawn. I felt extremely tall, a head and shoulders above the other boys, and I stood out when all I wanted to do was meld in with the crowd. I was stunned when one of the boys called to me, "You look like a spider." I was used to being called an arachnid in primary school, but was happy to drop it and couldn't believe my nickname had continued on into high school. Dad followed the directional signs and left me in a grand hall. It seemed to me that all the other boys knew each other, but on reflection, there were heaps of new boys just like myself. We all traipsed behind one of the boarding house masters and were shown where to go, how to settle into our dorm, and a few of the rules, which seemed to me at the time as being all about our dress code. Of course, I was as miserable as a chip in boiling oil, but I was not the only one, and gradually I made some friends. I was by far the poorest kid, surrounded by boys with $50 notes stuffed into the pockets of their pants.

When it came holiday time, it was a real scream what Mum and Dad would do to 'keep up appearances'. They couldn't come and get me in the ute, which was their only form of transport. Mum had a cleaning job at the high school in the evenings and would get varied shifts at the local Foodies during the day. If it was a drought year, which was just about every year, Dad would get work fencing, and some labouring work on properties in a region of about one hundred kilometres. If there were any roadworks, pretty much from The Mallee to Adelaide, he would hear about it and put his hand up for traffic control duties, which was really lucrative. The owner of the Foodies was a great guy and loaned them his late model Ford Falcon to come and get me and bring me home for the school holidays. Actually, the Falcon stood out like a sore thumb as all the other boys were being collected in 4-wheel drive Mercedes or Cruisers. A few jumped into European sports cars. Mum was dressed to the nines, compliments of a collective effort of the local ladies. Dad wore his wedding suit. The Foodies owner traded in his old car every two years and updated to the latest version, so it always looked good.

For me, the hardest year was the first and the last one, but by the time I got into Year 9, I was growing in confidence and had a group of friends. One lad, Clive, invited me to his place for the Easter break. I've never seen anything like it. His folks had a sort of emporium in the Barossa Valley and a very imposing old home with leadlight windows and a huge verandah all round. I'll never forget driving through the wrought iron gates along the paved driveway that was as wide as a road and just about as long, past the tennis court and massive gardens, and then entering a huge entrance hall. Even St. Lukes College hadn't prepared me for the vastness of the property. I think Mum and Dad were pretty miserable that I didn't go home, but I was having a ball.

Budgeting got worse when Raylee started at St. Hilary's. Mum and Dad encouraged her to learn a foreign language, which was a bit short-sighted of them. The 'school camp' was in Paris! Of course, Bugs had to go. That's when Dad went north for months to conduct extensive road works, and Mum had to manage the farm. The neighbours were a great help but I think they probably felt a bit cranky that their contribution was going to a very shaky cause.

Things started to unravel towards the end of Year 10. I grew early, hitting the old six-feet mark in Year 8. All of my mates were short arses at the time, but some of them shot up a bit in the last couple of years of schooling. I was the perfect candidate to get grog on the weekends. It was really lucrative as my mates were throwing $50 notes at me like confetti–sometimes even $100 notes. If I offered them the change, most of them would wave it away as though I had insulted them. We were allowed out unsupervised and we would toss down the drinks at the farthest playing field away from the college. It was that year that Clive asked me back to his house for the September holidays, but we got into so much trouble sneaking his parents grog out and trying to hide being off our faces, that Clive's dad rang my parents and they had to come and get me from a meeting point in Adelaide. I was causing ructions at home and, at one stage, Dad smashed every beer and wine bottle and poured the contents down the sink.

I got through Year 11 being mostly grounded and strictly supervised as, early in the year, I became more and more conspicuous to the staff, particularly the house master. I should have taken the opportunity to study harder, but all I can remember of that year was sleeping a lot and I was just scraping a pass in my exams, which is not satisfactory at St. Luke's College. When I did go home for the holidays, my old friends from primary school were not particularly friendly and I didn't help with my phony posh accent–which I hadn't realised I'd acquired.' Tarantula put on his posh voice: 'Like, we went to the cricket and ... like ... had to stand there with all these feral people with … like … cheap Target clothes, and they smelt … like … disgusting. It was positively foul.' Hamish and Watsy cracked up.

**I could feel his 'out-of-controlness' at the time.**

'When I was in Year 12, it all came to a grounding halt when we had the annual sports day whereby we competed against other top private schools. We had our grandstand, cheer squad, and my mate and I had snuck in a bottle of vodka in the guise of water. I was competing in the 100-metre sprint, and the 400-metre and 1,600-metre relays as I had long legs and was a pretty good runner. I was as full as a boot and wandered over other lanes, causing a huge disruption. I dropped the baton twice in the 400-metre relay before chucking it to the next runner, thinking it would make the game more interesting. He, of course, didn't catch it. I was removed from the ground well before the 1,600-metre relay was run and escorted back to school. The next day, I was expelled. Mum and Dad had to come and get me after seeing the principal. They didn't want me back as the chances of my failing exams at the end of the year was almost guaranteed, and my behaviour was the final straw as far as the school was concerned.

Mum and Dad were furious. They may as well have thrown all their hard-earned money down the toilet. There goes the pipe dream of a barrister/politician in the family. They were convinced that a private school education was a ticket to an elite club at university and an illustrious career. Dad decided that I would have to work on the farm. By this time, I was drinking way too much and, looking back, being a pain in the arse at home. I felt completely misplaced. I hated the farm and the community. My mates from primary school had cemented their friendships as they got older and I felt very much the outsider. My only source of contentment was through a bottle and that was short lived as I got angry about my lot in life. One night, Dad grabbed the bottle out of my hand and hurled it out the door, smashing it on the concrete path. It was like taking a bone from a very hungry pit bull. I threw a punch at Dad and knocked out a front tooth. The next day, he took me to a nearby town where his mate had a furniture removal business and I was employed on one of the trucks as a removalist. I wasn't there long as I was simply not reliable and wandered down the coastline getting odd jobs picking fruit and working in vineyards. I stayed in backpacker accommodation and never returned to the farm. I saw Clive once when I was pruning grapes. He was walking out of the very expensive restaurant attached to the vineyard with a group of beautifully dressed people. It looked like he was attending a 'special occasion' function. I kept my head down so that he wouldn't see me. I haven't seen any of my old mates from St. Luke's, and I'm sure they wrote me off years ago.'

After a silent pause, Tarantula mused, 'I wonder where they are now.'

'Wherever they are, I'm sure the phony, posh accent has disappeared,' replied Hamish. They continued walking down the road. Tarantula was thinking of his old school. I wonder what it is being used for now. Hamish thought of Freddie, picturing him swinging his arm over in a bowling action as he was walking along—Freddie could never keep his arms to his side. Watsy was regretting that he hadn't spent some of his hard-earned money and lashed out on an overseas holiday—and stayed there.

# The Search

Beags and Bagsy were arrested by the police and put into custody. They were charged with possessing a banned substance. They stuck to their story that they thought they were making a fruit punch in the laundry of one of the blocks, and it must have fermented. The police, of course, didn't believe them, particularly as they both said the laundry was in a different block number. The police were not really interested in collaborating their stories; they were after a killer, not a couple of miscreants. They did not link the hooch with the murder. They decided to give the guys a bit of a pasting and tell them they were in for 'life' to scare them, and then release them in a week's time to get them back to work pronto. They decided to make frequent raids on the laundries in each block, but all they found was washing powder and dirty washing. When they were returned to the building site in a police car, they were greeted with as much enthusiasm as the GRAPS would allow—no talking, just huge smiles and a pat on the back. When Gibbo's truck pulled in and he saw Bagsy, then Beags; his smile was so wide, his face looked as though it would split in two. He could not get near them, but waved from the window of the cement truck. Bagsy had to spend all day on the building site before he could get home to Nat.

However, he got home that night and Nat wasn't there—probably shopping as she wasn't in the laundry. When she swung in the door and saw him in the chair, she almost upended him in her rush. They clung together like glue in case it was just a dream. Nat was sobbing, Bagsy was shaking. Later on, he described his time in jail. 'It wasn't a jail, Nat, as there is no jail on Kangaroo Island. We were in cages in an old car park. I think it may have been an old supermarket car park, but it had an automatic grid gate. The ablution block was a bucket in the corner. The bed consisted of two pallets pushed together that quickly separated, with a thin piece of foam–like that exercise mat we used to own–on top. I could feel every bone in my body as soon as I sat or lay on it. The only natural light was a distant glimpse through the grid that used to be the automatic gate. We only saw the police when they came with morsels of food and a message that we were there 'for life'. Even the police, who spoke no English, could say, 'You here for life'. It was instilled in us and we believed it. There was no use pleading that we didn't make the hooch as they found it in our possession, and dobbing on Gibbo would have been futile as it wouldn't have changed our situation. The only good thing was, I could talk to Beags, who was a long way away but the acoustics rebounded off every wall. It was like communicating in a tunnel. We found out that we had given different block numbers when we said we were making the fruit punch in the laundry. On reflection, I don't think the police coordinated our statements. We were so scared, Nat. The thought of spending the rest of our lives in a cage was just too much to bear. I thought of you all the time and was convinced that I'd never see you again. I thought about you so much that you were often in my dreams, which was the only good thing that happened to me. As long as I have you, Nat, I can live this life, but I would rather die than return to that hell hole.'

The police were extremely active hunting for the murder weapon. They would go through blocks at any time, day or night. They would bang on a door, which meant the resident/s had to stand in the corridor while they undertook their search. They left the premises in a state of total chaos that had to be cleaned up before heading off to work the next morning. It was preferable if the raid coincided with a half day off work, but that was rare. The bullrooms and the brain banks fared better as their beds were stripped, drawers upended and wardrobes emptied. There were no other hiding places. However, the communal kitchens were targeted with plastic cutlery, basic utensils, plastic dishes, saucepans, and frying pans littering the floor. The contents of the fridges were emptied onto the corridor floor minus the container or plastic wrapper. After a couple of these raids, the food was scraped off the floor and divvied out for a collective, but scant, meal. The thought of more shopping and budgeting was just too hard to bear for weary bodies.

Life trudged on with no spare time for social interaction. This was the aim of the police force—one or more dispirited person would soon lead them to the killer.

Hamish did not share a half day off with Sonia, but he did with Kaitlyn, who was able to pass messages on so they could coincide their shopping from time to time.

*I fear that jealous trait rising to the constantly bubbling.*

One evening, Kaitlyn was telling Gibbo about being the conduit between Macca and Sonia. Gibbo responded with, 'Are you sure the link is between Macca and Sonia, and not you and Macca?' Kaitlyn stared at him long and hard. 'Holy shit, Gibbo. Don't start this one again. I cannot believe that your tiny, pea-sized brain could conjure up such a ridiculous suggestion.' Gibbo said, 'Only joking.' Kaitlyn stormed off to the bedroom, shouting, 'Which part of the joke was funny? I don't know where you're going to sleep tonight, but it certainly isn't in here' as she slammed the door. Gibbo shouted through the door, 'I'm tired and not thinking straight.' There was no answer.

*I felt his wretchedness. He wasn't thinking straight. He had contained his jealousy in the past, but he inadvertently let it slip out. He would have to make amends.*

In actual fact, Gibbo was tired and not thinking straight as the GRAPS were combing the land with metal detectors and he was scared that they would find the mobile phone. How much metal is in a mobile? He didn't know. The phone was buried close to a wall on D Block, under an old basketball ring that had left a rust mark and was wrapped in material. Were his fingerprints still on it?

Maybe. The GRAPS were concentrating on the open land as they were convinced the knife was buried. They combed the beaches. The island was now rattling along to the sound of metal detectors. More detectors arrived on the ferries and their workforce increased. They piled up their findings and forensically tested all the fishing knives that had fallen overboard, washed up on the beach and were buried by more sand. There were also kitchen knives that had been thrown out in the past that had to be scrutinised. Nothing matched the knife that inflicted the fatal wounds.

**I felt my countryside being combed. It's only a matter of time.**

# Discovery

The first people to get home to the blocks were the wrinklies, particularly the ones that worked as kitchen hands for the Power Houses. They were frisked on leaving every afternoon to ensure that not one morsel of food would leave the premises.

Two ladies went to their block and walked round the back to bring the washing in off the line. The first thing they saw were legs and shoes, and they ran over to help the poor person who had fallen. The body was lifeless. They looked up at the open windows on the top floor. They ran to get help from their friends. It was not until a group gathered that a tear was shed. They did not want the GRAPS to get to this young girl first, and they had the distressing job of telling her parents. The word spread quickly and it was decided that they would have a burial that evening outside the home block. They could not erect a cross or any sign, but they could place flowers. The small gathering grew larger, with everyone watching for signs of the GRAPS who would come and disband them. The parents of the girl turned to Gibbo for support.

*I felt the air as a young one fell to the ground. I felt the body bounce on the cement path. Then I felt her heartbeat stop. I had felt suicides on this island, but this was a youngster.*

*In the past, I had grieved for the young of my first people.*

The parents made a speech together, helping each other out in between sobs.

'Our girl was a happy-go-lucky kid right from the word 'go'. She wasn't brilliant at school –just average (when you think about it, so is the average kid), but she always saw the funny side of life. She certainly wasn't perfect –at times, she would throw a real fruity if she couldn't get her way. As a little one, we had to bribe her to pack away toys and tidy her room. But I reckon we weren't the only ones. Bedtime was always a problem, and cleaning teeth almost impossible. As she grew, she loved being the entertainer – she could mimic her teachers, particularly in the playground, which the other kids loved. She would demonstrate her mimicry for us and we'd crack up, even though we didn't know the teacher's traits. She would never tell us what she had learned at school, but she would tell us about playtime. No, she wasn't perfect –sometimes she overstepped the mark. She wrote an essay, which she thought was screamingly funny, about her school and teacher. This was definitely not appreciated by either party. We got hauled up to front the headmistress for that one. However, there was not a nasty bone in her body. She was very sensitive to her peers and always backed the underdog. She just thought life was fun. We reckon she would have made a great radio DJ or a stand-up comedian as she sure did have the gift of the gab. But who knows, she might have become an office worker or a landscaper. That of course, was in the old days, but now we do know—she could not face the future.

Our girl was nearing the end of her schooling, and could see her future plain and clear. There was no light at the end of the tunnel. Her ready laugh became almost non-existent. She no longer saw the funny side of life. She did write us a note, which was found in her pocket, but neither of us is strong enough to read it to you. She took matters into her own hands and decided she would be better off dead. A future in a factory was just too hard to bear. She decided to jump.

**I felt the enormous grief from this youngster's family, and one young girl whose face was a torrent of tears. She'd always remember her mate.**

'We have to stop others from following in her footsteps,' continued Maddie's father. 'We have to make sure that all the doors are locked on the upper floors. I know no one locks their doors as there's nothing to steal. We have to give our kids HOPE.

The only way to do this is to believe that international intervention will ultimately prevail. We have to believe this ourselves, so that we pass on our passion to our youngsters. It hurt us deeply that we couldn't afford shoes for Maddie. We were trying to save but the price just kept going up. Gibbo kindly gave her a pair of sneakers, and we know it meant a lot to her. I know she would want them to go to another child, so we removed them and would like to give them back to Gibbo. Perhaps you could say a few words, Gibbo.'

With a croaky voice and misty eyes, Gibbo responded, 'I haven't known Maddie long—well, not many of us have known each other long. I think the cricket match was the first time I saw her. However, we did have a little chat outside the shop after that and she struck me as being a kid with a big heart. Guys, we have to stick together and ride out this trying time. We will NOT give in to the GRAPS who are making our lives intolerable. I know they have the numbers, but they must be feeling pressure too. Don't get me wrong, I hate the bastards but they are in a foreign land without their old way of life. They are conducting raids day and night, which must be tiresome. I know we hate the cleaning up process, but they have to work hard to turn over all our possessions on a regular basis. We know they want a strong workforce so we have to do everything possible to reduce production so they have to rethink their strategy. We know this has all come about because one of them was killed. Word has it—stabbed—so I presume there was a knife involved. Another way to get these new regulations to cease is to locate the murder weapon. Given we are now not allowed anything sharper than a plastic knife, if anyone finds a metal one, we should leave it in a prominent place for the GRAPS. That way, we look as though we are trying to assist with their efforts without any one person being a suspect.

Australia, as we knew it, has been involved in pretty much every war known to man, starting, I think, with the Boer War. Over the centuries, we couldn't get our hands up fast enough to send our troops to foreign soil. Our recruitments were mostly naïve young men visualising victory parades abroad, but never the reality of muddy trenches. They were willing to grab the dangling carrot. We have been there for other countries and now we must believe that our allies will come to our rescue, and we must pass this belief on to our kids so they can have aspirations again.'

They all cried, whether they knew Maddie or not. They cried for their young ones.

Gibbo continued, 'Oh, and don't forget to lock up your penthouses!'

The GRAPS investigated why Maddie wasn't attending school. They were told by neighbouring kids, who could speak the lingo, that she was dead and they were shown where she was buried. They dug her up and took away the body. Every parent feared copy-cat suicides and were now on high alert.

*One young girl left the adults talking and walked home. I felt the tears splash on to my earth. The adults did not realise the enormity of her feelings and the impact on someone who had just lost her mate.*

# The Cantinnis

Gibbo's Op Shop continued. Just one evening from 6.00 pm – 7.00 pm every three weeks. It became the only highlight and was dropped into many conversations. 'See you at Gibbo's Op' became the new 'goodbye'. It was always a struggle to get enough stock and couldn't be held more frequently. Added to the fact that tokens were so scarce there was very little loose change for 'luxuries' like home-made biscuits. Wages were stagnant but the rent was increasing. Production in factories increased on Op Shop days, as no one wanted to stay on site longer. The final siren on the roads, building sites and factories was controlled by the GRAPS and was never predictable. Going to the Op Shop wasn't just the thrill of sometimes being able to buy something without queuing, but the social interaction that went with it. So far, the GRAPS had not come at the right time to upend the tables and send them all packing. It was a time when decisions could be made.

It was the wrinklies who volunteered to organise activities for kids, but they needed help with the collective ideas that came at breakneck speed. Learning the guitar was the most popular with the older kids, with craft for the younger ones. Because there was a huge shortage of children's books, it was decided that a 'serial' style storytelling would help fill the gap. 'We want the kids to remember the old days when Australia was Australia,' butted in Gibbo. 'You know, if we can get our hands on some Aussie stories, or even a bit of that poetry stuff like Banjo what's his name, and Henry something … and stuff like that. You kids need a big mob of culture.' The kids laughed and rolled their eyeballs but were secretly pleased with any suggestion to disrupt their monotonous lives. They never dreamed that they would get excited over a wrinklie reading a story, when in the past they cracked up if their tablets and phones were taken away. The message went out to the community that if anyone could lend a guitar, they could leave it in one of the kitchen cupboards for the wrinklies to collect and use so the kids could have lessons. Of course, there was not enough, but the kids were now very good at sharing. There was plenty of toe tapping, hip slapping, muso wrinklies to go round.

Sonia was asked for help with ideas for cheap craft activities. She came up with making paper mache decorations. 'All we need is old newspaper, and we can get that from the bins. We also need flour and water to make glue.' The kids were happy to scour the bins for paper. They started off small, covering plastic saucers, but they grew in size as well as popularity as time went on. The older children took weeks to make a collective model of no specific gender, which prompted their gleeful sniggers about dicks and tits. The activities and music lessons took place in one of the laundries, and the storytelling in the communal kitchen. The first session saw just ten children turn up, all looking very doubtful. However, the word spread quickly and even the storytelling was a hit, particularly as it was Anh Do's, The Happiest Refugee. The kids loved the bit about the younger brother being mistaken for a girl and decked out by the Vinnies in pink frills. The kids identified with Anh being in a strange environment, as they had been thrust into. Some of the kids had never been into an op shop pre-invasion and now it was an important part of their lives. The wrinklies had the same amount of expertise among their rank as any generation and they relished their new role at providing enjoyment for the kids. It was a win, win.

It was on a Gibbo's Op shop night that Silo fell off the makeshift 'scaffold' comprising two milk crate-sized boxes on top of each other at either end of a narrow plank, as he was fitting in windows on the ground level of the new building He had lost his job as a painter as the paint had run out. It was with much elation that he was assigned to Hamish's building block. He told Hamish that the painting job was a 'piece of cake' as the paint supplies were intermittent and the GRAPS turned a blind eye to him working very slowly. 'I couldn't believe it, Macca. Perhaps it was because of holding the camera steady all those years that I was able to paint straight lines as, of course, I had no aids, such as masking tape, to guide me. But it was a lonely job, and I had way too much thinking time, which is not a good idea on this island. I couldn't understand the rare conversations that went on around me and tried to guess whether they were agreeing with each other or having a full-on verbal fight. I was always in empty rooms, and I was ecstatic when I got allocated to your building site as I knew my days were numbered. Knowing that the paint was running out and more supplies were not coming in, made me shit scared that I'd be sent to a factory.' He had only been on the building site a week when he hit the ground fairly hard and was winded. The supervisor signaled for him to get back to work as he tried to get his breath back. That evening at the shop, his mates looked over his bruises and wound on his leg. There were a couple of ex- doctors and some ex-nurses on hand to give advice, but Gibbo was the most vocal. 'You need antibiotics and some anaesthetic cream, mate.'

'Yeah, and how am I going to get that?' retorted Silo. 'Reckon if I trot along to the medical centre, they will give me the nearest thing to hand—cough medicine and hemorrhoid cream—and I wouldn't know the difference, then cut off my dick for good luck. Nup, I'll be right. A couple of days and I'll be fighting fit.' He was right in one respect—the bruises faded, but the hole in his leg caused by a sharp stone was getting angrier and spreading. He was pale and breaking out in a sweat or shivering cold at work. His peers knew he had to be home in bed. 'Tell the GRAPS you have a new strain of Covid and forget to breathe' was their advice. Silo was eventually signalled to leave the premises to start the trek back to his block. The GRAPS came the next day and pushed him off the bed, but he collapsed onto the floor. They left him there in disgust.

It was a combined effort to provide food and water for Silo, who alternated between profusely sweating and shivering. The leg wound was spreading further and getting angrier each day. His roommates frog-marched him to the ablution block before heading off to work. They filled every plastic cup in the kitchen with water and placed them by his bedside. Any food they left behind was untouched at the end of the day. Hamish came over every evening with a vegetable soup that he had made from old stock at Foodies and scrounging any discarded leftovers from the Power House bins. He got Silo to sit up and he spooned the soup into his mouth. He washed him down with a towel before heading home to get in by curfew. It was as though Silo's blood had been poisoned and was making its way through his body.

On the building site, Silo was replaced by a new arrival. He tried to introduce himself, but the GRAP made a 'zip your lips' motion to him and barked instructions that he didn't understand. He looked completely lost. Hamish waved up a hand and showed him the ropes. During their lunch break, he told them his name was Sergio Cantinni and that he had arrived in Australia when he was four years of age. As he had cousins in South Australia, his parents headed straight for Adelaide. They saved enough money to fulfill a lifetime dream, and that was to own a farm.

They were all incredulous. 'Where were before you got here? Surely not in your own home.' Sergio explained that his parents bought a property near a large forest that was a favourite bush camp holiday spot for families near the coast. The property shared a driveway with a neighbouring farm, and the family never got round to putting up a sign or road number. All his aunties and uncles knew where they lived, so they didn't bother. The Power Houses did not know they were there as the house was hard to spot by air due to the surrounding tall trees. As soon as his father heard about an impending invasion, he gathered up the whole family as the thought of being split up was unthinkable. 'Looking back, he did the right thing, but we all knew it would be impossible for us all to stay on the farm indefinitely. We knew that all our neighbours had been relocated. If we ventured outside the track in, we would have been too conspicuous. Just like the days during the pandemic—we were locked in and too scared of the consequences if we went out. The Power Houses found us by mistake. We lasted in the farmhouse until last week when some officials missed the front property and continued down the dirt track to our place. I don't know who got the biggest surprise, but although we knew all along our days were numbered, it was still a shock. It didn't take long before we had to pack our bags and head for the ferry. The best part is that, although we have separate accommodation, we are together as a family.'

The cement truck swung into the site and Gibbo climbed out, with his lunch, to join the group. Sergio introduced himself, but in typical Gibbo style, he quickly renamed him 'Bill'. The group looked at Gibbo askance, but he just shrugged his shoulders and said, 'He looks like a 'Bill' to me.' Sergio now had a new name and laughed. Gibbo asked him why it took so long for him to get to the island and so he had to repeat his story and then continued with, 'Before we were invaded, us kids were scattered across Adelaide, working. My older brother and sister were married with kids. They were in the hospitality industry, but I had my own small dental practice.'

'You must have the smarts,' chipped in Bagsy. Bill smiled, flashing a mouthful of straight, white teeth. 'Well, I had a bit of a slow start. You see, when I turned five during the year, I had to go to Grade 1 at the local school. However, with hardly any English, I was put into a special class to learn the lingo. I didn't get much schooling before the long summer holiday break, and I had to return to the special class for another six months. I was then transferred into a Grade 1 class for the remainder of the year and the following one. When my mother went to the school for parent/teacher interviews at the end of that first year and got a glowing report at how well I had done, I couldn't see the big deal, so I piped up, "I should be okay, I've been in Grade 1 for three years!"'

'Gees, I reckon I could have done with a few more years in Grade 1,' responded Watsy.

'You're a lucky bugger, Bill, having your parents here.' Gibbo paused. '... but then I'm not so sure—my mum could be a weapon of mass destruction when she put her mind to it.'

The next day at their lunch break, which was also at the discretion of the supervisor, Watsy asked Bill about the meals he had at home. Bill was more than happy to describe his mama's home cooking. His eyes misted up just thinking about it, and his heart ached that his talented mama was now washing dishes and cleaning kitchens. He described the platters of antipasto, including individually stuffed olives that took days to prepare. His mama sniffed at supermarket pasta and made her own, so fine and delicate. Her cannelloni was paper thin and contained three different types of minced meat, with the seasoning infused during the cooking. The varied 'secondi' meals of fish, chicken and meat. The desserts of tortes, cannoli crêpes, bomboloni, and Baci gelato. Bill described some of the dishes in detail and the group couldn't get enough. They reckoned they could put on weight just listening.

The word got out that Mrs Cantinni made the best meat balls and, although kangaroo mince was regarded as a delicacy, it was still relatively cheap and the only affordable meat option. As time went on, the wrinklies called her Lucia, but everyone else called her 'mama'. Hamish told Sonia about the delicious food they indulged in at lunch time, thanks to Bill's vivid description.

'It's like watching one of those TV cooking shows. He talked about her famous meatballs, and they decided to try to organise a dinner. If Mama would make the meatballs with everyone pitching in to supply the mince, they would have a combined dinner in one of the camp kitchens and bullroom. However, they decided they would wait until Silo got better. It would serve as a 'welcome to the Cantinni family' as well as a 'welcome back to life for Silo', who was showing signs of slight improvement. The leg wound had stopped spreading and was gradually shrinking. He was out of the hallucination stage induced by an extremely high temperature. He was eating slightly more and was able to get himself to the ablution block. The GRAPS had visited from time to time but wrote him off as burial material.

Kaitlyn and Hamish visited the Cantinnis on one of their half days off. They introduced themselves and talked about Bill, which caused a great deal of confusion. Bill had talked about his parents every day since his arrival on site and everyone felt as though they knew them—even Sonia and Kaitlyn, who got the stories second hand. They called Lucia 'mama' and Sergio 'senior papa', which took the Cantinnis by surprise. The Cantinnis' English was heavily accented, which caused even more problems, but Mama eventually understood the proposal and was delighted to be involved. The idea was that everyone would pitch in to supply the mince, and the wrinklies would help Mama make the meatballs.

'We do 'Italiano' night—something to which …'She looked puzzled as the words were not forthcoming, so she clutched her heart. Papa picked up the enthusiasm. 'Buona, I do musica.' Mama laughed and said, 'You can no sing or play' as she mimed a guitar or banjo. 'No, I get other to make musica.' Kaitlyn and Hamish left feeling confident and light-hearted. We need a highlight, and this just might work—as long as it doesn't coincide with a raid.'

The raids were getting less frequent as the GRAPS had thoroughly combed through every building and every room. The Power Houses could see the futility of the exercise and decided to change tack. They decided to get the help of the Big Feet and Long Noses. They put up printed notices in every corridor:

**REWARD**
**TWO YEARS' FREE RENT**
**FOR ANY INFORMATION OR EVIDENCE**
**LEADING TO THE ARREST**
**OF THE KILLER OF LIU LI JUN**

When Hamish read the notice, he turned to Beags. 'They have a new Power House official who can write and presumably speak, perfect English.' He did not know that Jia Chen and his sidekick, Yi-Jun, had arrived on the island. 'I don't know what they want from us as we know as much as they do. But a couple of years of free rent would be on the top of everyone's wish list.'

Silo was recovering, but very weak. He was visited by the GRAPS and ordered back to work. However, despite the barking orders of the supervisors, he was too weak to be of any use on the building site. His mates tried to cover for him, but it wasn't working. He knew it was inevitable that he would be sent to a factory, but he was gutted when it happened. It was a life sentence. He went to Hamish and poured out his abject misery of spending the rest of his days in a factory building as opposed to manual outside work. Hamish tried to cheer him up by painting a vivid picture of what it would be like in winter standing on a rickety, slippery scaffold with no protective clothing, open to the elements of gale force winds and sheeting rain. 'We will probably be joining you one by one as the accidents become a regular occurrence.' Silo felt better.

# The Dinner

The pending dinner was shrouded in secrecy and had to be by word of mouth as any notices would have certainly attracted a raid. Anyone wanting to participate was to leave their mince in the fridges for the wrinklies to collect. Pasta and garlic were left in the communal kitchen cupboard. Straight after work, the kitchen was a hive of activity. The Cantinnis supervised and were also hands on. They stored the meatballs in the oven and decided that if there was a raid, they would eat them straight off the floor. Sonia made little red, white and green flags to decorate the walls. The menu was Polipetti con olio e aglio penne—meatballs with an oil and garlic pasta. Everyone came with plates. It was amazing how many meatballs came out of that kitchen—plenty for everyone, and even seconds for some. Watsy knocked back 'seconds', saying he was breaking his diet. 'Watsy, you could jump off a ten-storey building, land on scales and still not move the needle,' chipped in Gibbo, '…and that goes for every other bastard on this island.' They talked about past diets and clutched their stomachs with laughter. They decided to accompany the meal with aqua—'a nice dry white wine.'

The bullroom was alive with diners, including children, sitting on beds or on the floor. It was such a special treat. It was not a drudge to queue up as everyone was in a great mood and enjoying the chat. Light bulbs had been removed to all but one dangling fitting, so that the room would not attract the attention of the GRAPS. Sergio Senior organised a barber-shop style quartet and they sung 'O Sole Mio' in subdued tones, once again, so as not to attract attention. They got two encores.

Hamish and Sonia sat on the floor with their meal and were joined by Nat, Bagsy, Beags, Gibbo, Kaitlyn, Tabasco, Tarantula, Watsy, Silo, and Patsy. Bill floated in and out as he was helping in the kitchen. 'You must meet my extended family before you head home.' They promised they would. The circle got bigger as everyone got their meals. They had a lively conversation about all the restaurants they had been to and the wonderful food they had enjoyed in the past. They agreed that this one was up there with the best—even if it was partaken on the floor with a glass of water. They couldn't believe that the amount of mince collected could make endless trays of meatballs. Sonia asked Hamish to thank the Cantinnis and someone called out, 'Make a speech'. Hamish faced the diners.

'I know nothing puts more flavour on food than hunger, but I think you will all agree that this has been up there with one of the most delicious meals ever.' The room hushed as he thanked all the workers, particularly Mama and Papa, who made the meal so memorable—and not one grain of rice! The meatballs were delicious and the pasta a delight—a very special treat. The Cantinnis beamed. Sergio Senior put up his hand and said, 'Gratia Mac-ca, but you and your bella wife (pointing to Kaitlyn), made this night ... come si dici ...'

Bill called out, 'Possible.'

'Si.' Kaitlyn cracked up over the error as she was older than Hamish and was delighted with the compliment. Gibbo looked dark before he recovered and sported a big smile.

**I feel the old jealousy rising up. Calm down, son, it was a genuine mistake.**

Bill brought over his family to meet the group and there were introductions all round. They were unanimous in their praise for the meal and couldn't believe that Mama could produce so much food with the amount of ingredients at her disposal. Bill's sister smiled and said. 'I'll let you in on a little secret. Mama bulks up the amount of meat with boiled rice, but don't tell anyone.'

'I couldn't give a rat's clacker if she plumped them up with laxatives. I could still eat a truck load of Mama's meatballs,' was the response from Tabasco. Even Silo agreed, as his appetite was gradually improving.

As they were returning home before curfew, Beags, who lived in the next block, told Hamish that he was frightened to go to bed. He was having recurring nightmares. He was always locked up in his cage.

'Macca, I know I wasn't in for long, but I was convinced that I would be there for the rest of my life. I couldn't shake the conviction that my life was over, and I would either grow old in a cage or end it myself. The latter option, of course, was far more attractive, but I had no means of carrying it out. The thought of every second, every minute, every hour, every day, week, month, and year in a cage was the heaviest burden I've ever had to carry. Looking back, the GRAPS were instructed to instill in us that we were there for life, and they did a bloody good job. It never, at any stage, crossed my mind that they were wanting us to be shit scared before releasing us. I couldn't imagine endlessly walking around my cage like a wild animal. It was doing my head in big time and just about every time I close my eyes now, I'm back in there.'

Beags described the conditions. The makeshift jail in an underground car park, he thought could have been an old supermarket, with an automatic gate to stop nighttime hoons. The rows of metal bars that formed the cages. The darkness. The pallet bed and bucket. He didn't know the location of the building as a blanket was thrown over his head in transit.

'They came in twice, looking like astronauts with space outfits and breathing oxygen from a tank on their backs. They had pressure hoses. I was told to strip while they hosed down the cage and me. It stung, but at least I felt clean. I felt more animal than human. I thought about caged birds and imagined setting them free and seeing them soar off into the sky.'

'Yes, I feel for any animal or bird cooped up in a cage. I feel it's even harder for a person not to be able to roam free. Any other punishment than being caged.'

'I think every wall had a line of cages, but I couldn't see anything more than the cages across and beside me. There were way too many for me to count. The only light came from the metal grid that was once the automatic gate. Bagsy and I were the only occupants and the only sanity saving factor was that we could communicate. The sound bounced off every wall, so it was like answering an echo. Bagsy was pining for Nat, and there was nothing I could say to help him. We tried to exercise together, marching round our cage in unison which, for some reason, was calming. I cannot imagine what it would have been like had I been there by myself. I think I would have started head banging.'

'When I get into bed, I start thinking of the GRAP who was killed. I imagine the police coming to get me and accusing me of murder. They could just pick anyone at random. I don't reckon they'd be too fussy. Another scenario—they are now offering a reward. What if I got up someone's nose and they decided to try for the free rent and get rid of me at the same time? Macca, I'm losing my brain with all the stuff that's whirling round my head, and it doesn't let up—day or night. Any little thing I saw, smelled or even thought of in that cage can trigger me off and I'm back in there.'

Hamish knew that Beags's concerns were genuine, but without any credibility. 'Why would anyone pick you, Beags? There are so many of us and, at the moment, I think we are of more use to the GRAPS than being jail fodder. They want a labour force, and we are providing just that. You and Bagsy would be the last people to be accused. Anyone dopey enough to accuse you is virtually saying to the GRAPS, 'You had the killer under your noses, and you let him go. Egg on face for the GRAPS and you know what that means—maximum jail time for the dobber. Don't forget, the notice says "Any information or evidence" that leads to an arrest—what possible info or evidence can anyone conjure up against you? No, Beags, it couldn't happen. Rest easy.' He made a few suggestions to help. 'During the day, if your mind goes to a dark place, try singing a song, making up the words as you go along, and always about something you enjoyed pre-invasion. At night, tell yourself a really repetitive story in bed—The Three Bears, anything—bore the socks off yourself like my dad used to do to me with his monotonous tone when I was a kid. If your mind starts to wander to darker places, start all over again. Give it a try.'

Beags was not the only one worried about the reward. Gibbo knew his friends had linked the hooch to the shed and were suspicious. He was not sure how well he had convinced them of his innocence. Of course, he could trust Kats, but what about the others? Free rent was a very lucrative offer. He made up his mind that he would slowly convince everyone that the reward was a sham and the person claiming it would, more than likely, end up in jail themselves. His motto would be 'Can we trust the GRAPS?' He started to feel better.

Strangely enough, the reward was rarely mentioned, which made it more sinister for Gibbo. It was as though everyone was plotting how to get their hands on it without giving away any secrets. In actual fact, no one had a clue as to how they could find evidence to convict a killer. Added to the fact, no one really wanted to dob in one of their own. The free rent was just something to dream about. Gibbo tried to raise the subject many times—on the way to and from work, in the laundry and shopping queue—but there was little or no response. He could not use the op shop as a forum as it would draw attention to himself. It was as if all the adults on the island were staying mute but looking at each other with suspicious eyes. Gibbo had no doubt that any evidence would be handed in and that could take the form of the mobile phone. He could not chance moving it as he had a tracker on his ankle that could alert the GRAPS and there was always too much traffic round the housing block. He was not worried about the knife. That was safe.

# Visitor

The next day, Gibbo was in for one of the biggest shocks of his life. He was sitting at the table with Kats after their noodle meal when there was a commotion down the corridor. He heard voices shouting his name and then a knock at the door. His immediate thought was 'a raid' but they would have heard their neighbours being raided, so it must be a one-off. Gibbo's heart was pounding as he opened the door. There were two policemen standing there with a piece of paper. 'Jack Gibson?' they asked, and with that a body came bursting through, clutching him as hard as she could. It was his mum.

**I feel pending turmoil.**

'Oh, Jack and Kaitlyn, I've had the most terrible time.' 'Where's Dad?' Gibbo butted in. 'I don't know—they broke him.' The tears rolled down her face as she told them what happened. 'We were sent on a bus with no seats, crowded in, holding on to straps for nearly five hundred kilometers. The little children tried to sit on the floor while the others held on to their parents' legs. We set off in the evening and travelled all night.' She paused. 'Except at meal time or tea breaks, when the driver and his crew, sitting up front on the bus, stopped at Kurdnatta' (we know it as Port Augusta). The Power Houses used only the First Nations names for outback places, unlike the cities and larger towns that had two names—the original First Nations name and the new Power House name. They locked the door, and the windows were locked in a partially open position. We didn't know whether they would leave us there all night in that almost airless hellhole.

They stopped for a shorter break, with the same conditions, at an outback roadside service station. We had no idea where we were headed, but we knew we were on the Stuart Highway for a while and thought, Darwin—or whatever it's called now. However, we turned off and knew that we would be somewhere in the outback, a long way from the city and the sea. We were sent to Woomera, which retained its name. It was hell on Earth, and the Chop Sueys quickly recognised that and did everything possible to improve their own lifestyle. There was housing there, but big blocks like this one were being built when we arrived. We shared a house with two other couples and four children. Dad and I were fortunate to have a small bedroom to ourselves. The Chop Sueys set about building a leisure centre for themselves. They already had an outdoor swimming pool with notices saying, 'Power House Officials only' which, of course, is everyone but ourselves. They had plans for a golf course wrapped around a huge resort, which was being built when we arrived. A sports centre was nearby with an air-conditioned undercover tennis court, badminton courts, basketball, table tennis, and an indoor pool. Massive works were being done to map out the golf course, which incorporated extensive paved pathways in between fairways.'

'How were they going to get water for a resort pool and keep a golf course green?' asked Kaitlyn.

'I have no idea. Bottled water? The only reason I know all this is because your dad saw the plans. There were no young men in Woomera. They were sent to Piya-piyanha to work in the uranium, copper and iron mine. Majority of the boys over the age of thirteen were deemed strong enough and sent there to begin their new 'career'.'

*I feel the inexperience of these new conquerors in my outback. I hoped the digging would stop, but my scars may get deeper.*

'Dad showed up on the Power House computers as owning a paving company in our previous lives. The only reason he retired was because of his bad back that made it too painful for him to continue. He was happy to hand the business over to you, Jack.

The Power Houses didn't want him as a supervisor ... oh no—one of their Chop Sueys, who had probably never laid a brick or paver in his life—got that armchair job. Do you remember how fussy he was? Everything had to be perfect. Well, he changed, as he just wanted this mammoth task with such a small and inexperienced crew to come to an end. He was hurting more and more every day and then one day he just could not move. He said it felt as though his spine had snapped and was on fire. The Chop Sueys kicked him to get him up. He told me he saw the boot coming but didn't feel any extra pain. The next morning, they came for him and escorted him to a bus. That was the last time I saw him. He waved from the window, and I waved back.'

Tears rolled down Kaitlyn's face, and Gibbo had a hard time swallowing.

'I decided I would do everything I could to educate everybody, including the Chop Sueys, to the benefits of a healthy diet and a sensible exercise plan.' Gibbo and Kaitlyn sighed in unison. 'The Power House kitchens were full of low-grade oil, food additives, white rice, fatty meat that could easily be replaced with tofu, and a lack of vegetables, particularly of the green variety. I made a potion with turmeric to relieve inflammation pain. I was running round the kitchen doing stretch exercises and jumping on the spot with arms akimbo to show them that exercise was fun. I was doing a very good job, throwing out the sugary drinks and unhealthy ingredients when I was put on a small bus that had seats on it, and taken away. There were Power House officials on that bus, but they were sitting up front. I headed straight for the back and was able to lie down and sleep through most of the trip. I think they forgot that I was there, because when we got to Kurdnatta, they didn't even shut the door. I could have walked off, but where would I go?

Remember the city of Adelaide? Now called 'Xin Chengdu'/'Kaurna'? We travelled up what was called King William Road, and I could see down the old 'Rundle Mall'. Although the buildings are the same, there are new, huge flashing signs, banners and large television screens, but I couldn't see what they were showing—we were travelling through too fast. I know I haven't been to Shanghai, but I have seen pictures and that's what it looked like. It was a mass of red and gold. I felt like I was in a different country ... well, I suppose I am. I had to transfer over to another big bus, which had no seats and was packed to the rafters. The journey was only about one hundred kilometres, which was easy after the long haul to Woomera. I couldn't believe it when I saw the ferry and worked out where I was going. I was hoping this was where they took your dad, but the inner me knew that he would be with the infirm. As soon as I got here, I had to line up and register. When I got to the top of the queue, one of the officials was going to allocate me housing, but I asked if there was a Jack Gibson on the island. The official tapped on the computer and nodded. He had a smattering of English, and I was able to get through to him that I didn't need accommodation as I could come and live with you.' Kaitlyn and Gibbo's eyebrows almost shot off their heads. 'Mum, why were you sent away from Woomera?'

'I have absolutely no idea,' she replied.

At the building site, at any opportunity, Gibbo whinged for the following week. He always began with, "It's getting worse. You won't believe this but ..." (they did believe it) or, "You don't have to be dead to be stiff" —the GRAPS don't want to employ her, so no extra tokens are coming in and they're charging us extra rent because she's sleeping on the futon! As you know, you can't swing a cat without getting blood on every wall and she seems to be filling every centimetre of the little space that we've got. She threw out the tin of tuna—apparently it may contain mercury. We had to virtually empty every bin to get it back.'

Someone asked how he could afford tuna. Gibbo smiled and said, 'Compliments of the Power Houses, but don't tell Kats.' Kats cried so hard when the fish got tossed out that Mum promised she would not throw away any more food, no matter the contents.

You won't believe what she said to Kats the other day. "Well, dear, it might be just as well that you didn't have children. This is not the best environment to bring up little ones. But if you hadn't run in those marathon races, things might have been different!" You know Kats has a tongue sharp enough to cut old boot leather, but she was too speechless to reply.'

Someone asked Gibbo if he would bring his mum to the next op shop so that everyone could meet her. Gibbo looked doubtful and said that his mum knew all about the shop before they had even mentioned it. Anyone she met in the corridor or laundry, and chatted to, would sign off with, 'See you at the op shop'. Mum couldn't believe that anyone in their right mind would go to an op shop. As she says, "Wearing second-hand clothes and buying food with no labelled ingredients is my idea of punishment. No, I think I'll give the op shop a miss."

Last night was the only night that Kats hasn't cried. Would you believe? Mum cracks up about another noodle meal and wants to do all the shopping! We had to get through to her that there's no tokens. She took that rather well. In fact, she looked quite pleased with herself and announced that she had quite a lot of money. We were gobsmacked. She asked for scissors, then brought out some clothing and started snipping away at the pockets. "Immediately after the invasion, I was busy sewing pockets into my clothes, packing in the money and then sewing the pockets up, so that no one would know," she beamed. She produced a bundle of $100 and $50 notes. "There. When you were tapping your phone for every little thing that you purchased, I was using cash and saving." she said with a big smile. Kats just stared and I knew it was up to me to put her on the right track.'

'Mum, when we got searched before and after the ferry trip, the GRAPS did not ask us for our wallets or purses. The reason being, there could be nothing in there of value. Our credit cards, medical, library—even driver's licences—were obsolete as they were issued by the Australian Government and this money is now extinct. You can keep it as a souvenir.' Mum's face fell and this time it was her turn to cry. The next day, she was busy mending her clothes.'

It was busy on the building site, and Gibbo was backwards and forwards in the cement truck. Every time he drove in, he would wave out the window with a huge smile on his face. He couldn't wait until their lunch break to tell them the news.

'You won't believe this. Mum went to see the GRAPS. She said she got a very nice official and convinced him to give her a job as she wants to 'pay her way'. Well, the next day, she goes back, and he has a piece of paper that he thrusts into her hands and points to the hospital. Not the medical centre, but the one that we're not allowed in. She is told to come back at 7.00 pm. We hadn't got home when Mum left, but she left a note. It turns out that she has been employed at nighttime to clean all the bathrooms. She's over the moon with excitement, reckoning that once you get your foot in the door, you can kick it even wider.'

# Highlights

The next Op Shop evening, Gibbo regaled everyone with stories of his mum and her travels. This was the first time anyone had heard of mainland Australia since arriving on the island, and they were all ears. In a way it made them feel more satisfied with their life, particularly the men, as they voiced their preference for working on a building site or in a factory, rather than at a uranium mine in the outback, known for its harsh weather conditions. The hot, dry, windy summers that can reach over forty-eight degrees Celsius. The dust storms that blind you when walking to and from your workplace. Houses with air-conditioning units that have been dismantled by the Power Houses. The out-of-bounds swimming pool.

He described and embellished his mum's account of travelling down King William Street in what was called Adelaide. In reality, the glimpse only took seconds, but he talked about the shops, the new flashing signs and the huge red lanterns shining in the dark sky. This brought a barrage of reminiscences about the shops, pubs, discos, restaurants—entertainment that was once familiar.

'Remember the Adelaide Festival of Arts?' Everyone chipped in with their memories of the 'Fringe' shows held at The Garden of Unearthly Delights and Gluttony. The comedy, music, circus, and variety acts.

A soft voice asked, 'Why don't we have our own "Fringe"?' They all looked at Soula, who was normally a little shy. She looked up and added, 'I reckon there is some talent among the lot of us, and it would give us something to look forward to. Remember when we were going on holiday? Sometimes the anticipation was better than the holiday itself. We need a highlight.' Gibbo jumped in with, 'Great idea, Sools.' And the decision was unanimous. They were running out of time before curfew, so they decided to write down any ideas they had and hand it over to a convenor. Gibbo was the first to be asked, probably because of the Big Bash cricket match, but he declined. 'Nah, I'm not much use at collating and organising that sort of thing. I know I'm full of culture, but fair crack of the whip, that's beyond me. The girls are better at that sort of thing, and for starters, it wasn't my idea. What do you reckon, Sools?' She immediately turned to Sonia and Kaitlyn, who agreed to pitch in to start the ball rolling.

Meanwhile, the wrinklies were looking for more activities for the kids. 'Remember the billy carts we made as kids? Let's get them cracking making their own.' They could have been talking a foreign language as far as the kids were concerned. 'What's a billy cart?' 'A highly dangerous and, at times, very fast vehicle with no brakes, that you can sit in.' **That** got the kids' interest. 'Just think,' someone mused, '…these are the same kids who, not long ago, were whinging if they got a scooter that was not electric and wanted a hoverboard with Bluetooth and lead lights!'

The problems arising from making billy carts were knocked down one by one.

No nails or hammer. One chap overcame that hurdle. 'I've got some tubes of liquid nails.' They all stared at him. 'Who in their right mind would pack liquid nails into a suitcase?' 'Well, my wife packed a small first aid kit, so I decided that I couldn't be without my liquid nails.'

No wheels. 'We can scavenge. The GRAPS like seeing us at the dump site, picking over their rubbish.'

No wood. 'There's always offcuts from the building site. We can't take it home with us, but we can retrieve it from the dump, which is probably not out of bounds on purpose. It provides entertainment for the GRAPS.'

Rope? 'Reckon we can find enough rope to hang every GRAP on the island!'

The biggest problem the Aussies faced was time. The wrinklies had shorter working hours, which worked in with the school kids. However, the younger workers had to cram their chores and shopping into half a day per week. The pendulum swung at night when they faced the monotony of sleepless hours after the 8.00 pm curfew and mandatory lights out. The girls had a new project, which they called the 'KI Fringe'. They knew it could not be advertised but the success of the Cantinnis' dinner proved that this was not necessary. They decided that it would be 'adults only'. The bigger kids would be able to look after the little ones for a couple of hours. They needed as much diverse entertainment as possible, and this meant a time limit of five minutes per act. The message went out that they needed participants. Gibbo and Hamish had to spread the word and be the talent scouts for the guys. The best time for this was in the shopping queue. All entrants were to put in their written or verbal submissions to Kaitlyn as they could be shoved under the door if face to face was not an option, so that a program could be arranged. Kaitlyn was to pass on any contributions to Soula and Patsy as they were in the same brains bank.

The inevitable happened. The wrinklies came forward straight away with their contributions. The younger folk started with a dribble, but as the enthusiasm grew, the ideas set down on paper started to flow. The girls had to work out a date, a venue and a program. They decided that the bullroom once again would be the easiest and most convenient venue. They suggested that the guys could remove mattresses and make a stage out of the slatted beds. Any robust physical movement would have to be on the floor. The girls would act as usherettes, greeting guests with a 'Welcome to the KI Fringe. Please be seated in the front stall.' (Sitting cross-legged on the floor). Or 'Welcome to the KI Fringe. Please be seated in the Royal Balcony.' (Chairs for the wrinklies were at the back). The stars of the show would make their entry from the communal kitchen.

The kids were commissioned to make drums out of old containers and thick packing plastic that was lying around the island. They made shakers out of drink bottles partially filled with rice. These instruments would accompany the guitar players and there were plenty of people with their hands up to form a band. Although the kids were bribed with biscuits by the wrinklies, they were always looking for activities to relieve the boredom of the long evenings. There were no parks, playgrounds or sporting equipment of any kind and the beaches were out of bounds. With a shortage of reading material, the kids had time on their hands.

After a call went out for torches to be placed in the kitchen cupboard, four were collected. Sonia covered these with coloured cellophane to provide the lighting. Although the girls organised the program, they had to delegate the setting up as they were never sure when the siren would end their working day. The date had to be word of mouth as the GRAPS would have relished disbanding the Big Feet. Sonia made up one large program to be displayed inside the entrance for all to see.

> The KI Fringe
> Block C – Bullroom
> 6.00 pm commencement
> 'My Country' – Granny Smith
> Kisser's juggling act
> Big Kitty – song and guitar
> 'The World's Wonders' band
> Honey-bun's yarn
> Banjo Patterson Poem – Chilli
> Tarantula's yarn
> The Wobbly Legs band
> The Italian Quartet
> Song and dance by the Slinky Slick Sisters
> Men on Site (a skit) – Gibbo and the Gang
> Open mic – (if time)
> Lighting by: Patsy, Sonia, Kaitlyn, and Nat

Block C was selected as it was fairly central. Word got around to wear socks over the ankle trackers that evening in the hope that the GRAPS would not pick up on their computers the number of people heading for the same block. The GRAPS were very suspicious and felt threatened by large groups congregating.

On the afternoon of The Fringe, the wrinklies and kids were busy getting the bullroom ready. They pushed some bed frames and slats together to make a stage, but it was definitely not for dancing. A microphone was fashioned out of a piece of wood with a ball on the top and some electric cable leading to nowhere.

It was a rush to get home after work, toss down some noodles and head off to Block C. The 6.00 pm start had to be flexible, but time was running out before the 8.00 pm floodlights came on to highlight any curfew breakers.

Gibbo got home to find a GRAP sitting on one of the kitchen chairs. His heart pounded for an instant before he realised that the girls had given the paper mache model to the kids, and they had made a Power House-coloured shirt and fashioned a cap out of cardboard. 'Holy shit, Kats, you know how to pump a fellow up!' The model was to be used in, what the girls hoped (as they wrote it), a very funny skit with Tarantula sitting behind, activating the arms and talking gibberish while the guys from the building site were having a lively conversation with their GRAP supervisor.

Gibbo was the emcee. The bullroom filled up and they were underway. Gibbo greeted everyone with a, 'Welcome to the KI Fringe'. He looked at his wrist, which had once sported a watch, and with a flourish he announced they were running a little late, so they would just have to talk, sing, play, or dance a little faster.

**Yes, they do have to hurry. I feel different vibes from inside another building.**

A Power House official was having a lively discussion with her co-workers while watching the monitor for any suspicious behaviour. Monitoring activity on the island was monotonous. It was easy to go into the twilight zone and slip into a deep sleep.

The discussion was keeping her awake and as she was chatting, the movement of many Big Feet caught her eye. She decided to track one couple, followed by a group of three. They went into Block C. She waited for the next few, confident that they would go to the same building. She alerted her co-workers, and they came and watched the screen. She rang the police.

*Oh oh, an attempt to entertain and provide some light relief is being threatened. Their morale is low – they need a boost.*

Gibbo introduced the first act – one of the wrinklies who could remember, 'I Love a Sunburnt Country' from her school days:

> An opal hearted country,
> A vivid, lavish land
> All you who have not loved her
> You will not understand,
> The earth has many wonders
> But wherever I may die,
> I know that it's to a brown country
> That my homing thoughts will fly

There was a silent pause and then soft clapping from an audience with misty eyes. It enforced the realisation that they were home—but they were not.

Kisser came onto the 'stage' and threw three old tennis balls up in the air—a very uninspiring piece of juggling. However, when he caught one ball in his mouth and closed his lips, the audience couldn't believe it. They knew he had a big kisser—but not THAT big.

Big Kitty came on stage with her guitar and sang a very sexy song called, 'I Was Faking It'! That got everyone smiling.

'The World's Wonder Band' were too many for the makeshift stage with their drums, guitar and percussion. They played Kenny Roger's 'The Gambler' and had just started when the police arrived.

*I feel the joy turned to fear. Is there anything incriminating in the room?*

Sonia was on the floor with a torch as part of the team providing the special lighting effects when she heard the commotion of the police cars pulling up and doors slamming. They poured through the ground floor doors. They came through the laundry and front door. Sonia raced to the kitchen, ripped off the shirt and cap adorning the paper mache model and stuffed it into the oven. She ran back into the bullroom as the heavily armed police stormed through the laundry, into the kitchen and through to the bullroom as more police were entering via the front. They were shouting for everyone to get down on the floor with their arms in the air. They were convinced that it was a political meeting that had to be disbanded and perpetrators arrested. They circled the prostate gathering, shouting and brandishing weapons. However, all they found were some musical instruments. When the dust finally settled, Kaitlyn mimed playing the guitar and started to sing, 'You've got to know when to hold them … know when to fold them …' Others joined in as they sang Kenny Roger's gambling song. The police started to relax. There were too many to arrest and it was before curfew. They shouted for everyone to disband and go home. They took the guitars, makeshift drums and percussion instruments with them. The next day, there were notices in every block:

INSIDE AND OUTSIDE GATHERINGS
OF MORE THAN TEN PEOPLE
IS A CRIMINAL OFFENCE AND HENCEFORTH
BANNED

That was the end of Gibbo's Op Shop.

# Something Fishy

Kaitlyn was miserable. But then, she wasn't the only one. The failure of the KI Fringe was a huge setback as it had been eagerly anticipated. Morale was low. Gibbo knew that Kats had put a lot of work into organising what should have been a fun evening. She had been stoic when the block was raided on many occasions, but this one had left her silent and brooding. The repercussions of banned gatherings were just too hard to bear. Gibbo tried to cheer her up, but it fell on deaf ears. He decided on his half day off that he would prepare a special meal. He bought some potatoes and made some fish cakes. He decided that he would have a go at lightening up Kats's mood and then produce his gourmet meal. He knew it would be a hit. A meal without noodles or rice—what a treat! His mood was buoyant as he virtually danced round the tiny kitchen. He had scavenged some stale bread from a Power House's bin and made breadcrumbs. He tossed the fish cakes in the crumbs and heated them up in a frying pan. He would keep them in the oven out of sight and reheat them for just a few minutes, and bingo!—one mouthwatering meal would be ready. He listened out for Kats, but she didn't come home at the normal time. He set the table. If he had had a candle, he would have put it in the middle, but he used a small footy trophy—the only one that had made the ferry trip over—as a centrepiece instead. A cut-up plastic shopping bag was used as placemats. He set out the plastic cutlery and neatly folded two tissues to use as napkins. He looked at his handy work and was impressed. At last, he heard the door open.

Kats came in looking despondent. It had been a long day in the factory. The anticipation of the final siren continued for over an hour. She left the building and caught up with Sonia. They were both gutted by the failure of the fringe. 'I saw you fly into the kitchen, Sunny, and I didn't work out what you were doing for a short time. If that model dressed in Power House official clothing was found, it would have caused outrage and, probably, a harsher response. I should have joined you, but I wasn't quick thinking enough.' Sonia told Kaitlyn how she ripped off the cap and shirt and stuffed the model into a cupboard. 'There was nothing that you could have done. Two people rummaging in kitchen cupboards would have caused more suspicion. I was only glad that I got away with it.'

When she got home, Kats was surprised to see Gibbo so lively, and a table set as if for a special occasion. He was grinning and ushered her to the futon to rest. Gibbo started talking about The Fringe. 'I couldn't believe Kisser could put a tennis ball in his mouth and close his lips. What a big mouth! Who was that girl who played the guitar and sang, 'I was Faking It'? She called herself something.' Kaitlyn had seen her before but didn't know her. 'I think it was "Big Kitty". She had a good voice and really knew how to play a guitar. It was hilarious.' Gradually, Kats found Gibbo's energy contagious. She told Gibbo how Sunny had disposed of the GRAP model. 'As soon as she heard a commotion at the door, she flew so fast into the kitchen that in the old days she would have picked up a handful of frequent flyer points.' For the first time since the concert, Kaitlyn started to relax.

Gibbo put a tea towel over his arm and held a glass of water up high. 'I'm taking you to a very special restaurant.' As he helped her off the futon, he said, 'This way, Madam.

Is there anything special you would like to order?'

'Anything but noodles or rice.' 'I'll just hop into the kitchen and tell the chef. He won't be long.' Gibbo took two steps into the kitchen and 'spoke to the chef'.

'The lovely lady would like a special meal.' He kept up a tirade of chatter as he heated the fish cakes. He removed his footy trophy and placed the pan in the middle of the table.

'One special meal for a very special lady.' Kaitlyn was impressed. She took a bite, put down her knife and fork and said, 'What sort of fish is this?' 'Salmon,' was the response. 'What sort of salmon?' 'I don't know. Just salmon out of a tin.' 'I want to see the tin.' 'Bloody hell, Kats. What's this all about? Where's the tin?' Gibbo produced it and Kaitlyn stared at him. 'Where did you get this from?' 'Kats, just like the tuna, I brought it from home. I thought you'd enjoy it, savour every mouthful—not interrogate me. I think you are getting just as paranoid about food as my mum.' Kaitlyn looked at him. 'Gibbo, this is red salmon—the most expensive tinned fish you can buy. I *know* you did not bring it from home as I did all the shopping and I never bought a tin of red salmon, let alone one with foreign labelling. Don't forget, I re-packed your bag after you initially filled it with football memorabilia. I *know* there was no tinned food in that bag. When you told me that you had brought the tuna from home, I let my suspicions slide as I was in a state of shock with your mum arriving on the island. Now I know that you did NOT bring this with you. You had better tell me the truth as I also know that there is no way known to man that we could afford a tin of red salmon from Foodies. Don't try your usual method of 'attack is the best form of defence' like you did when everyone questioned you about the hooch shed and, for your information, I'm still not convinced. Just tell me the truth. Where did you get the tin of fish?'

Gibbo went into appeal mode. 'Kats, I did it for you. I've watched you getting so despondent lately and I just wanted to lift your spirits. I thought a nice meal would help and I tried my darndest to provide it. It wasn't stealing—they've stolen from us. Holy shit, Kats, they've got our business, our home and our dogs. I just wanted something back in return—a fair fucking go for both of us.' Kaitlyn pushed her plate away and stood up. 'You would be prepared to go to jail for one tin of fish? Gibbo, you need a new brain. Hasn't Beags told you what the conditions are like? If the GRAPS came in now and raided, we would both be sent to jail and then we'd find out who is feeling despondent! I suggest you put that tin in the bottom of the bin and make sure it is well covered.'

She went into the bedroom sobbing. Gibbo kicked himself for not thinking to tell her that he bought it with the hooch tokens. He hadn't thought fast enough. He'd also lost his appetite.

'I'll never shoplift again,' he yelled at the door. And he meant it, which was a good thing as he had a 'high alert' sign after his name on the Power House computers.

**I felt the danger every time you went shopping, son. Keep your promise.**

He had been monitored by the surveillance camera re-entering the store. He was seen hovering in an aisle, but the camera could not pick up what he was doing. When he emerged from Foodies for the second time, he was searched but nothing was found. He was a person 'of interest'.

Two days later, as they were eating their noodles, Gibbo's mum came in looking dejected. Although she slept on the futon during the day, they rarely saw her as she worked at night. Her half day did not coincide with either of them. She didn't wait to be asked. 'I've been sacked. Two Power House officials came to me with papers in hand and removed me from the building. I went to the Power House office but was not allowed inside. One official eventually came out and told me that I had not had a Covid vaccine and therefore can no longer work there. I cannot believe it—I was doing such a good job.' Although she had only been at the hospital for a few weeks, she told everyone she met she was a 'superintendent'. She felt as though she had broken the barrier by working for a purely Power House organisation. What she didn't understand was that the Power Houses had no problem with a Long Nose pushing a trolley full of toilet paper and carrying a mop and bucket. She was not allowed to talk to any staff or patients on her night shift. She turned to Gibbo. 'Now, I don't want to be a burden to you both. I will go and see the authorities tomorrow to get work.' Another thing she didn't understand was that her son and his Kats hadn't spoken for two days.

Gibbo tried to cheer her up. 'Are you hungry, Mum? I've got some fish cakes.' They sat and watched as she wolfed them down without asking any questions.

It wasn't long before she felt the frost in the air and decided to help. When Kaitlyn had her half day off, it was the perfect opportunity. 'Well, dear, I know I might be a bit old fashioned, but sometimes a little wisdom from past experience can be a help. You and Jack seem a little out of sorts and I know that marriages don't always run smoothly. As you know, Jack has a very kind heart. I wasn't here when he organised the cricket match on that public holiday, started the activities in the evenings and instigated the op shop, but I heard all about it from people who were very appreciative. I know there are times when he mixes with the wrong crowd and can be a little easily led, but he cares about people, and I know he cares very deeply for you … for some reason. He would have loved children, and I think that had you changed your name to 'Gibson', it may have made a difference.

Believe me, Dad and I had our moments in our marriage, but I knew that if I put my feelings to one side and pandered, he would eventually come round to my way of thinking. I would cook a nice dinner and tell him how much I admired and appreciated him. I would remind him that he was not always 'right', but then nobody is. You can stroke his ego while telling him the error of his ways. I always managed to get us back on an even keel and I think that you can do the same.' Kaitlyn glared. 'And where am I going to get the tokens from to cook this special dinner? Do I also provide a nice bottle of Grange Hermitage to go with it?' Gibbo's mum didn't know that pre-invasion, 'Grange Hermitage' was a very expensive wine, so she let that one slide. He loves fish and I know you buy some from time to time, so perhaps if we pool together, we may be able to get some.' 'Perhaps you could go to Foodies and check out some prices of tinned fish, so we know how much we are up for.' Kaitlyn responded. While Gibbo's mum was gone, she packed her bag.

**I've felt a lot of tension in the air from this building and it's not getting better. This couple are on a collision course.**

That evening, Gibbo stormed into the bullroom, shouting, 'Where's Macca?' Hamish had just finished his noodles and was sitting in the communal kitchen with Watsy and Tarantula. Gibbo took one look and ran back to the door. 'What was that about?' asked Watsy. 'I have no idea,' Hamish responded.

*I feel the rush of air as this fella looks for the love of his life. He suspects one person in particular. He feels intense but he's off on a tangent.*

Kaitlyn went to Sonia's block, sat on her bed and waited for her to return from work. She had no idea what she was going to do with herself, but she knew she wasn't going back home. She didn't know how Gibbo would respond to her absence, but she was rather hoping that he would get angry, which would make her decision easier. Sonia was shocked to see Kaitlyn with the travel bag that she had brought over on the ferry, sitting on her bed. 'I've left Gibbo.' A statement that covered all her questions.

'Sunny, I didn't appreciate my parents' honesty until my early teenage years. I don't think I recognised it until I reached high school. Over time, I would hear stories of how other parents would fleece large organisations, such as insurance companies and taxation. It was considered a 'given' thing to do—almost honourable! If you could work for cash and cut out the tax man, it was the way to go. If you lost a piece of jewelry, claimed on insurance and then found the jewelry, it was a bonus. You were in luck if you were undercharged for an item. My parents were the opposite. If there was an honesty box and they didn't have the right money, they left more. When I was a kid, Dad found a $50 note and immediately took it to the police station. Unbelievably, they notified him some months later that he could come and collect it. They didn't preach honesty—they just did it. They couldn't understand why anyone would evade tax. "We all have to pay for schools, roads and hospitals" was their motto.

Gibbo has been less than honest with me, and I don't trust him anymore. I know he has been shoplifting and runs the risk of being caught. I've always known that he likes to live life on the edge, but his actions could be fatal. We all wondered how some Foodies items would appear at the op shop with hugely marked down prices, and now I'm pretty sure I know the answer as I also know that he loves to please others and get the accolades. I admired him for his outgoing nature, but I sometimes feel that there is a hidden festering anger that he manages to override. Perhaps he is not even honest with himself!'

Kaitlyn paused, looked at Sonia, and added, 'But that's not my biggest worry. You see, I've gone over and over it in my mind. That night when Gibbo said he had finished making hooch and was cleaning up a mess as something had burst and the smell was a dead giveaway. It was dark and he had a bucket with rags in it. I heard him running water in the kitchen sink. It wasn't until a few days later that I noticed a red stain on the inside of the cupboard that looked like blood, and a week or so later, I heard that a Power House policeman was murdered in a shed. Do you remember when you all confronted him with your concerns, and he went ballistic, and everyone backed off? Well, Sunny, that is a typical Gibbo response—go straight to attack! His mum would fall for it every time. If he was accused of anything (mainly by a policeman at the door) and his mum later questioned his actions, he would make her feel guilty for not trusting him and it would always be someone else's fault.

I haven't seen you since his mum lost her job. They found out she was not Covid vaccinated so goodbye "hospital superintendent". This hasn't helped the situation with me and Gibbo. She obviously could feel the tension and gave me a little lecture this afternoon about "how to keep my man". She's had a few theories in the past as to why we didn't have kids and, of course, they all lead back to me. The latest one is that if I had changed my name to 'Gibson', we would have a bunch of kids by now!' Sonia's laugh was so infectious, that Kaitlyn joined in.

Sonia was worried as there was no spare bed in their communal room, which was now filling up as the girls returned from work. They all knew Kaitlyn from work or the op shop. 'Come into the kitchen and we'll have some noodles. This was the new word for 'dinner', no matter what you were eating. They were all surprised that Kaitlyn had left Gibbo as they appeared a very supportive couple. They all decided that the best place to go was Mama's—she'll know what to do. After some lively chatter, Sonia and Kaitlyn went upstairs. Mama took a little while to work out what was happening, but she was very welcoming. 'Si, si … Katerina … you stay with us.' Kaitlyn had a new home.

Gibbo was angry, but he knew he could not force Kats back home. He also knew that the future living with his mum would be very bleak. He thought back to his early days of marriage and decided that if he could do it once, he could do it twice. He would try to win her back. The only problem was that, back then, he had the time and opportunity. Now, he could probably go weeks without even sighting her. The repetitive nature of work and his mother's constant assurance that 'she will come to her senses' depressed him. He didn't realise that this constant longing was affecting him. The short lunch break to catch up with his mates wasn't enough to energise him. He felt lethargic but knew that he would have to put in a solid day's work, or he would be replaced. The future was bad enough but that thought made it even worse. His mates, of course, noticed a change and knew the reason. They watched as this fun-loving larrikin became sullen. They tried to stir up the old Gibbo, but it was falling on deaf ears. They decided they would try to get him interested in the kids' billy carts. They recognised Gibbo as a 'people' person and helping others was in his DNA.

On his half day off work, Gibbo went to see how the kids were progressing with their billy cart building after school. Some were so big they could have been horse drawn. This went against them as they could only go on the road, and they were far too conspicuous. The kids were good little scavengers, and the carts were coming along nicely. Their new playground was now the dump, and they poured over it meticulously. The wheels were hard to find, particularly multiples the same size. They were always on the lookout for small, dumped bicycles and prams. They scoured the dump for rods that could be utilised for axels.

They had no power tools and had to use a hand saw. It was a long project but after a few weeks, the older kids produced the first billy cart and decided it needed a name before road testing it. Names were being bandied round—Zoomer, Crasher, Hurricane … but Lucy was thinking about the ferry trip and remembering what Maddie said about the bike she got for Christmas. Her father said something like, 'Hey buddy, it's a …' With misty eyes, but a firm voice, she said, 'We'll call it "Trek".'

There was a narrow concrete path incline between the laundry wall and the housing block. They walked Trek up, turned it around and the biggest boy jumped in. He went three metres before hitting a wall. There was little room for error and the steering was very touchy, but the race was on to reach the bottom of the incline without crashing. The kids took turns with varying degrees of success. Gibbo fancied his chances, and the kids gleefully watched him jump in as they held onto the back of the cart. His knees were in the air and his feet were placed precariously on a single plank of wood. They let go of Trek and chanted a ticking clock. He lasted six seconds. The kids were delighted. He had a second go before giving up and he lasted nine seconds. He got a loud applause as most of the kids could beat that record. Gibbo jumped out with a huge grin and took a bow.

He went into the block laundry to watch the billy cart building. He was flummoxed to hear the younger kids talking to each other. 'Hey guys, you're speaking the wrong lingo. Where's your English?' One little kid looked up at him and said, 'We speak the official language. You had better learn it.' He left confused. He knew the kid was right, but he had no opportunity to learn a new language now or anytime in the future.

Gibbo took himself off to Foodies. He had no intention of shoplifting, but he did have on his boardshorts with the concealed waterproof pocket that originally held his mobile phone while swimming. He got some powdered milk, sugar and noodles, and exited via the confectionary aisle. He didn't recognise the security guards in the aisle as they were dressed as typical shoppers. They were watching him as they were pretending to scrutinise the products on the shelves. Their shopping bags contained a silent alarm device to alert the armed security at the front of the shop. They had been warned as soon as Gibbo entered the shop, and his photo had popped up on their mobile phone screens.

Gibbo got to the blocks of chocolates and paused. He had a teaspoon of coffee at home and the thought of combining it with something sweet was very appealing. He deserved it. It would lift his spirits. He knew he had promised Kats he would never shoplift again, but she was gone. He had nothing to lose.

**I can feel your despondent mind. I can also feel danger. Go home!**

The security guards at the front were familiar to him and usually enjoyed his banter, even though they only understood the odd word. But they were amused by his gesticulations and mimicry. He wouldn't have any problem getting past them. He fiddled with his shorts and opened the zipper compartment of the plastic pocket. One bar had a picture of multiple fillings, and he could imagine himself with feet up, a coffee in one hand, slowly sucking on a chocolate square, trying to guess the flavour. He needed comforting, and what better way? He quickly took the block of chocolate and put it in the pocket, zipping it up. He didn't rush as that would draw attention to himself, but he couldn't wait to get home. He didn't know that there was a security guard walking behind him. He was in the checkout queue, chatting to the folk ahead of him when he was suddenly surrounded. Two uniformed, armed security guards shouted at him to raise his arms. Two plain clothes security guards were behind him. He did what came naturally and tried to talk his way out of a sticky situation. 'What's this all about? I have come into the store for a few provisions. I was looking for some drinking chocolate but couldn't find it. Can you help me?' He waved his arms in the air and shook his head. Security drew their weapons and shouted at him to stand still with his arms above his head. They shoved their hands into his pockets and found nothing. They frisked his upper body. They motioned to him to drop his shorts. Gibbo placed his feet wide apart so that the impact of the chocolate would be lessened when it hit the floor. He undid his shorts and let them drop to his ankles. His lower body was frisked with no result. One of the guards motioned Gibbo to put on his shorts and, as he was bending down to retrieve them, the other guard stopped him as he wanted to frisk his shorts. The first guard shook his head as they already knew there was nothing in the shorts. They went to walk away, with the second guard following. Gibbo almost audibly sighed with relief and promised himself that he would never put himself in that position again. He was not interested in the chocolate—he would choke on it. The second guard suddenly turned round and came back, motioning Gibbo to remove his shorts again. This time he found the chocolate.

Gibbo knew he would be shown no mercy. He was not in the hands of the Australian police dealing with a troublesome teenager. He was alone and had to get himself out of this mess however possible.

# Hades

The word spread through the community that afternoon. There were many people in Foodies at the time and he was probably the most recognisable person on the island. The cry went up. 'Gibbo's been arrested for shoplifting.' It was not so much a surprise but a shock that hit hard. The island loved him and knew his absence would impact on their own wellbeing. He had been a pivotal cog in touching and enhancing day-to-day living. The cricket match was still talked about, and the memory relished. Not everyone had been to Bagsy and Nat's wedding, but they had heard all about it. He had been the enthusiastic organiser of activities to relieve the boredom of long summer evenings. He was credited with organising Mama's meatball dinner, although it was Hamish and Sonia's idea with Kaitlyn's help. In fact, anything that was considered slightly favourable was attributed to Gibbo. If a washing machine was repaired, the consensus was 'Gibbo must have worked his magic'. He had a knack for lifting people's spirits and making their dreary lives more bearable. His op shop was gone and now he would no longer be with them. The heart and pulse of the island for the Aussies had disappeared. They held little hope for a quick release as this was not a misdemeanor, but a criminal offence and they had no doubt it would be dealt with harshly.

His mum was inconsolable but not sure who to blame. If she blamed Kaitlyn for leaving him, then she acknowledged his guilt. She convinced herself and cried to everyone she met that the item was planted on his body by corrupt police. However, there was no motive and, of course, it was met with scepticism.

Many in the community remembered those unaffordable grocery items that popped up from time to time at Gibbo's op shop at very cheap prices.

Kaitlyn was devastated and blamed herself. Gibbo had promised never to shoplift again and had she stayed, she felt that he probably would have kept that promise. She knew he would be a mixture of anger and depression, which was a very poor combination for rational thinking. She also knew that the consequences of his actions flew out the window when he acted on impulse. She flew to her friend, Sunny, for consolation, who held her friend tight and cried with her. The two friends felt as though they had been hit by a train.

Help was on its way. Hamish was one of the first on the scene. He was closely followed by an entourage of mates: Bagsy, Nat, Tarantula, Beags, Presto, Watsy, Tabasco, Patsy, Bill, Silo, and Soula. There were too many to fit in the communal kitchen, according to the new 'maximum of ten' laws, so they had to split up into two groups. They reminisced and told stories of Gibbo's antics—their first meeting and the humour that he exuded. They were all there to support Kaitlyn. Bagsy and Beags were very quiet. They knew the conditions that Gibbo would currently be in and could not find any words of consolation. His friends mourned him as they would mourn the dead.

Notices went up on every building when the new rules were introduced. The Power Houses were aware that factory production was decreasing and recognised that a half day off per week was making the workers listless. They would not only change the factory rules but substantially improve the output. The following day, all factory workers were made to stand outside the fence line. They were then divided into two groups. They were issued with instructions written in grammatically correct English.

**YOU WILL WORK EACH NIGHT AT THE
FACTORY FROM 6.00 pm to 6.00 am
YOU WILL HAVE ONE DAY OFF PER WEEK AND YOU
WILL BE ADVISED OF THIS BY YOUR SUPERVISOR**

**YOU WILL WORK EACH DAY AT THE
FACTORY FROM 6.00 am to 6.00 pm
YOU WILL HAVE ONE DAY OFF PER WEEK AND YOU
WILL BE ADVISED OF THIS BY YOUR SUPERVISOR.**

Kaitlyn and Sonia were not only delighted to be working nights together, but sharing the same day off was a huge bonus. The factories were now working round the clock with four-hourly rotations of the numerous supervisors.

After household chores, the two friends spent their first free day trying to plot a way to help Gibbo. They did not know where he was being held. Bagsy and Beags had described the underground car park site beneath a building, but they did not know the location. The two friends spent their days off trying to seek information from administration, but after hours of waiting, or being quickly waved off, they were sent home. Hamish knew that that there was an official on the island who had a very good command of the English language, and Sonia was trying to access this person. However, the 'no fraternising with Big Feet' policy so far had made this quest impossible. Hamish also knew that he had mixed feelings with Gibbo now in prison. The memory of the night at sea was fresh in his mind and still caused him to wake up at night in a sweat. He could never truly trust Gibbo, but with him incarcerated, he could feel for his demise.

The whole community was affected by Gibbo's absence. Newcomers were streaming on to this large island as more housing blocks were completed. They quickly heard of Gibbo's arrest, and it didn't take long before they felt that they knew him personally. They all talked of a quick release but held little hope that this would happen. The Aussie population felt that without his presence, the only semblance of their past life had been taken away from them. Somehow, in this numbing, monotonous mess, he had shed a ray of light.

Gibbo woke up on a pallet. His face throbbed and a large wad of congealed blood was attached to his nostrils. His puffed and bruised lips hid one wobbly tooth. He carefully removed the blood and pushed his tooth as far into his jaw as possible, holding it there as he tried to recall the events that happened since entering Foodies. He remembered being handcuffed and thrown into the back of a police car, flanked by two policemen, and a blanket thrown over his head. He recalled the interrogation room and the officers screaming at him in a language he could not understand. He didn't know whether a full day had passed as it was dark. The last thing he could remember was lying on the ground and a boot coming down on his face. Thankfully, he must have passed out. He felt his nose and presumed it was broken. He sat up slowly, looking for more damage to his body. However, rearranging his face was as far as they went.

Eventually, a guard came with a small dish of plain rice and a glass of water. Gibbo was desperate to engage in a conversation with the guard. 'Tell your boss I can help find the killer of the policeman.' But the guard threw his hands in the air and retreated. Gibbo knew that his only hope of an early release was to collaborate with the police without implicating himself. He had got himself out of many scrapes in the past and he was determined to get himself out of this one.

Guards came and went infrequently, and Gibbo had the same message for all of them. He kept pleading to faces that were devoid of all movement. Not even a blink of an eye. He didn't know how long it took before he was once again handcuffed and escorted into the interrogation room. He sat before three mute policemen until the door swung open and a fourth plain clothes official entered. He sat down and introduced himself, speaking very precisely with a slight English accent. 'My name is Jia Chen. I am told that you can help us with the capture of Liu Li Jun's killer. Is this correct?' Gibbo responded and said that before he would say anything to help the police, he had to know how long his prison sentence was likely to be. Jia conferred with his colleagues, and they decided that the minimum punishment for a criminal offence against the Power Houses would be three years—'But tell him ten.' 'And if I lead you to the killer, what can you offer?' Again, there was a long discussion before a consensus and Jia announced, 'Six months.' He then went on to tell Gibbo that if he had any information, the police had ways of extracting it per gratis. The offer of a six-month sentence was extremely generous and had to be taken very seriously. 'If I agree, how will I know that you will honour this bargain?' Jia was deeply hurt to have his honour questioned by this common thief. 'Don't you dare talk about honour. You and your kind are like feral animals roaming the countryside, destroying everything in your path. You have no grace, discipline, dignity, or history. We are descendants of an ancient and highly respected society. We cannot teach you honour—it would take centuries.' Gibbo had no choice. He knew he could not survive ten years in Hades, but he could survive six months.

Jia asked why he did not respond at the time to the offer of a reward for any information that would lead to the killer. 'Because I thought I could be implicated and was frightened.' Jia did not believe him.

Gibbo was now a collaborator.

He told his story to Jia, who raised his hand from time to time so that he could translate to his colleagues.

My friend wanted to get married, and we planned to have a ceremony on a Sunday when we all had a day off work—before the new rules kicked in. My mate suggested that we make some hooch, as he knew all about it. My mate found a shed and asked for my help. Of course, I was only too happy to oblige as we both wanted the wedding to be memorable. When I heard about the killing of a police officer in that same shed, I was in deep shock and also denial. I convinced myself that someone else may have had access to that shed, which was the reason I did not come forward beforehand. As I said, I was scared that my slight involvement might implicate me, and I did not dare come forward with this information. However, I now feel that this person should be investigated.

'And the name of your mate?'

'Hamish McIntyre—"Macca."'

# Incarceration

Hamish was torn before he set off to work. He had been to Foodies every night after work in the hope of meeting up with Sonia. Even a glimpse would do. So far, he had no such luck. However, he was down to his last token, which would not even buy him a packet of noodles. This could be the very day that she could be standing in a queue. He knew he would cause suspicion if he joined the queue to buy something small and totally unnecessary. Security would immediately hit the alarm button, and he would have them swarming all over him. Was it worth it? No, but he knew in his heart that he was going to go.

He walked to work with Tarantula and Watsy. Of course, they talked about Gibbo, which had been the main topic on the island for days. No one was surprised that Gibbo had been arrested for shoplifting, but everyone was in shock. They all suspected that Gibbo had shoplifted items for the op shop as he was at the forefront for risk taking. They knew Gibbo hated the GRAPS and would do everything in his power to hit back. But somehow, they thought he was bulletproof and never envisaged him languishing in jail.

Everyone told 'Gibbo' stories—how he would march behind a government official, over emphasising a silly walk. If the official turned quickly, Gibbo would pull something from his pocket as an offering, which was always refused with disdain. He would then continue his antics as soon as the official's back was turned. He was fearless. Everyone loved hearing Gibbo's version of his mother's latest obsession. He would always start with, '…you won't believe this, but ...' His stories about his mother were the only ones they did believe as they did not need embellishing or exaggeration. Nothing would be the same without his company. Even when he was upset and angry, he was regarded as a 'character', which most people could not get away with. Hamish had mixed feelings. In some ways, he felt more secure with Gibbo in jail, but he missed him at the same time. He knew the island would not be the same without Gibbo's enthusiasm and dogged persistence in making their existence somehow feel brighter than it was.

They discussed the length of prison term that Gibbo would have to endure and even the most optimistic guessed a lengthy stay. It was clear that they would be without his company for a long time to come, unless their prison mate could produce some 'Gibbo magic', which they didn't believe in, but hoped for all the same.

**I felt the heaviness of the island. How could one being have this much effect?**

Watsy and Tarantula teased Hamish along the way over his incessant shopping. 'Have you been shoplifting, Macca?' However, Watsy worked out the reason and they both laughed as Hamish shrugged his shoulders. They also wondered aloud what he was using for money. He admitted that he was down to his last token and his mates dug deep and offered him two more. Hamish couldn't accept their generosity but relished their good intentions as everyone was scratching to have enough tokens to last until pay day.

Hamish worked on the building site efficiently and quietly. At times, he received a token bonus, which caused him embarrassment. He never spoke to an official, even if his instructions were severely flawed. The day flowed on as he thought back to his previous lifestyle by the sea.

That afternoon, two police cars screamed into the building site. Everyone on the building site downed tools and stood in fear. The supervisor pointed out the person of interest and Hamish was handcuffed and shackled. He was led out to the car and pushed into the back seat. The officers covered his head and raced back to the police station. There was no conversation. The journey was undertaken in an eerie silence. Hamish was trying to think of any way that he had disobeyed an order, but his mind was blank. This had to be a terrible mistake. He was pushed out of the car and, while being flanked by policemen, he tried to walk as fast as possible with shackles that allowed for little movement. The police were dragging him forward.

Everyone on that building site, including the officials, were stunned. It was the collective opinion of his workmates that the last person on the island who would be guilty of any misdemeanor would be Macca. The number of police and the manner of his arrest suggested a very serious infringement. They had no idea what Macca could possibly have done to deserve that treatment.

At the same time, four police cars arrived at Block D armed with metal detectors. Two officers were scouring the outside of the building, and the rest poured into the bullroom. They found many metal objects, particularly in toiletry bags—scissors, mirrors in metal frames, nail clippers. They were instructed to search every millimetre of space. They ran the metal detectors along the walls and under beds. They threw all personal items from the wardrobes and doors out of the entrance so that the room was bare. Watsy and Tarantula arrived home from work to find their room invaded. They were waved to wait outside among the debris that had been thrown out. They listened as the beds were stripped and metal detectors were placed along the top of the mattress. However, the detectors were singing in tune as the metal springs registered. The raid instructions were clear: 'Do not exit the building without evidence.' One of the policemen had a knife. He sliced through the thin mattress material and inspected the contents. They systematically sliced open all the mattresses and did the same. One of the officers outside was investigating the cause of his metal detector going off when his colleagues poured out of the building, grinning in triumph. They had found a hidden knife. Watsy and Tarantula watched their departure and were not only shaken to the core by the destruction, but by the fact that they had witnessed the discovery of the knife and realised that Macca had been arrested for murder.

It was only a few days prior that the friendship group, minus Silo, who was working daytime in a factory, gathered to console Kaitlyn. However, Kaitlyn and Sonia had already departed for work. Watsy and Tarantula described the carnage and the police findings to the group. They were able to describe the mattresses being ripped apart and the glee on the faces of the police when the knife was uncovered. Tabasco had tears pouring down his cheeks. The group was very somber. They remembered their meeting with Gibbo when they confronted him with their suspicions that he was involved in the murder of the policeman that took place in a shed. They remembered Gibbo's heated denial and their embarrassment at even contemplating his involvement. Tabasco and Watsy were now in no doubt as to the truth. What would they say to the girls? They decided that Beags and Tabasco would tell Sonia. Watsy and Bill would tell Kaitlyn separately. Patsy and Nat were working during the day and there was no time for them to be able to get together with their friends, who were working nightshift.

The whole island was abuzz when the news of Macca committing murder spread through the community. At first, there was disbelief, but then the recollection of Gibbo naming Macca as a traitor kicked in. There was a growing consensus that Gibbo was a good character judge and must have seen something in Macca that everyone else had missed. Tabasco and Silo were appalled when they heard this line of thinking on the building site the next day. 'Gibbo was cranky with Macca well before the murder took place,' Tabasco countered. 'We don't know when the murder took place. We don't have the privilege of that information,' was the response. Tabasco was stymied. He knew there was nothing he could say that would sway the accepted collective opinion. He knew that Watsy also had doubts about Gibbo's innocence and was astounded when Watsy declared that, although it was hard to understand, Macca must have been the guilty party. Tabasco argued that it defied logic that Macca would kill a policeman and hide the knife in his own bedding. He was talking to blank faces. The thought of Macca stabbing anyone was most certainly beyond belief for everyone on the island, but Tabasco realised that logical thinking did not come into the equation. The majority of people on the island wanted Gibbo back—guilty or not. Macca was well liked, but expendable. Sonia was gutted when she heard the community reaction.

Sonia and Kaitlyn were walking home from work when they were passed on the road by the incoming shift. When they saw Sonia, many quickly expressed their condolences about Macca's arrest before moving on. All these people could not be wrong. They arrived home together. Kaitlyn went upstairs to Mama's unit and Sonia to her quarters in the brain bank. They were met by the men. Sonia felt the life leave her body when Beags and Tabasco told her what had happened. Tabasco had tears running down his face and promised his support. Kaitlyn was in a state of shock and did not utter a word.

Sonia walked to and from work by herself and didn't see Kaitlyn who, she knew, was avoiding her. She only saw her friend from a distance during their lunch break. Her two closest friends on the island were now gone. If it wasn't for the continued support of Tabasco every night visiting the communal kitchen, she would have been totally alone. She knew that Silo was hurting too, but he worked day shift and didn't have the same day off. Their only quick chats were when they passed each other going to and from work. Her roommates kept silent as they did not know what to say.

On her day off, Sonia was in the laundry when Kaitlyn appeared. 'Sunny, we have to talk.' They went into the kitchen and Kaitlyn looked at her friend. 'All of our lives turned upside down when we were invaded. But when Gibbo was sent to prison, I felt I had landed on my head. For the last two days, I have gone over in my mind all the recent events. It seems that we have been on this island for years, but it's only been months. I cannot believe our lives could have spiralled out of control to this extent in such a short time. I feel as though I have been put in a washing machine with the spin cycle going full pelt. Sunny, I just want you to know that I am deeply sorry for what has happened to Macca, and the effect it has had on you.'

Sonia had tears splashing down her face. She responded with, 'I know I haven't known Hamish very long, but I just can't believe that he is a killer.' Kaitlyn held her friend tight and, in a whisper fraught with emotion, she responded with, 'He's not.'

Hamish was marched to the interrogation room and confronted by three policemen, one of whom was translating. Hamish did not know that his name was Yi-Jun. They were all convinced that they were facing Liu Li Jun's killer, and they wanted a quick conviction. The officers fired questions in the official language like bullets coming from a machine gun. Name, residence, the position of his bed in relation to the entrance door. They asked him how he had made the hooch. 'I don't know how to make hooch.' Yi-Jun translated: 'I'm good at making hooch.' The officers were puzzled that he had not answered the question but were pleased that he had substantiated Gibbo's story. 'Did you go to the shed with ...' He looked down at a piece of paper ... Jack Gibson?' 'I did not.' Yi-Jun translated: 'I did.' The officers were smiling. This was going very well. 'Did you kill Liu Li Jun? This was translated to: 'Do you know who killed Liu Li Jun?' Hamish thought for a moment and answered, 'Yes, I think so.' Yi-Jun knew that every person on the island with no or minimal command of the English accent, knew the words 'yes' and 'no'. He didn't have to translate for the officers to beam. Hamish could not understand what went wrong. Why were these policemen delighted with his denials?

Yi-Jun left the room to get a printed statement for Jia as one of the police officers got a baton and swung it into Hamish's ribs while yelling a tirade of abuse. He heard a crack. He felt another blow, another crack, and he slumped to his knees. This continued until footsteps could be heard, and Yi-Jun appeared with a statement written in a foreign language. He held out a pen for Hamish to sign. Hamish furiously shook his head, but the pen was placed in his hand with another atop as he signed the statement. His past identification was obsolete—he now had a new signature.

Hamish was taken to his cage. He remembered the night he and Beags were walking home from the Cantinnis' dinner and the vivid description of the makeshift jail conditions in an old underground car park described to him—but the reality still came as a shock. His eyes had to adjust to the enveloping darkness, with only a vague light filtering through the grid of an old automatic gate at the far end of the building. The fluorescent lights were only turned on when the guards pressure hosed the cages and their occupants or delivered food, which consisted of a broth with a few noodles in the morning, and steamed rice in the afternoon. Although it was blinding, this was the only time the prisoners could see others and their surrounds. The walls were lined with cages, giving the impression of a large nocturnal zoo enclosure. The emptiness and vastness of the room made every sound bounce round the huge space like a rotating pendulum hitting walls. Hamish located the ablution bucket in one corner and the pallet with its thin rubber lining. He tried to lay down, but the pain from his ribs was swift and he let out an involuntary cry of anguish. He got on his hand and knees and lowered himself on to the pallet, laying on his back whilst his ribs screamed in agony. He dreaded the thought of having to stand up in the morning. He heard footsteps. A guard came into the cage with a torch, forced his head up, and placed a tablet in his mouth, followed by water. Hamish tried hard not to swallow, not knowing if the pill in his mouth was lethal. However, a part of him said 'just rest in peace' and the water slid down his throat. As he fell into an induced sleep, the same guard returned with a knife, placed it in Hamish's hand and closed it tight. They now had his fingerprints.

# News

British Intelligence picked up the satellite photo of a shackled and handcuffed Hamish, flanked by policeman, walking to a car. They notified the press secretary, who was given the directive to email the image to the media. They supplied a brief text but knew that the media would grab it in both hands and blow it up as there was a lot of interest in the plight of the Australians. Most people had friends or relatives living in 'Nan Tudi' and were deeply interested.

The next morning, Aunty Bev woke up and flicked on BBC News. She was in the kitchen making a cup of tea when she heard the words, 'Australia as we know it.' She rushed into the lounge room and got a glimpse of a man shuffling along to a police car, surrounded by policemen. It was grainy and long distance, but the man did not look like Jack. She went over in her mind what Jack's instructions were over the phone. She did remember him saying, 'Cut the Christmas photo of me and supply it to the media. I want a fair trial.' However, she was not at all convinced that this man was Jack, and if she submitted his name and photo to the media, it could cause him grief.

It wasn't headlines as there was plenty of local news, particularly about the royal family and the latest divorce, but it did make Page Three of The Sun with a caption above a photo:

### 'It's not G'day for this Aussie mate'

**Despite assurances from the Power Houses that the Australians would have a better future under their rule, this image showed a**

**man shackled, handcuffed and bearing a GPS tag on his ankle, being led to a police car in Daishiu Dao—or Kangaroo Island as, until recently, it was known.**

The article went on to describe the island, renowned for the devastating bushfire that destroyed almost fifty per cent of the land prior to the pandemic, that touched the hearts of people around the world. It showed satellite photos of housing blocks, shops with guards at the entrance, and the lines of people, all wearing an ankle GPS, going to and from the factories that they knew, operating round the clock. They called for the United Nations to put pressure on the Power Houses for information. Television stations picked up the story and ran it for two nights in a row, the second night under the heading: 'Mystery Aussie man being led like a lamb to the slaughterhouse'. It went on to describe the likely fate of the person depicted in the photo image and achieved the desired effect by sending shivers down the viewer's spine.

Jia was worried. Everything had been going along so easily—perhaps too easily. A killer captured and a speedy conviction guaranteed to follow—all wrapped up nice and neatly. However, he was worried about the written interrogation that was placed before him. 'I think so' was a very strange response to the question: 'Did you kill Liu Li Jun?' He also knew that this prisoner had no command of the official language. That was his own fault. He felt something was wrong, but he was dealing with evil and massaged his niggling doubt with the knowledge that he could not only use any means at his disposal to eradicate it but was honour bound to do so. There was another problem: How did the British press get the information in the first place? He found it hard to believe that it was a haphazard coincidence. Two military lawyers arrived from Nan Tudi, and Jai supplied the signed statement. They were shown the knife on a sheet of paper with Hamish's fingerprints. The lawyers, defending and prosecution, were happy that this was going to be plain sailing, and no amount of international intervention could change the course of events.

Sonia and Kaitlyn spent the next two evenings waiting outside a building they believed was a police station. They were waved away by angry officials, but as soon as they got into their cars, the girls went back. The third day, Kaitlyn was upset that she could not accompany Sonia on her day off as Mama's back was troubling her and Kaitlyn promised that she would take over where Mama left off—by scavenging food items from The Power House bins. Mama could remember as a little girl her grandmother finding delectable items of food out in the fields or at the beach. Mama didn't have the luxury of being out in the countryside or at the beach, so it had to be the bins. Kaitlyn hated this job, but she had grown very fond of Mama, and vice versa. She could often understand Mama when she forgot and slipped into her first language.

Sonia made it a priority on her day off work and set off early in the morning. At 10.30 am, Jia came out and headed for his car. Sonia approached and was met with the usual wave of disgust to get out of there, but the tirade was different: 'Get out of here, you have no right to be standing on this ground.' Sonia knew she had found an English-speaking official and she was not going to back away. She knew he was a police officer, and his uniform suggested that he was of a very high rank. She approached slowly, saying, 'What is happening to Hamish McIntyre?' Jia stopped in his tracks. He could not believe that the English language had just poured out of his mouth. He was opposed to fraternising with Big Feet, but this girl brought back very strong memories. He recognised the expressive eyes. He could see the pain. Physically, this girl looked nothing like her—but looking into her sad, expressive eyes—Jia could see Bridie.

Jia walked with Sonia away from the building. He angrily motioned Sonia away from his presence, but his voice was softer. 'I can tell you that the person you speak of has admitted to killing Liu Li Jun. His fingerprints on the murder weapon are sufficient evidence for any court to convict him. He has signed a statement declaring his guilt.' Sonia stopped to digest this information. 'How did he come to be arrested?' Jia said the information came from a very close mate and could not be faulted. He told her he had no more information as he got into his car and drove off feeling deeply disturbed. He was responsible for upholding the law and he had just flouted the first rule of allegiance to this new country—if there was any suspicion of any alliance to anyone of European background, the culprit would immediately be sent back home in disgrace. He thought of the impact on his parents if this should happen and immediately felt the flush of guilt coursing through his body. His father would never forgive him and his mother would be torn between her husband and son. He resolved to get this trial wrapped up quickly so he could return to the mainland of Nan Tudi.

That evening, Tabasco called in to see his friend. Sonia told him about the conversation with the English-speaking official. 'I think he's a very highly ranked police officer, but I'm not sure.' Tabasco was quick to respond. 'I believe the informer must be Gibbo. He is being held in prison and has access to the police. He's really got it in for Macca—has for a long time. I was a witness to that. Sonia, if you can get to this police officer again, try to find out the name of the informer and, if I'm right, convince him that Gibbo and Macca are not mates.'

Sonia went back the following evening and watched the police cars coming and going. She kept in the shadows and waited. If 'her' policeman returned, she was going to see him. She felt that this person was a conduit to Hamish, and she was going to do everything in her power to keep this connection alive. Kaitlyn wanted to accompany her, but Sonia said she would have a better chance alone as it was easier to hide one body in the shadows than two. Jia did exit the building before sundown and Sonia walked towards him. Jia was furious. He should never have spoken to this girl and now she was being a huge nuisance. Sonia called out, 'I just want you to know that Jack Gibson and Hamish McIntyre are NOT mates. Jia threw his hands in the air with an 'I don't care' attitude when Sonia continued, 'Jack Gibson tried to kill Hamish McIntyre by setting him adrift in the sea with no land in sight. If you look up your records, you will see that Hamish was picked up by a police car and driven to the station for questioning before being released. He did not name the perpetrator, but I can tell you categorically that it was Jack Gibson.'

Jia pretended that he had not heard a word before he entered the building. However, he did check the records and Hamish had been picked up by a police car. The description was that he was wet, shivering and walking as if intoxicated. He told the police that he had been caught in a rip. However, that did not explain how he had come to be so far away from Block D. His niggling doubts about Gibbo's information were increasing.

The next day, Jia had Macca brought into the interrogation room. This time there were only the two of them. Hamish was suspicious that his answers may be used against him and requested a verbal interview. He was astonished when Jia turned off the computer and turned it round to show what he had done. He could sense a softening in attitude. Jia asked, 'Jack Gibson tells us that you are good mates. Is this true?'

'No.'

'Has Jack Gibson ever tried to harm you?'

'Yes.'

'In what manner?'

Hamish described how he had helped the site supervisor when he dislocated his arm and Gibbo had accused him of being a traitor. He didn't mention the word 'GRAP'. He described the cement truck, the boat, and told how he had strapped a polystyrene lid to his body for survival. Jia stood up saying, 'We will check your information.' Hamish was dismissed.

Jia called for Gibbo, who was led in. He said he had heard that Gibbo had tried to harm Macca, who he now described as a 'mate'. Gibbo gave a soft chuckle and, sounding wounded, replied, 'Fair go, mate. So, Macca denies our friendship and makes up some cock and bull story about me. If we're not mates, ask him why we were sitting side by side handing out the hooch to paying customers. I bet he even denies making the hooch with me. I'm surprised that you would listen to a word he says. He's obviously in a very desperate situation and will say anything to help his cause. I can prove that we are—or were—the best of friends. Your Power Houses have removed a digital camera and there is evidence on it of how close we are … or were.'

Jia was surprised that there were two digital cameras still being kept with a lot of other peripheries that had been confiscated during raids on the housing blocks. It was a lot of junk—home-made basketball rings, old carpet, old golf clubs, a home-made baseball bat, old tennis balls, and a home-made football among an assortment of useless outdated items. It didn't take long for him to find an image of the two mates beaming at the camera with arms around each other's shoulders. Another photo showed Macca behind a table serving drinks and, at what looked like the same location, Gibbo with his arms round Macca's shoulders, the two of them smiling for the camera.

Jia did check Macca's story with the site supervisor. Yes, one of the site managers had dislocated his shoulder and a workman quickly put it back into the right position and showed him how to hold his arm steady. He was not sure who that workman was. Jia showed him a picture of Gibbo and Macca on his mobile phone and the supervisor smiled and pointed to Macca. Jia was continuing to smell a rat. However, Yi-Jun did not share his compatriot's concerns.

# Caged

Gibbo and Hamish were not the only ones in the makeshift underground prison. Between the two men was Lucy, a twelve-year-old girl. She had been caught shoplifting a box of washing powder that she had placed at the bottom of her bag and had not declared it at the checkout. She kept repeating that she had simply forgotten that it was there. Across from their cages was a fifteen-year-old boy, Jason, who had tried to smuggle out broken biscuits from the factory where he worked. His pockets yielded a small number of loose sultanas and some broken biscuits. His parents were not told of his arrest but found out from the labourers returning home that he had been searched and taken away in a police car. They were distressed because of the hopelessness of the situation. Jason walked round his cage non-stop and every now and then he cried out for his mum and dad.

The one thing they all had in common, was hunger. Hamish's ribs were so painful the first day that he gave his bowl of rice to Lucy. He could not understand why the police would place a young girl in between a shoplifter and a murderer. On the second night, he woke to a tidal wave of hunger that smothered his body. He hallucinated about food and imagined eating a whole apple—slowly. He could almost taste it. He vowed that from then on he would savour every mouthful that came his way. The next morning, he would take a sip of broth from his bowl and hold it in his mouth for as long as possible, before slowly swallowing. In the evening, every grain of rice was eaten individually. This not only lengthened the meal, but made it feel more substantial.

As Gibbo's swollen mouth healed, he spent his days chatting. He called out to Macca: 'No hard feelings, mate. We've always been buddies and it's just bad luck that we have ended up in this place together. Talk to me, Macca. We're in this together, we can work our way out of this together. We have to help each other now. I'm happy to do anything I can to make life a bit more bearable in this joint. Macca, Macca, talk to me please. We both need company and we can make this place a bit better if we can communicate. Macca, Macca, talk to me. How are you feeling? You seem to be walking with difficulty. Macca, Macca …'

Hamish remained silent. Yes, he was having trouble walking. The pain of his broken ribs eased a little when he was lying on his back. However, he knew that he had to exercise and spent short periods walking in squares round the perimeter of iron bars. One morning, a guard put all the lights on and instructed the inmates to throw bedding and all their clothes out of the cage door. Two guards in full body suits, breathing oxygen from a tank on their backs, entered the cages with their high-pressure hoses. Behind them were two more guards pointing machine guns at the prisoners with a finger on the trigger—one gun was aiming at Hamish and the other at Lucy. When the avalanche of water hit Hamish's naked body, the pain was excruciating. The second time this happened he tried lying on his stomach on the wooden pallet, but they motioned for him to turn over. He did not cry out.

Gibbo gave up talking to his 'mate' and chatted to Lucy, who he called 'kiddo'. As Jason was barely visible from the other side of the dark, vast area, his constant footsteps echoed through the underground building. Hamish did not know how long he had been in prison as he was there when he arrived. He had trouble keeping up with the days, although he could tell day and night from the distant light that came through an old gate grid. He knew his chances of survival were extremely slim and a fair trial with the weight of evidence against him non-existent. He would have loved to have ended his plight and knew that the only way to a quick and sudden death would be to rush at the armed guard with the gun aimed at his head when 'the cleaners' came to pressure hose his cage. However, that would compromise Lucy, and she was too young. 'Rest in peace' sounded like music to his ears.

He was concerned about Lucy, being in this terrifying place at such a young age. Hamish tried to reassure her that she would get an early release. 'They let Beags and Watsy out within a week.' However, Lucy replied, 'Yeah, but they weren't accused of shoplifting. I think I'm going to be made an example of so that all my co-workers will not end up in this hell hole. I worry about my mum and dad. Even though we fought, I also worry about Lucas, my younger brother. I don't know what the officials have told my family. They may not even know that I'm still on the island. I know they will be fretting and feeling completely powerless, just like the way I'm feeling. I think I know how my grandparents felt.'

Over the next two days, Lucy would drift over to the bars separating him and Macca and tell him snippets of her background.

Her grandparents came from Cambodia and were placed in a detention centre in Sydney. They did not know whether they would be allowed to stay in Australia or how long they would be held in detention. Her voice was choked with emotion. 'I feel as though I am in their shoes. I can feel their pain. The Australian government, at the time, was trying to encourage them to return to Cambodia. However, my grandparents were released after a while. We heard the stories, but we didn't listen. I wish I had been more tuned in. We were too busy leading our own lives. I feel now that I can share my experiences with my grandparents and that's a help.'

Lucy would drift back to her pallet and Hamish did not know if she was crying.

**She was. I felt her tears. She was crying for her family, and she was crying for her dead mate.**

When they were having their rice that evening, Lucy took her bowl over to Hamish's bars and continued to relate the hardships that her grandparents suffered. 'My grandmother gave birth to my mum when she was in detention. Mum said she could remember the huge surrounding fence and the huts in which they lived.

191

When they were released, they moved to South Australia as they had relatives there and were told that there was not only work, but cheaper housing.'

'How long were they in the detection centre?'

'I'm not sure, but it must have been many years,' was the response.

Lucy looked at Hamish and asked about his grandparents.

'I didn't know my grandmother as she died of cancer when I was a baby. My grandfather was an electrician, which was probably why my dad continued in the same trade.'

'That's funny,' Lucy responded, 'my grandparents worked hard and bought an electrical business. I know it's not the same, but they might have known each other.'

Lucy's voice sounded lighter. 'My grandmother was terrific at selling. Very often people would come in for one item and walk out with two or three. My grandfather drove the delivery truck and helped with all the deliveries. He was very strong.' Lucy's voice took on another tone when she talked about her mother. 'My mum loved school, and my grandparents encouraged her. She was a teacher and met my Australian dad at the same high school. That's how come we were living in the Fleurieu area. After the invasion, we were split up as they lived close to Adelaide, so I don't know where my grandparents are now. I don't know how they will feel—whether they feel that they are once again in detention, or that if they can survive once, they can do it again. They won't hear "Here's Lucy" ever again. They are getting old.'

The next day, after being pressure hosed, the two inmates stood close together with their slim sliver of rubber mattress wrapped round their bodies. They had learned to use them as a towel and hoped they would dry off before nighttime. Hamish had asked Lucy about her school life.

'My friends felt sorry for me having nerdy teachers for parents. They thought my home life was just an extension of my school life. Of course, I never told them that I loved going to school. It wasn't cool. I probably wasn't the only one who pretended to hate the joint … I bet there wouldn't be a kid now who wouldn't give their right leg to go back to school now. I didn't like homework much, but Mum and Dad never pressured me … well, not too much. If I needed help, they were there. I'm not saying that life was perfect every second of the day. Mum and Dad often disagreed and us kids could feel the undercurrent. Sometimes, I think, if Dad said one thing, Mum would disagree just because she felt like it. I also had the usual hassles with older and stronger kids, particularly those who blamed the teachers for their bad marks and tried to take it out on me. But I had a good group of friends, and we looked after each other. Yep, I liked school.

Macca, when I found Mum crying in the laundry because she had a bundle of washing and no washing powder, I thought of my grandparents. What would they have done? Somehow, they would have overcome adversity. That's when I decided to take matters into my own hands.'

Lucy's voice became a coarse whisper. 'It's hard to accept that I will never enter another school gate. In Australia, we worked towards our future. Now … we just work towards our death.'

Hamish could not believe the astuteness and desperation of this kid and knew that the only thing he could do to help was to keep asking Lucy about her life pre-invasion, particularly about her parents. She spoke much more lightheartedly about the past. During the long hours, she talked to Hamish about her escapades with her friends. How they used to hang out in the skate park and on the soccer field. The endless text messages that bounced from one to the other. Some of them were now on the island, but long working hours, different days off, and apathy had eaten away the fun of friendship. She did not tell him about Maddie—that was still far too raw.

Hamish could also hear Lucy talking to Gibbo at times, but despite the echo, or perhaps because of it, he could only catch the odd word. He worked out that it must have been a more lighthearted conversation, as he could hear an occasional chuckle from them both. Gibbo would have been sending up the GRAPS and Lucy would enjoy that.

Jia would not admit it, even to himself, but he made sure that he left the building at the same time each afternoon, knowing that Sonia, and sometimes Kaitlyn, would be in the shadows. He was well aware of the strict 'no fraternizing' policy and never disclosed any information about the prisoners other than commenting that 'they are being well looked after'. He could honestly answer her question that he did not know the date of the trial, which was a mystery to him, as he presumed that the Power Houses would want a quick trial and conviction. He could not tell her that the United Nations had images of a prisoner in shackles and were putting pressure on the Power Houses for a fair trial. However, one of the school children overheard a conversation between teachers about the United Nations interfering with their justice system. 'That killer deserves everything he gets with no mercy,' was their consensus. The community was still reeling from the shock of Macca being held in jail for murder and was pleased to hear the news that the outside world was aware of his plight. It didn't take long for the word to spread.

Jia didn't walk with the girls but had a routine of going over to where they were standing in the shadows and only ever having a very quick conversation. He then shouted at them and waved them angrily away. Sonia seemed brighter one afternoon and asked if the United Nations knew about the plight of Hamish McIntyre. Jia was taken aback but responded with, 'It won't do him any good' before he shooed them away. Sonia took that as confirmation and, for the first time, she felt uplifted. She knew it would be a closed courtroom to Big Feet and Long Noses as any representation of misplaced people would undermine the integrity of a superior justice system.

# Trial and Error

*I feel authoritative footsteps collecting a caged person. I do not know what they will do to the person, but I'm getting very negative vibes.*

No one saw it coming. Hamish heard the footsteps coming towards the cages. He knew it was night but didn't know the time. He had been lying awake on his pallet and guessed that it was well before midnight. The guards came to his cage and opened it. He was escorted out of the building and into another. This was not another interrogation. There were armed police dotted round the wall and a table set up at the far end of the room. A military official walked over to him and Hamish thought he said he was a lawyer and would be defending him. Hamish found him difficult to understand. The three men, also in full military regalia sitting behind the large table, must have been judges. Hamish was told to stand before the judges. He got the impression, as they looked at their watches, that this would not take long, as their night had been interrupted. Jia was present to act as translator and placed himself between the lawyers.

The judges had Hamish's statement before them. They also had the knife on a sheet of paper. One of the judges held up the statement and asked Hamish if he recognised it. 'Yes ... but ...' The judge held up his hand to silence him. This is all going at lightning speed without any preliminaries or ceremony, he thought. He felt resigned to the fact of a quick trial and knew that, perhaps even in minutes, he would know his fate. The knife was held up and the prosecution lawyer stated that the fingerprints belonged to the man facing the judges. The judges asked Hamish directly if he had been to the shed where the body of Liu Li Jun was discovered. 'No.'

*I can feel the life draining out of you. That optimistic outlook on life has gone. I can feel your spirit leave your body as you resign to your fate.*

The prosecution stepped in. 'In his statement, this man admitted to killing Liu Li Jun. There is no way that he could not have been at the murder scene—the shed. He was asked if he killed Liu Ki Jun and he answered, "Yes, I think so."'

Jia whispered to the defending lawyer, who stood up and countered, 'This sounds like a statement from someone who did not understand the question. "Yes, I think so" is a very strange response.'

One of the judges said to Jia, 'Your fellow officer was interpreting. Are you telling me that he cannot translate a simple question?' Jia bowed his head and retorted that the written and spoken word may have become confused.

The judges conferred with each other and announced that they were in unison in their judgement of the case. They were ready to deliver their verdict. They went on to say that their priority was to protect their own. All The Power House officials had the right to work in a safe environment. Liu Li Jun was a policeman, who had his life cut short in a barbaric act by this person standing in front of them. Evidence showed that, although the body was charred, Liu Li Jun's face was mutilated in what could only be described as an act of despicable savagery. The autopsy also showed damage to the head plus stab wounds front and back. This man being held in this courtroom was a despicable, evil killer—more animal than human—and should be dealt with accordingly. Jia did not translate.

Hamish did not know what they were saying, but from their body language and tone, he was certain that the judges had made their decision. He was ready to hear it. He wanted to hear it. The only thing he would miss was his constant thoughts of Sonia. He relived the cricket match where he first met her. If he couldn't remember the exact conversation, he made it up. He could picture her on those Sunday afternoons before the rules changed and everyone had the day off work. He closed his eyes and watched her kicking the home-made football and teasing him when she hit the goal posts that had been painted on the wall. 'That was a fluke,' he would retort. 'Ok, Hamish, do better than that.' And at times he did, and they laughed. He could see her throwing the same ball at a basketball ring and passing it on to the next person. He thought about the wedding when he told her about being tossed about in the sea waves and could see her intense face with the silent tears flowing. He revisited the op shop and the lighthearted banter that flowed between them. He could feel the pleasure of both of them sitting on the floor with their Italian meal that Mama Cantinni had provided. It didn't matter what sort of day he had endured, Sonia's presence made him feel alive and optimistic. The world and its problems disappeared in her presence, and he hoped she felt the same. Hamish did not know of Sonia's stubborn and often futile daily vigilance, standing for hours in the hope of catching a few words from Jia. Knowing her background as a teenager, of helping her mother gather up the children and relocate to another state to support her younger siblings, he would not have been surprised. He knew she had grit.

The judges asked the prosecuting lawyer if he wanted to say anything further. 'No.'

They asked the defending lawyer if he wanted to say anything further. Jia whispered in his ear, 'Yes. All our policemen carry mobile phones. However, none were found on or near the body of Liu Li Jun. I feel that a vital piece of evidence has not been located, and I would like a week to take time out to try and find this piece of equipment.'

The judges looked at their watches and conferred. In their minds it would not make any difference to the judgement and would only prolong proceedings. They had more important things to do with their time than being up another night. However, they did have a directive from their mainlands 'to ensure the appearance of a fair trial'. The Power Houses may even contemplate submitting the court hearing transcript to the United Nations. It would be a triumph to prove what sort of base creature they had justifiably convicted. It would silence any interference from abroad. They would supply photographic as well as written evidence of the mutilated state of Liu Li Jun's body. They gave forty-eight hours in which to locate the phone and dismissed the court. This was later amended to seventy-two hours as the judges did not want a night trial after a day on the golf course.

Hamish was disappointed. He knew he was condemned and would have preferred a judgement rather than waiting and contemplating for another two days. In his mind, he was working out his execution and was hoping for a firing squad. He knew nothing about the law, but somehow, he felt that he would not be committed to a life in prison. Why would they go through that hassle? He did not know that his photograph was on Page Three of The Sun and had been beamed around the world. He also did not know that the United Nations was pressuring for a fair trial. He knew nothing about a mobile phone and, after Jia described the decision to him, he could not understand how it could have any bearing on this case whatsoever.

As soon as he was back in his cage, Gibbo called out, 'What's the verdict, Macca?' He didn't answer. Lucy was awake and also wanted to know the verdict, but Hamish thought that this question would have come via Gibbo, so he remained silent. They both presumed that he was in a state of shock. Hamish knew that he only had forty-eight hours and was happy to think his own thoughts. Despite the late hour, a guard came with a torch and put a bowl of rice outside his cage. Hamish thought it must have been a mistake as he had already had his evening's rice. However, this time it was different. He could not believe it when he picked up a small cube of carrot. He was going to make this last for as long as possible. He then found a pea and chewed it into minute particles. There was more. He couldn't believe how happy he was to find the vegetables in his rice and savoured every mouthful. Perhaps this is what happens before facing the firing squad.

The search was on. The metal detectors were in operation once again. The community had no idea what was going on, but they knew what was coming. More raids. Jia and Yi-Jun ordered a thorough search of Block B and particularly number twenty-seven. Gibbo's mother answered the door to a group of police some with metal detectors. She was ordered out into the passage. She could see from the set look on the invading faces that any questions would be futile. She had heard neighbours being raided and for once, she kept her mouth shut. Despite a thorough search, lasting hours, they went away empty-handed.

Sonia and Kaitlyn had no idea why the raids had commenced again. The police seemed to be looking for a specific object as they threw items out of cupboards. Every mattress was ripped apart with the springs and stuffing exposed. Everyone had to make up coverings using any materials, whether cloth or plastic, that came to hand. There was a mass exodus, including children, to the dump to scour for anything that could be used to make patchwork covers.

The raids inside the buildings ceased. Jia now had a huge problem. A day had passed, and time was ticking away. Yi-Jun was convinced that Jia was on a wild goose chase and did not share Jia's concern that they could be convicting the wrong person. Jia had told him he wanted a quick trial so that they could return to Nan Tudi and could not understand why Jia was extending their time on 'Daishiu Dao'. The mobile, if there was one to be found, could be anywhere outside. It could be in the middle of an empty paddock. Jia knew that Yi-Jun was not the only officer who sensed that this search was useless. The next morning, he was in two minds as to whether to call it off. However, as he was contemplating this decision, he resolved to channel all his resources into searching the outside of the building blocks, concentrating on Block B. He sent the bulk of the police on this mission, with just a few to randomly scour the land nearby. With no result at lunch time, he called in his team and gave the order to concentrate on Block D. If Macca had disposed of the mobile phone, he could well have hidden it nearby. Jia decided to enlist some help and called in teams of workers from building sites, armed with shovels, to dig the dirt surrounding the cement paths that connected each housing block. The police half-heartedly had to swing into action.

Once again, the sound of metal detectors filled the air. After forty-eight hours with no result, Jia returned to the police station to hear the news that an extra twenty-four hours had been granted. He knew that Yi-Jun and his team were questioning his actions, but an innate hunger to find out the truth, forced him into action. 'I have become my father,' he mused. But that thought made him proud.

Tarantula, Beags, Bagsy, Presto, Watsy, Tabasco, and Bill were among the crew digging up dirt. They had no idea what they were looking for but knew that it would not be the beginnings of a flower bed. They worked in silence but gave the shrugging of their shoulders, 'I give up', signal to each other. It was getting late, but the digging crew was not worried as they were rather enjoying being away from the building site for a change, and they were much closer to home. They didn't care what the police were looking for, nor were they worried whether they found it. Before knocking off that night, Watsy mimicked shovelling and throwing his hands in the air in a 'what are we looking for?' sign. A policeman returned the mimic by pulling out his mobile phone and pointing.

That night, word went out to the community that the police were looking for a mobile phone, and they all tried to guess the significance. Sonia waited for Jia that evening, but to no avail. She and Kaitlyn were at work and didn't hear the news until the next morning when Tabasco hurried over to the brain bank, telling them that the police had ceased raiding the inside of all the housing blocks and were now concentrating on the outside areas in order to find a mobile phone. Jia had ordered all possessions belonging to Hamish to be taken to the police station. The police were surprised to find an esky lid at the bottom of the drawer, but Jia did say ALL possessions, so they threw it in. When Jia saw it, later in the day, he knew why it was there.

Neither of the girls had had time to patch up their mattresses and had spent a sleep-deprived day lying on exposed springs. Tabasco informed them that crews of Aussies had been enlisted, armed with shovels, to dig around the outside of the housing blocks—so far Block B (Gibbo's) and Block D (Macca's) —and told them of the previous night's meeting.

***Yes, I felt them coming together – they were banding as a
group, but they were powerless.***

The previous night, Tarantula, Beags, Bagsy, Presto, Watsy,
Tabasco, Silo, and Bill gathered in the kitchen to discuss what was
happening. Bill suggested that it must have been the murdered
policeman's phone. 'They would not be going to all this trouble
if it was not of huge significance,' he added. They all agreed. 'The
thing is, they will probably be looking for fingerprints. I don't think
Macca's will be on it.'

They all knew who it would implicate, but it was Watsy
who verbalised. 'Yes, I agree that the chances are that they are
looking for evidence, namely fingerprints. We were all suspicious
of Gibbo's movements after the wedding and—I'm speaking for
myself—he almost convinced me that he was innocent. However,
do we want the police to find this phone? Macca has been charged
and we can't help him, but we can help Gibbo if we find the
phone first. We'll destroy it. What do you think?'

'If I find the phone and get caught with it in my possession,
I will be sent to jail,' responded Beags, who was still having
nightmares of his week in a cage.

Bagsy, all fired up, joined in. 'We are Aussies—dinky di, true-blue
Aussies. We stick together. We help our mates—not the GRAPS. We
are not sure where Macca's allegiances lie. He did come to a GRAP's
aid, but we do know for certain that Gibbo is one of us. The question
is … do we want Gibbo back in our community? The way I see it
is, he has dragged our miserable lives out of the gutter and provided
some relief. I, for one, would find these living conditions intolerable
if it wasn't for Gibbo. I don't care what he did or didn't do. I say if we
happen to find the phone before the police can get their hands on it,
we hide it and smash it into minute pieces. Why should we assist the
GRAPS? All that would do is help convict two of our mates instead
of one. The worst-case scenario is that as many of us as possible put
our fingerprints on the phone before the GRAPS get hold of it. Are
we collaborator GRAPS or do we stick together?

They all agreed, except for Tabasco and Silo, who stayed silent. They had been confident that no one in the Aussie community could influence a court of law. However, now they were not so sure.

*I now feel divisiveness in the community. They don't want any of their number in custody, and one person in particular was more important to them than anyone else. Perhaps they were not so powerless.*

Silo felt helpless as he could not be part of the digging crew the next day. He was a factory worker. He wanted to help Macca, but that was impossible.

Bagsy continued: 'We must pass on the information to everybody with a shovel tomorrow —finders, keepers.

Sonia was appalled to hear Tabasco's news. 'The GRAPS have removed all traces of Hamish from the building and now his mates have erased him as well. I cannot understand why no one will stand up and try to help him.'

Kaitlyn was confused. 'Why would any of us want a mobile phone when we can't use it? The batteries would have run out long ago as all cords and chargers were confiscated before we left for this island. The only way we could get our hands on a Power House issued mobile would be to steal it.'

Tabasco was thoughtful. 'Or kill for it.'

Hamish knew that time had run out and waited to be escorted back to the make-shift courtroom. He listened in the night for the footsteps that didn't come. He woke in the morning confused. The judges said forty-eight hours and that had passed. Perhaps something more important had sidetracked them.

Jia was on the scene the next morning at dawn. Officials had roused the Aussie crew and work was swinging into gear. The whispered instructions were passed down the line. 'If we find the mobile phone, we keep it or destroy it.'

'I don't mind hiding it from the GRAPS, but I don't want it on my body' was the general verdict. 'Give it to Bagsy or Watsy,' was the response. 'They have made the decision.'

The crew shovelled all morning. The sound of metal detectors once again filled the air. Johnno Vallorani was shovelling outside Block D under a rusty mark on the wall. There was many shovellers who stopped to pick out stones, rocks, pieces of crockery, but Johnno dug up the mobile phone, wrapped in an old piece of cloth, covered in dirt and grit. He looked up at the guards scrutinising their every move and partially removed some of the cloth to take a peek. What he suspected was true—it was a mobile phone—but he didn't know that he wanted it. His first thought was, Not me. I'm in trouble. I will attract attention if I put it back, and I can't hand it to a GRAP. He waited for a shout from the guard as he put the phone in his pocket, knowing that he would offload it at the first opportunity. He couldn't wait until the lunch break. Every time a guard walked past, he could feel his pocket burning.

The lunch break came, but it was different to the building site. Jia had the Aussies sitting against the wall and three metres away a line of guards was facing them. Jia walked between. 'You will have a ten-minute break. There will be no talking.'

Johnno kicked the Aussie next to him and pointed to his pocket. It took a little while to click in and the message was passed down the line with the same signals. As the information travelled down the line, everybody knew that the mobile had been found but no one knew who had found it except Johnno's neighbour. Johnno spent the rest of a very long afternoon digging and anxiously waiting for the final siren so that he could, at last, offload the phone. He was hoping that someone would find an object of interest and cause a disturbance so that he could chuck it into the pocket of someone else. This did not happen. Why did he not just leave it where it was buried so that someone else could discover it, or deny its existence? There were supervisors haphazardly raking the soil, but by this time he could be well away from the scene. If only ... like everyone else, he had heard about conditions in the makeshift prison and he knew he didn't want to put his hand up to go there. Now, here he was innocently caught up in the biggest dilemma of his life. If only he could hand it to the GRAP, everything would be okay. But then, he would have to return to the community, and that thought was almost as unpleasant. He really was between a rock and a hard place. He knew his fingerprints would be on the cloth and every now and then he would rub the phone with the dirty cloth to erase any fingerprints that may be on it. It was a warm day, but he was the only one sweating profusely.

The sun was setting, and still Jia did not call a halt to the workers. Yi-Jun was intently listening for any English information that would come his way. However, the workers were mainly mute throughout the day with just a sprinkling of indiscernible whispers. There was only one word that he picked up and that was 'Gibbo'. It was almost dark when the directive came from the supervising guards that they could down tools, but they had to stand still until further notice. Yi-Jun reported back to Jia the only piece of information that he had gleaned—the word 'Gibbo'. Jia issued a new order. The guards came along the line with torches and Johnno realised that everyone was being searched. He only had one option, and that was to drop the phone and kick it as hard as he could away from his body. He waited until the guard was searching the person standing next to him. He reached into his pocket and removed the cloth. He lowered the phone down the side of one leg and slightly crouched. He dropped the phone. There was little noise, and it was not noticed. He then kicked as hard as he could, which drew the attention of two guards. He pretended to have a cramp and jumped up and down, rubbing his leg. One of the guards used the butt of his gun to knock Johnno to the ground. Other guards flashed their torches along the trench of freshly turned soil. One of the torches picked up the glint of the glass. Then they pounced.

In the ensuing confusion, Johnno was not arrested. His mates picked him up and he was searched as he was swaying with concussed feet. The guard pulled out the piece of dirty cloth from his pocket and looked askance. Johnno took it from his hand and blew his nose. The guard turned his head in disgust.

Jia rushed to his car as he could not wait to have the mobile phone fingerprinted and the battery charged. Despite attempts to wipe it clean, there were two sets of fingerprints on the phone, one of them being Liu Li Jun's.

# Judgement

Hamish was not surprised when he heard the footsteps and, once again, guessed that it would be before midnight. Police lined the side walls, and the three judges were already seated. Hamish stood in the middle of the room, facing the judges.

The judges asked if the mobile phone had been located. The phone was placed on the table in front of them.

'Is there any evidence on this phone that would influence the decision of this court?'

'Yes.'

The defending lawyer stood up and told the judges that there was a call made to London, which he did not believe was made by Liu Li Jun. In fact, there was evidence that the call was made after the murdered body was discovered.

The judges looked up sharply and asked how this had any bearing on the case.

'It has been a mystery how the overseas press has obtained information and a photograph of the man in front of you. I think this phone has been used to communicate with London by an unknown person, who was probably the last person to see Liu Li Jun alive.'

Jia was translating, and Hamish could not believe what he was hearing. The judges sat back and stared at the lawyer. 'Have you got fingerprints from this phone?' 'Yes. We have the fingerprint of Jack Gibson.' The judges were pleased with this news as now they felt that they could bring two people to justice. Jia was ordered to contact the guards and bring in the prisoner. The judges looked at their watches, stood up and left the room. The lawyers also left the room, which left Hamish alone in the courtroom surrounded by police. His brain went over the information that only took minutes to deliver, but he could now see that the judges had two murder suspects. This realisation saddened him.

Gibbo was led into the courtroom and made to stand a metre to the side of Hamish. He gave Hamish a cheeky grin and a small 'thumbs up' signal. Jia, the lawyers and the judges returned to take up their position. One of the judges held up the phone and directed his question to Gibbo. 'Do you recognise this mobile telephone?' 'No.'

**I feel he's going to be caught out. He felt he had a lifeline, but that is now near breaking point. He's been able to wriggle out of trouble in the past, but can he do it again?**

The judges looked pleased with this answer. 'In that case, we will dial this number and hand the phone over to you.' Gibbo knew who they were dialing. Aunty Bev, don't be home. Oh God, what time would it be there? I think it's morning. She will be at school. Thank God this is a landline. He was having trouble breathing … unless it's the weekend.

A voice came through the speaker on the phone: 'Beverly Gibson, can I help you?' The judges motioned Gibbo to respond. 'I think I have the wrong num …'

Before he could hang up, the phone was snatched from his hand.

'Jack, Jack … is that you? I have been so worried about you. I did what you said. I saw the prime minister's press secretary and went to Scotland Yard to let them know that there was trouble on Kangaroo Island, or whatever it's called now. I went to all the newspapers. I was told that satellite images are constantly being perused, but to date there has been no sign of any maltreatment. They assured me that Kangaroo Island would be closely monitored in the future.

I had to provide your name to Scotland Yard and there has been a photo of a man in the paper from your island being taken to a police car. I'm sure it wasn't you. Jack are…?

They hung up.

Court proceedings ceased as the recorded conversation was translated to the judges. Gibbo had to hold his hands tight behind his back to stop shaking.

The judges were now convinced that they were confronting the killer and an accessory.

The judges directed their question to Gibbo. 'What is the relationship between the person answering the telephone and yourself—and don't consider for one moment saying, "None",'

'My aunt.'

'What is this "Kangaroo Island" that is being observed by overseas interference?'

Jia responded with, 'Daishiu Dao.'

'How many fingerprints are on the murder weapon?'

'One.'

'Who do these fingerprints belong to?'

'Hamish McIntyre. However, we have fingerprinted the mattress where the murder weapon was located and found two sets of fingerprints belonging to Hamish McIntyre and Jack Gibson.'

'Perhaps they were lovers,' retorted one of the judges, and they went into fits of laughter. (This was not translated).

The defending lawyer continued: 'We believe the murder weapon was placed in the bedding of Hamish McIntyre by Jack Gibson.'

'Why is it that the accused has fingerprints on the knife that killed Liu Li Jun?'

Jia stood up and answered directly. 'We may have asked him to handle the weapon when we were interrogating.' The judges looked intently at Jia. They recognised methods that everyone had used in the past for a speedy trial. The prosecuting lawyer stood up to object to this conjecture, but the judges waved him down.

The judges conferred and one of them directed their observations to Gibbo. 'We know you were the last person to see Liu Li Jun alive. We believe you removed his mobile phone from his dead body. How many people went to the shed where the murder took place?' 'Two. Me and Macca.'

The judges directed their question to Hamish. 'Have you ever visited the crime scene?'

'No.'

Jia whispered to the defending lawyer, who responded with, 'We have found Jack Gibson's fingerprints on a chair in the burnt-out shed. Apart from Liu Li Jun's fingerprints, there were no others. We believe that Jack Gibson alone knew of the whereabouts of that shed and visited it on many occasions. We believe that he was making an alcoholic drink but was discovered by Liu Li Jun.'

'Where does this information come from?' Jia stood up and responded with, 'I was not fraternizing with any of the Big Feet and Long Noses, but the information was called out to me as I was entering my car.'

After this translation, Gibbo instinctively shouted, 'Sonia!' One of the judges called out, 'Silence!'

Jia told the court that the information he had received had come from Kaitlyn—Jack Gibson's wife.

Gibbo fell to his knees.

The judges ordered the prisoners out of the building. Gibbo and Hamish were surrounded by police and escorted outside. Gibbo was ranting. His hatred and vitriol towards Hamish flowed. 'I know that I'm done for, but I'm taking you with me, Macca.' Even a gun pointed at his head could not stop him. It was not until Jia came outside and said that the judges had reached a decision and ordered the two men back into the courtroom, that he fell silent. They stood side by side.

The judges read from a sheet. 'We believe that Jack Gibson alone murdered Liu Li Jun in the shed in which the body was found. We believe that Jack Gibson stabbed the victim front and back. We believe that Jack Gibson mutilated the face of the deceased. We believe that Jack Gibson set fire to the building to erase evidence. Scrutinising the evidence of fingerprints, we believe that Jack Gibson placed the murder weapon—a knife—into the bedding belonging to Hamish McIntyre. He did this by piercing the material and pushing the knife in as far as his arm would extend.

Jia translated each sentence as it was delivered. The middle judge pointed to Gibbo and pronounced judgement: 'We sentence Jack Gibson to life imprisonment. It is the ruling of this court that Hamish McIntyre took no part in the murder of Liu Li Jun and is to be herewith released from custody.'

When he heard those words, Hamish's brain seemed to take on a life of its own. It went blank. He could not digest or believe what he had just heard. He didn't even know whether he was happy to hear those words, and then the cloud lifted, and he resolved to make the best of the rest of his life and he hoped Sonia would share his feelings. He could now look forward to seeing her again.

As they were walking out the door, Gibbo was surrounded by police, with Hamish behind and Jia coming up at the rear. Hamish turned to Jia and said, 'I cannot believe what you have done, and sincerely, thank you. Lucy is a good kid, and I hope for her early release.' Jia nodded curtly and waved Hamish on.

Gibbo half turned and shouted, 'You're a fucking snake in the grass, Macca. A fucking filthy, rotten worm that squirms up any hole it can find. I've hated you since the cricket match. I watched as my Kats threw her arms around your fucking shoulders to congratulate you on making a golden fucking duck. I saw the look on your face—you cunt. Yeah, I wanted you dead—back into the ground where a grub like you belongs. Thanks to you, I'll never see my Kats again. You think I'm fucking blind, not seeing the looks that passed between you two. I saw what happened when the Cantinnis mistook you for man and wife. I hope you die a slow, agonising death. You're a fucking arsehole, Macca.'

There was one insult Gibbo didn't throw Hamish's way—he didn't call him a GRAP.

As he was walking to Jia's waiting police car, Hamish, in a voice choked with emotion, whispered back, 'You got it all wrong, Gibbo.'

The end

*No, it's not. I can have the last word because I will be here much longer. Hopefully, many millions of years longer.*

*How will I fare with this new species now in control?*

*They have elevated my first people, but will they listen to their advice?*

*I don't know, but just like the people on Kangaroo Island – I'm fearful.*

***The end***

# Acknowledgements

Phillip Owen, for his brutal observations and helpful assistance. Karen Commerford—the first person to read my 'draft' and encourage me to continue. Ainslie and Dwain Buffett, for encouragement and assistance. Eddie—for being Eddie. And my Editor Julie Guthrie.